T0070408

ALAMEDA

DAVID RUSSO

ALAMEDA

davidmrusso.com
@davidmrusso

iUniverse books may be ordered through booksellers or by contacting:

iUniverse
1663 Liberty Drive
Bloomington, IN 47403
www.iuniverse.com
844-349-9409

ISBN: 978-1-6632-3554-1 (sc)
ISBN: 978-1-6632-3555-8 (e)

Print information available on the last page.

iUniverse rev. date: 03/04/2022

Sterling >

Run to her boy shes waitin for ya ~ Jay Lender

Alameda

Its interesting when people lie ~ Don Henley

What I remember most about that night is I love the way he laughs. There's more to say than that, but explaining it all is like analyzing something from every possible angle - it's smart to be able to, stupid to actually do it.

To get the picture, we were in Sterling's room now that his hair was all cut. "Hey, I missed a text from Amie saying she's waiting outside, so I'm gonna skip down the hall and run down the stairs, already late again."

"You won't go, you have to stay for your price adjustment," he reminded me.

"You don't think I should go?" His face was hidden under the clean shirt he was putting on. "You don't think I should go."

"If the answer has no affect on your decision, of what use is the question? It's your responsibility to anticipate your obligations." I just stood there looking at Platform Holly beyond the window behind him. "Are you gonna keep waffling?"

I'm literally leaving right now.

"You think if I asked she would - "

"Kleytjen." He stopped folding the discarded shirt. "We don't live in a conditional."

"I'll call you, Sterling." I picked up my backpack by the left ear.

"Stay vert," with his honest smile.

"I'll be up all night. I'll be up forever." I almost twisted an ankle turning from the hall to the stairs and decided not to run.

Patricia smelled like saffron, I could tell as soon as I walked down to the street and reached for the door. Four years and serious miles on it, three times around the world at the equator. Amie already replaced the spark plugs. My running shoes were about to hit four hundred. She likes everyone to watch her go, know that. The thing about Amie is there's always music on in her car. Even when no one's in it. "Hey Kley, why so fast?" She shifted to drive before my back hit the seat. "Sorry for the mess."

"You have crazy timing. I was right in the middle of a movie with four girls."

"Give me four names and a title and I'll believe you."

"Jordyn, Liz, Marie, Andera. *Midnight in Paris*." Green eyed girls.

"I don't believe you."

"The truth has nothing to do with your beliefs. I still say we make it there by midnight. So the good news is," unzipped the pocket on the nose, "I brought food."

"Goldfish!" She's crazy about those but looked down. "Shoes, huh? Always overdressed. What else's in the animal? Don't be so precious about it."

"Camera, yes, and clothes. By the way the food's a gift, not a bribe." So hard to keep her satisfied. "The other good news is, I don't have any bad news." She was about to honk at this car that wasn't turning on red from Lagoon Road, right on the edge of campus. "Hey, don't praise the messenger. Well, if you want to. How's your friend? More good news?"

"She's all right now. It's just that, for the next twelve hours or so, I don't know. But then she's usually fine for at least a few months." About to turn right on to El Colegio and this time she did honk. "Dude, *girl*, there are other forms of transportation than walking around in eight inch heels."

"She's just taking her time."

"Ours, too." Radio was playing Get Me Bodied and she lip synced along.

"Well I hope she's better. You catch that south that came through? I saw a girl at Casey's today who looks just like you and it freaked me out."

"I look freaky?"

"You didn't know? Just so you know, you're not taking me to my parents' house, my sister's having a sleepover and using my room." An incomplete truth.

"Wherever that is." Made it to the 217 and put the windows up a minute later when we got on the 101 with signs about the next nine exits and being shorter than fifteen feet to pass.

"They don't even know I'm coming down. If you drop me off downtown again that'd be awesome, I know it's out of your way."

"Whatever, weirdo. What would you do without me?"

"I honestly don't know." She'd left the moonroof open until this time.

"Yeah that should be fine, unless I get super tired." Amie never sets the temperature for the middle; all the way hot, all the way cold, back and forth every minute. "You can put the heat seater on if you want. Seat heater. So you're just gonna be gallivanting around town for the weekend?"

"Unless I get a better offer. Hey, there's the place Katy Perry wrote that song about."

"*All* her songs. Where have you been the last three years? Can you open that can in the cup holder for me?"

Normally not a difficult maneuver for her, but she was typing into her phone. "That's a forty."

"I only drink when I drive." She sped up to nine thousand rotations per minute.

"You need to take a good look at yourself and never drive again."

"I will after walking next Saturday. It's iced tea by the way." She finished the tea right away and switched to whatever was in her rosé canteen.

"I get the feeling you won't. Wait, you switched from Sunday?"

"Don't judge." She always says not to, being far more judgmental.

"Judging is inherently neutral and it is entirely likely to make a positive judgment. The brain only works with positives. My sister's Spanish teacher told her." She didn't want to hear about it, doesn't like to be told how to talk when she's better at it.

"You know, this song should be *Lie* Down Sally." I was about say that. "Are you gonna go to karaoke next week? You can just dance if you don't want to sing."

"Well you know how good I am at finger dancing." Thirteen miles in was a reprieve from the dark off to the right thanks to Fleischmann placing the harbor in such a weird spot, although he did a good job at creating a unique break.

"Halkirk said there are no wrong steps, only variations. You should go line dancing with us." Professor Halkirk, we're convinced, has taught every subject. She has six degrees.

"Square dancing is four times funner." Past Montecito and Tony Montana's place, to Summerland, seeing all all the money on that hill even in the dark.

"So stupid. Maybe on Monday so Jordy and I can both convince you." Santa Claus Lane is where I first caught myself thinking what a night this could be, something from Aqueous Transmission was playing. "Hey Meepface, look at that guy! He just jumped out of his car or something. Don't *stare*."

"I wasn't staring, I just turned around for half a fraction of a tenth of a. That's not even long enough to stare!" She spends way too long looking in the rearview mirror.

"Has anyone ever told you you don't make any sense?"

"Well, I did the other day, if that counts."

"You're so weird, it's unbelievable."

"You used to think I was funny."

"What? I don't remember that." She's the funny one. "Don't look at me like that. How bout I just stay at your fanciful hotel with you? I assume that's what you mean by downtown."

"And leave before I wake up? You're still switching stations. I thought you wanted to check on your friend."

"Well if she's asleep I won't want to wake her up. At least I'll be there in the morning. There are so much more songs for singles than couples, it's annoying."

"That was your favorite song."

"There might be something better."

We had both been up since six, or sometime between midnight and noon. “Since we’ve made it this far, let’s just stay up for the whole week. We can sleep after finals.”

“Yeah, good luck with that. My circadian rhythm will be back to normal by Monday. I kind of want to stop at Rincon on the way back. Best wave in California,” she said in a way that almost undersold it, even with her wetsuit in the backseat.

“Is it a right hander?”

“I like how you pretend to know what that means. Ninety minutes paddling out, fifteen seconds holding down, a few deep drops and bottom turns, and that’s what you ask.”

“You ever go when it’s dark?”

“Moonlight surfing? Only when there’s a full moon. Otherwise it’s, you know, lake status.” It was dark, too dark to see the Islands or even the water, especially not blue dolphins, or take a picture. “The next good swell isn’t coming til Wednesday, more time to prepare for finals.” And so we went in and out, like the tide. “It’ll be good. I have four and I’m only taking three classes.” Unbelievable. “Watch me toss this empty goldfish container in the backseat.”

It landed right in her unzipped back backpack pocket, so she celebrated her random precision. “Were you actually trying to do that?”

“I told you to watch. I can’t believe we drove all the way down to Ventura to play mini golf.”

“It’s hard to believe we only went once.” First time we slowed down with this coupe she was tailgating going half a mile an hour in the fast lane, “What’s his hurry?”

“Come on Camara,” she swerved, “you’re supposed to be fast.”

I looked to the left past her profile. “He’s asleep.”

“You don’t have to *laugh* at it.”

“It’s usually what I do when something is funny.”

“You could say something intelligent.”

“Aims, I know you like to say no to everything I ask, how’s this: wanna go to the scavenger hunt on Tuesday? There is a correct answer.”

"I do want to, but I have a meeting that night." Not allowed to do more than one activity per day.

"Let me know when you change your mind. You already know you're gonna have a good time. Okay, be honest: frisbee golf on Wednesday. Or free bowling. You know, like we used to." We always change our density, like lava lamps.

"No, thanks for asking."

"When I said I wanted you to be honest I wasn't being honest."

"I think you underestimate how much I have to do."

"I don't underestimate that. I don't underestimate it. I just overestimate how much you care. There are a lot of things you do you could skip in favor of something that doesn't happen fifty three times a year."

"You don't overestimate that. But it's more than me, it's about everyone else I go with. I didn't know this week meant so much to you." She gave me the truth increasingly rarely.

"You never do. I think they can survive without you for a day."

"So can you."

"Maybe that's not what I want."

"Maybe it doesn't matter what you want."

"Can't we just agree on something fun?" I know she could. "Don't say maybe."

"We'll see."

"What does that mean? Just say yes or no." Hypocritical me.

"Okay, I'll ask my roomies if they wanna go. You should too."

"So it's cool to hang out as long as other people are there?"

"Good God, damn. You are so sensitive." She swung her arm to switch the air back to cold and hit the canteen, spilling it all over my lap, and apologized before I even realized what happened. "If your sense of worth is inversely determined by how many other people there are, it's decreasing every second. You're so brittle, Kleytjen. I've got nothing but good memories with you, I see no reason to change that. If you would only listen - "

"I listen to you."

"No you don't! You don't listen at all, you just think of what to say. Seriously, you interrupt everyone. It's annoying. If you *did* listen, you might just realize I'm trying to do everything that I can. You can get out and run the rest of the way if you want." She's full of ideas, no doubt about that.

"You're just someone who gets annoyed. What you're missing is I don't think anyone knows that as well as I do."

"You're missing me - you're missing my point. Just sayin." She sure would like to change me, but I didn't mean to make it taut. Once we got past Carpinteria it was smooth sailing, like a peanut butter ship. "Wanna make lunch together? Maybe Tuesday or Wednesday at eleven." I acquiesced. Just two lanes still, with more in approaching Ventura, and she asked about summer. "You're not sure? There's nothing worse than uncertainty." Put both hands on the steering wheel for the first time, but they didn't stay long.

"To be uncertain is to be uncomfortable, but to be certain is to be ridiculous. I don't know who said that." I still don't.

"For once." She picked up her phone for the fifth time that minute. "Text me back," then tossed the rectangle behind her and it too landed in the backpack.

"Do you listen to yourself?"

Amie laughed and had what hadn't spilled from her canteen. That's the thing about water - it dries. "I listened to your story about Norman's party. What happened to Mason?"

Alameda

How the hell am I supposed to be ~ Usher Raymond

All good things start somewhere. Palmer's grey Corvette looked humid, slowed down to about ninety - the Carmel Valley streets were still slippery - then pulled over. Before the seat hit my back he started, "I have a story for you Kley. You know how I told you I came home with the hottest girl ever? She dropped her phone, we were *about* to hook up, then she remembered she had a boyfriend. I let her sleep on the couch and now the boyfriend's been texting me and thanking her for not fucking anyone. Bitch got did. I think with Amie, you're like a bug in a spider web. You just hope it forgets about you." His hair was dusky, looks wild through a neutral density filter.

"You kept her phone?"

"Dude I wasn't gonna get nothing out of this. I at least wanna see what she looks like. Tell me about my future school."

"Alright, for a minute. Jordyn Natalie was at the soccer game today too, turned to me and said, 'You didn't already know that? What did you see last night?'

'*Moonrise Kingdom*. At the drive in, we used their two for one weekday deal.' Today is everything that happens before you go to sleep."

"Thursday's a weekday?"

"Depends on when you wake up. Amie had sent,

Ready? I'm getting a court at the rec cen

'Jordyn, you're a person - you're an intelligent person, tell me if this makes sense. I said I would bike over to her place, like Einstein, she said Okay, then picked me up.'

'You probably would've been late.'

'Right. So yeah, I bought her her ticket.'

'You bought *your* ticket and gave her the free one.'

'That's what I said.' On the way back a Florence and the Machine song was playing and I've been running it over in my mind ever since to figure out which one."

"Dude, there's only like two songs it could be." That's not true at all.

"Exactly. 'Are you gonna join us on Taco Monday? We're working hard on The List, we only have a week.'

'I know, you're not gonna finish. I haven't told Amie, so I don't know how you feel about it, but Chase always has to have a girlfriend.'

'You told me that before. We have fun, I don't care what it's called.'

'That's *all* you care about, Kleytjen. You always get into a triangle. Not an equilateral, but a triangle just the same.'

'That's a great shape. I didn't mean for anything to start again.'

'Things started anyway.'

'All I know is last night I was so uncomfortable, and so happy.'

'Tell me why.'

'Her knee was wrecking my spine. Actually, it was super comfortable, like a really uncomfortable bed.' There was no room between cars for lawn chairs.

'No, the second one. Amie said they always knew they would break up when school ends. I couldn't do that, I have to think it'll last to go for it.'

'Which is why that was the stupidest thing to say.'

'But it was said by a smart person. Like the Taylor Swift theory.' "

"The hell's the Taylor Swift theory?"

"The Taylor Swift theory says, ask ten guys if they'd rather go out with her for a month or be friends with her for life. Nine out of the ten will say friends for life, and nine of them are lying. Even if they don't know it."

"Is that lying?"

"We don't notice any time pass. So it started out by biking back to my place and seeing her going inside Casey's Cafe on yesterday, followed her inside, she asked me what's doing for the weekend and if

I'd want a ride here, then told me about the movie. 'I gotta go. Got a group from Puget Sound, or Palm Springs. Here, take my tortillas.' They weren't mine to begin with.

Jordyn grabbed them. 'You're leaving? Way to be a fan. We're gonna score in a minute.'

'This is my fourth game today. And I'm already late, have to get there instantly, if not sooner. Let me know if Andera shows up.' I skipped down the stadium stairs.

'You gotta be fashionable some way. Wait, you're not late at all!'

'It's my last one!' Then the ol new phone rang. 'Hey Aims, I'm only gonna be there for five minutes. You know this gym date's three years in the making, right?'

'Jim? Do you wanna wait - '

'Okay, two and a half.'

'I don't know what you're referencing.'

'The first Tuesday we hung out, you asked me if I wanted to go on Wednesday and I said Yes, cause I knew there was soccer that night we'd go to instead.' Last year I asked and she said, It's eighty five degrees. I don't think she remembered my question.

'That's almost funny. I'm bringing two friends, but I'm on your team!'

'We're playing doubles? Twice the injury risk.'

'And you're riding with no hands, I can hear the wind. We should just do this later, aren't you already late? I'll let you know about San Diego.'

'You're actually going? I thought your friends couldn't make it.'

'Friends can always make it, it's just gonna be really late. You really wanna go?'

'Sure, I'll go.'

'You don't have to.'

'You asked if I want to. I do. Keep me posted, I say we'll get there before midnight.' So I stayed straight instead of turning left, parked my bike outside of South Hall. 'Hey everyone, so glad no one waited. My name is Kleytjen. I won't ask for a long introduction like Mick Jagger, I just want to tell you about us. The asking's all up to you, it's the greatest thing ever invented.'

'Are you talking about his song featuring Keith Richards?' "

"Dude, I love musicians. Why take acid when they can take it for you? There's no come down."

" 'That's the one. We're an amazing academic universe according to the Netherlands's top seven, except for my acceptance, always thought it was a misprint.'

'Does anyone pay attention to that? What's it based on?'

'I have no reasons for you, like what makes the Manhattan Chicken always win tick tack toe, so since we're here above the Earth's crust, let's keep moving. Let me begin a year ago. Lots of folks go home every weekend, but at Orientation you'll be told to start your new life at your new place. Where cost is less and fun is more. My policy is to not go out of town even for one night, always feel like I'm missing everything when not here. I've also been told to never leave any place that's super awesome. I'm just being honest. But that weekend I went down to - we'll just call it San Diego. Was only going away to come back. It's where my parents moved five seconds after I was in your position. They're like nomads. No need to bring your homework with you whenever you do go out of town, it'll be there when you get back.' Do you follow?"

"You talk too much, see if you can get the bluetooth to work." Cruise control worked fine, merged us on the 5 right by Mission Bay where the 8 begins. Palmer handed me some animal crackers, said he was full.

"Sure, lemme just hack the mainframe. You don't have a charger for this, do you? Okay, 'Okay, America's Finest City. I like traveling more than everyone in my family combined, yet each of them have been to a state the rest of us haven't, except me. If you look around you'll notice several fixtures that set our campus apart, according to my brother Ravi, he went to Davis, now has a gig on Broadway, which is that way. Here we go. From the top. Short Short Friday, first home soccer game of the calendar year, this golden yellow attire, field in great green condition. Season starts in August, what it was was just a scrimmage against the Fusion, a pro team. No Pep Band nor Cheerleaders, but the Locos showed. They're crazy. Same shirt as mine on the front, different on the back. I didn't have any tortillas, I'm prepared to be unprepared in all circumstances.'

'Did you know cheering on your team without preparing is bad for you?'

'But I left prepared. The team, guys team that is, was last ranked ninth in the country. The girls team has a lack of marketing, so please go to all of their games as well, we just want to carry the goal into the ocean again. It's not a tradition if you only do it once, but that ain't no matter though. We have the best fans.'

'Sports fans are terrible.' And a sports fan is amazing.

'So, me having to leave right in the middle. Much as I wanted to watch the second half, best of the year, I went to talk with a professor about a paper I thought wasn't graded fairly, but I haven't been right about anything since fifth grade. That quarter I had to get my grades way up so the Honors Program would keep me. Straight As make an A minus bad.' Marvelous definition of *bad*. 'I don't deal with pluses or minuses anymore, I'm kind of an absolutist. Simply difficult to get As because I originally learned the alphabet backwards.

'So you were late?'

'First half ran three minutes over. Priorities, you know. The standing, yelling Locos, maybe twenty two in total, "You're *leav*ing?" We're always surprised by extra ordinary things. Which is surprising.'

'Yeah, ten bucks is ten bucks.'

'What are you talking about?'

'Oh, take Brad Park. As a frosh he made our hall an album called *Big Frames With Tiny Pictures.*' I'll send you the link for it. 'Bradshaw, when he asks how long you were thirteen for, and you answer, One year, he gets real surprised. Gets extremely interested, then tells you, January is carbon monoxide awareness month! Tells you that in November, too. On the regular. On our door he put: You go to school where other people go to vacation, glory glory. Every new person he meets doesn't know the real surprise. The night we met he gave everyone his digits in case anyone wanted to borrow his bike, I hit him up that night and had my first drink, got drunk as an elephant and slept in a - slept on toilet paper roll. I bought this one two weeks later.' The bike, the flask I gave away.

'We meant the ten bucks part.'

'Ah. It was my former future roommate Carson's paper, I didn't care about my grades. "Kley, I need to rewrite a paper. It's stupid, though, I - "

"Maybe you should've written a better paper." Often times the simplest explanation is the best.' "

Cruise control lasted a whole three minutes, Palmer had to pass these cyclists otherwise he'd crash right into them. "Where'd you get your stupid backpack from anyway?"

"Who do you think? 'Why don't *you* talk to my professor since it's so simple? I emailed her I'd be there at four, she doesn't know who I am. Her name's Klurton.'

'What's it about?'

'Nothing. I'm a politician. Just do it, you'll never see her again.'

'That subject is notoriously difficult, it's so full of cliches. I won't do it for free.' I'm getting ahead of myself, here we go again. 'My madcap mission began like the first law of motion to South Hall, this greenish purplish orange building right here in the eastern north part of campus, we'll go inside in a minute. Our film department resides there and Michael Douglas recently donated two trillion dollars, so it'll have a different name. I passed the softball and baseball stadiums, baseball had an away series and softball's finale wasn't until Sunday. More blustery on the path by Ocean Road as I approached the crowded Rec Cen, some dude brushing his teeth as he biked to the racks. That gym, add nasium, still doesn't make sense to me. I once rode over there just to ride the stationary bikes. Haven't gone back because I confused myself so much. Run on the beach.' Someone asked about the air. 'No, I don't smell the saltiness, you get used to it, for better or for more better. A cluster of girls were digging volleyballs in the sand and more were serving tennis balls on the courts, so I allowed myself to slow down. It's a great school, no matter how you look at it. Or where. Bumpy patches on the bike path by that roundabout, but other than that. Open minded kids. Also, before you find out, know that by accident or otherwise, I interpret the things that happen to me too cautiously, so take everything I say with a gram of sugar. Aside from our athletes it may seem pretty empty in the heart of campus, Friday is prime for professors to ditch. Everyone's at Campus Point enjoying the south coast. And splashing in the low tide along the bluffs and slippery rocks, twisting in the water. If you go toward the park, there's a sunflower growing in the middle of the sand, the ugly part where there's a ton of rocks, right here on the edge of the continent. The other point, a mile west, has the surf and more chances to see creatures. I should know more about sea creatures, like sea monkeys. I don't know ethology, I just know if you record a sea star and speed it up, they move all over the place.'

'You should or you want to?'

'Both. We attract out of towners. From other states, bring your friends. How you party's how we pre party, it's commensurate. Take Halloween, that's a week long, spills over into April.'

'Have you been to Spain?'

'Not physically. Almost every building has a secret tunnel. This is our library, I've never been inside. Well, that's not true. Few days after I met Brad I was mapless, didn't know where my fourth class was. So I went in and to the top, four years ago my guide said there's a model of campus up there. It's nice when we're told true things. See, it's too sterile. Textbooks have crazy covers that make you believe you're going to do calculus in a forest and that all of history took place on a boat. Accounting is best, costs nine thousand dollars, but at least it has a great picture of a girl riding her bike up a huge mountain. We know all accountants ever do is ride mountain bikes all day. Should be a picture of jumping off a cliff or something. Astronomy gets it, you can tell by its cover of colliding galaxies. Except, the opening sentence: In the beginning there was nothing, then it exploded.' If there's nothing there, how could anything go right? 'I don't need to tell you that doesn't make any sense, but I will tell you when you see it then - okay, that burst of cheering means I already missed a goal. With Carson's paper, I got to these rusty racks, locked up, then walked into the vortex of the second floor,' out of six, 'I never knew, but I do now. Backwards mapping. Carson is originally from Secret Town, wanted to go farther away than a few marathons, that lasted two years, transferred from Kalamazoo or somewhere where it's only all right.' Smelled like beige paint. 'All this renovation has the building being shared amongst departments, but you'll know which part is what thanks to the professors who post blurbs on their doors, like a fortune cookie. Or Brad. "Learning isn't fun, it's hard work." A falsehood universally acknowledged. "Asking a meaningful question is harder than giving a good answer." Film, obviously. "Don't let your cardiac muscle eat your cerebral cortex." Didn't want to be a biologist, that's what happens when you hear politics. "I didn't choose the accounting life, the accounting life chose me." That, before now, never seemed so clear. I don't want to sound like a bad student in case I'm not, but I didn't have my backpack, just Carson's scroll held together by a staple, in my back pocket. The one I have does lend me credibility seeing as she is sculpted into the shape of a puppy and barks when you grab her left paw. As soon as I got to his professor's door she was walking out alongside Andera Butterfield, sweet shorts.' Andera looked good, too."

"How do you tell?" From the outside Palmer's new ride was way louder than Patricia, but from the inside you could hardly tell it's on, couldn't hear any outside air.

"By the rigidity of her shins. Andera and I nodded to each other. 'So much for being late. "I'm not blaming anyone, I'm just giving the truth. Hey look, a chicken!" Buttery voice. "It wasn't meant to be inclusive, just representative." Peachy lip gloss. "My main point is it was a reduction in assets, not a distribution, and I didn't get that from anyone else."

"And that's good. Once you get rid of your fatalistic attitude you'll be fine. I only say this because I know it's true. You can do better. I look forward to it."

With that Andera was completely out and I in. "Sorry I'm late, I was drinking tequila."

Klurton left too. “I’ll be back in a sec. You can sit anywhere.” ’

I dont know where my phone is ~ Nelly Furtado

In case you haven't been, Santa Barbara is a great party school, whatever that means. "Mason was staring at the white gold spoon ring around Liz's finger. Norman told him she transferred from Berkeley and they'd been married for eleven and a half months. 'Are you seriously kidding me right now?'

'Have I ever lied to you?'

'About twice a day.'

'There's a hundred sixty dollar receipt to prove it. It sounds ridiculous, like a sponge, but it's pure truth.'

Mason asked her directly. 'Dude spent a hundred sixty dollars on your ring?'

'Yeah. Well, no. For both of ours.'

'You know he's supposed to spend like three months salary on that, right?'

'He did.' I don't even care, that's awesome. 'And Highway to Hell was our wedding song.' Mason upped and walked away. 'By the way, we're kidding.' "

"Last wedding I was at, eight thousand dollars were spent on spoons that match."

"I know, and none of the food required spoons. You could at least get Super Bowl tickets with that."

"I said they *match*."

"Next spate of arrivals included Chase's brother visiting from San Luis, Mason asked what he's majoring in. 'I'm in a frat and I party a lot!' To be fair, what a stupid question.

'Any of them got sisters?' Norman, Torrey, and Eli said they were about to go gamble. 'You're going to the casino *now*? Where you really going?' Torrey works at the hotel you might drop me off at. She's special, best at every subject, and things that aren't subjects. Trained both her bosses.

'Mason, we haven't lied to you all day. Why would we start now? By the way Kley, you by far have the best photographs of anyone in the group. Everyone else should be taking fucking notes.' From that Leadership project we had with Liz."

"Whatever, Man Ray. You take the most *ran*dom pictures."

"Well yeah. 'Kley, I probably shouldn't tell you this, but I'm drunk so I'll tell you.' She likes gin, no tonic. 'Sorry I talk reallyfast when I'm drunk.'

'That's okay, I listen fast. What were you saying?'

'Huh? I don't think he's fat.'

'What did you say? I've been meaning to ask you this, Liz. I heard it's really hard to transfer here. What they make you do, walk over coals?' I took a few more swigs of Jack.

'Yes, you should. Only in school once,' looking down at her phone. 'I never go on Facebook anymore. Only like once a day.' Goes hours, even minutes, without checking her notifications. We found ourselves at a table, 'Is this cocaine?'

'Hold on, I'm the drug dog,' Jordyn sniffed. 'That's not coke. Believe me, that's *not* coke.' She showed it was alka seltzer, much cheaper. 'Let's get crossed.'

'On red and - hold on babe, my girlfriend's calling.' Norman stepped outside. He got mono twice the same year. 'Sup Babe. I'm watching some dude eat grasshoppers. How you doin?' Walked halfway downstairs, marched back up. 'No, I'm not talking to mermaids. Carson says Hi. Yeah, no. He's not naked this time. Babe, it's a normal distribution. Babe. No, H as in hola. Wait, I can't hear you, you sound like you're underwater. Call me back when you reach the surface.' He hung up. 'I don't think - I don't think she could tell.' His shirt was inside out when he came back. 'I hugged a bush!' "

"He ended the call, there's no hanging up anymore."

Glad she noticed that through all her singing. Once we were past Rincon and out of the county the station switched, so the splyric was something like, Having fun but seriously - Baby we ain't the first. Just sang right through the static.

"I told him he embarrasses himself."

"From the one who couldn't give up vodka for forty days. Not consecutively, just cumulative throughout a year."

"Forty sounds about right. 'How come you don't want her to know what you're doing?'

'She makes everything a big deal. I should get a girlfriend with a mute button.'

'They're called guys,' Carson joined.

'It's like, thanks for making me feel bad for loving you. I don't play that shit. Let's go, Babe.'

Even with two couches Mason claimed the love seat. And Circus was on. 'Why've y'all got to go so early? You're not gonna turn into pumpkins.'

'Great party. No whiskey? We go home.' Walked into his room. 'At least we were embarrassing.'

'To more anarchic moments. Good night.' Mason meandered over to the Beer Barn, the party within. Bunch of crap in the sink, as well as dinner dishes. 'Are you gonna clean this?'

'It cleans itself, dawg,' Carson explained. 'Our rule is, clean your dishes before you go to bed. If you don't, clean them in the morning.' "

"They had very strict rules." Then the station went out altogether and instead of changing it she turned the thing off.

"They impressed Jordyn. 'This is a nice place for a bunch of dudes. Really. You don't keep your cereal in weird places, and you can see the floor.' And you can look at the bathroom without throwing up. 'You guys have any ice cubes?'

'Oh shit, who closed the freezer? No wonder it's so hot in here. Whoa, is this Spanish?' Carson was trying to read the orange juice carton. 'Fuck ice cream.'

'What? Why?' Cut my hand on a broken bottle of Stevens sitting on the counter. More blood arrived with Chase's brother, dripping from his face. 'What happened to you?'

'A girl happened. And I asked her out in front of her boyfriend. Cars c'n I borrow some of your bread?'

'Sure, here. When're you gonna give it back?'

'Whenever you want. Wait. What color was this when you bought it?'

'There's no way of knowing,' I said. 'Let's see if it passes the perpendicular smell test.' He ate it all, so it passed something. 'The more the más. See that girl over there?' He raised his eyes. 'Yeah. I went on a run with her.' The eyes rolled. I always need to prepare before going on a run.

'Beer me, I need a chaser.' For Jordy's econ thesis proposal she used game theory to discuss the correlation between milkshakes and boys in the yard. Challenge accepted, contingent upon her letting Halkirk assist her. She declined. 'I don't know why our department doesn't teach about beer.' Carson poured a drink for us. 'Scotch and soda is my shit. Or just scotch. You're spilling.'

'No, it's only overflowing.' Pretended to look away from her. 'See Kley, melting point and freezing point are the same, it's just a matter of which direction you're going. Drink up. Anyone else?'

'Scotchka for me, thanks.' Instead Jordyn poured him milk, straight up. She sifted through the cabinets for the makings of Brandy Sour, Woodstock, Slippery Pete, James Bond and the Giant Peach. I had it all. Quite the plunder in Yoda shot glasses, everyone became dizzy. 'I'm still rallying from this morning.'

'Here's a margarita.' On the rocks, no ice.

'That won't help. Delicious, though!' Carson looked back to the sink. 'How come you're not partying?'

'I already have enough serotonin, you shouldn't have broughten me,' Mason said.

'Your hair's looking nice,' one thing Torrey notices.

'I know. Thank you though.'

'Yeah Mason, nice haircut. What do you use, tangerines?'

'Why don't you grab that cinnamon sugar and I'll show you.' So sozzled but trying to keep up with the playlist. 'Say Watermelon, it'll look like you know the words.'

Norman reentered society, 'Watermelon is my favorite color! This rum is oddly intoxicating.' Still up on the quote wall. 'Kley, you ever go skinny dipping as a kid?'

'All the - oh, not when I was a kid.'

'Me too.' All part of his meek, misleading demeanor. Exceptionally quiet, after two sips he starts rap battling, rhythmically insulting us and everything. 'Are you drink yet?'

'Don't worry, I'm more sober than all you all combined," Mason said. 'Jordy, I hope you're a utilitarian because if you say yes to me, the happiness of the world will increase by much more than if you do to someone else.' She put the great wall of body language up between them."

"I don't think she realizes how pretty she is."

"Everyone else does. 'Kley, you're living with Cars next year? Just embrace taking Norm's place, he does the weird stuff. Here, take my phone so I don't drunk dial.' I heard of another way to prevent that. Torrey acts incredibly normal drunk, sending seventeen texts to every contact, especially those she hasn't talked with in months. Another song was interrupted and after a minute we realized it was her phone.

'I didn't bring my number. When's Florida?' Florida's a good idea, my mom's been there twelve times.

'August first! With Marie.'

'The girl with the hair?' Yep, Miss Arabella.

'Three years and still in love with the same woman. If Liz ever finds out, she'll end me. You'd think I could trade her in by now.' Norm sets the bar for fidelity.

Mason couldn't let it go. 'I just feel like Jordyn's settling. Why can't she settle for me?'

'He was basically two timing me the whole time.' She took off her light jacket to put on him. 'You look sexies in these.'

Norman smacked his face into the living room wall even though it looked like he was looking right at it. 'Who the hell put this here? Hey, Kley, think I can punch a square hole in this?' Fractured his right thumb. Liz returned from wherever she was, changed the subject with her appearance.

Mason let it go. 'Where else have you been? Florence is my favorite city in Italy.'

'You're allowed to go to Italy? Lock up your sororities, Tenaya's on the loose! Where's the bathroom?'

'I don't live here,' I shrugged.

'You never knock when you come over,' Carson pushed his glasses up while focusing on Mason and Torrey, they're monozygotic. 'Hey. Mason. You turned down Cornell?'

'Yep. Torrey, she - what's the word, encouraged? That's what she did for me to go here. Yo, lemme take a hit.' What a guy. Yes, from the one who went a whole weekend, at least forty eight hours straight, with alcohol over point two one, drove Torrey to her boyfriend's, in his car. I got pulled over cause Palmer Szczesny's car had a broken headlight. That's all they noticed."

"I still can't believe you did that."

"But I don't anymore, and you still sleep drive all the time. Have you ever been to Ojai?"

She saw the sign too. "Naw. Let's go on the way back."

"Well that might be never. In Connecticut, fourteen years ago. Balderdash, homemade pizza, grandparents visiting for the end of summer, they had to go and not return until Thanksgiving. My brother Ravi and I were sad but our grandma outlined, 'You could survive *tor*ture for twelve weeks.' Eighty eight days later, I remember looking out the living room window so I'd be the first to see them. Furious flurries of snow all day and then we got a call saying they were in an accident. Yep, people had phones back then, I didn't know that either. Drunk driver, right in the middle of the afternoon. Strange definition of *accident*. No one's sure if our grandpa remembers. He doesn't remember anything recent, which drives everyone around him crazy, such a selfish reaction. What he does remember is all the things that happened when he was a kid, and each of his friends from the Army and ping pong baseball and poker."

"Because he has pictures of it all."

"You really should listen to yourself. But yeah, he has his priorities in order."

"That's why they're priorities. It's crazy how distracted you get. It's like if I paddle out and think about the water that's gonna go up my nose instead of where to position."

"Just trying to pass the time. Alright, Mason said, 'You're a real inspiration. You're blinking so loudly.'

'Come back on Mojito Tuesday. You want some sugar?'

Carson jumped in. 'Shore! I'll smoke anything you give me. Dude. Hey, guys. I can fly.' What a smart human. 'Here, it opens you to the mind.'

'There's no such thing as the mind.'

'Yeah, that's what it shows you.'

'Well I already know it.'

'Why are you so closed minded, Kley?' Song now was Out of My Head. I told him about a text conversation with Jordyn that morning and he sneezed. Rude to sneeze at a party. 'Wait, you have Jordy's number?' I got it from Marie's phone."

"You stole it?"

"Well, she still has it. 'They wanna get my - where'd Norman go?'

'I don't know, out the back door.' I forgot we were upstairs. 'How are we not out of jungle juice yet? I already had six cups.'

'Have another six, balance your diet. How bout you, Jay Nat?' Indistinguishable. 'She said Yes. What time is it?'

'Right now? It's uh, leven. What are you doing here, Kley?'

'I live here.'

Jordyn looked confused. 'Where's my foot?' Too drunk, still drinking. 'Not gunna lie. I'm feeling pretty.' Wobbly.

'How drunk are you? I re - I remember you the other weekend at Marie's margarita bash.' Cinco de that was a kickback.

'One to ten?' She likes scales or something."

"Does she like snakes?"

"No one likes snakes. 'Sixteen being the highest.'

'Zebra.' Fell face first onto the open side of the love seat."

"When you drank you only talked about how drunk you were."

"Very subtle guy. 'Where'd you go?' Like William Adams said, Fergie parties harder than all of us, which is dope. Marie's sister really liked to dance with anyone who could keep up."

"To say dancing is what they were doing is disrespectful to words."

"You weren't even there. You could tell she's good, she just did what she was feeling. Didn't care what song or who was there. I like that, just dance if you want to dance. 'Whoa, if you're spilling liquor on my floor you're not drinking any more. Oh, it's water? Ferry on.' She really enjoyed the Kesha song, for its social commentary. One guy, Mel, tried to move with two left shoes. Didn't know she was much younger."

"Are we actually supposed to believe Kesha wakes up in the morning?"

"The wait for the bathroom, everyone lining up to puke our guts out, got too long, so partiers started going next *door* to get sick, with the single girls, and so that bathroom turned into the express lane for ten beers or less, with the exception of no walk all limp Liz. 'Carson, you know that bike we saw in a tree?'

'I remember it like it was yesterday.'

'That was this morning. When's the last time you took yer shoes off?'

'I haven't tied these in years.' Then he noticed. 'My toe nails! Both of them.' Jordyn painted them all."

"She didn't draw on his face?"

"Oh, she did. Marie exited the bathroom, starting to glow. 'Wanta hang out tomorrow? We can get lunch, play soccer, exchange fluids, whatever.'

'Maybe, yes, definitely, whatever. I'm going to San Diego if I can.'

'Bring pesos!' Like I was going on vacation. So used to getting rides, I invite others to wherever I'm going before realizing there's no room. 'Make sure to tag me!'

Liz, hands in her dress pockets, 'Who tagged my car? Oh hey Kley, I liked those skating pictures.'

'Gimme your number and I'll send em your way.'

'They're not *that* good.' She turned around and Norman appeared. Too much tongue, they don't care who sees. Sounded like macaroni and cheese. Everyone knows when he proposes it'll just be a formality. But Mason didn't know that." And he didn't know where I went after dessert.

Where did you go? People are starting to ask questions

I told him I was after someone who makes you hope life is real. "You just gave me a cavity." Where were we - the road turned inland away from the negative space and we passed sign posts for Ventura, Reseda, and Mulholland, like you're driving through a Tom Petty song, with no traffic. One difference from driving back east is the lack of street lights, couldn't even see where the fire burned back in April. Amie had to avoid a twin mattress that was dropped right across our lane. If you took the freeway along this stretch and turned it upside down you would be amazed at all the furniture that falls out: desks, couches, ladders, cribs. No doubt there is enough each day to furnish an entire house.

"Those who can make jokes and those who can take jokes, 'Two girlfriends, huh?'

Obviously neither remember any of this, if I explained it it would make perfect nonsense. 'What are you talking about?'

'You're not gonna marry your girl?'

'Sit down, man.' Already was. 'Are you crazy? I don't believe in marriage. Or decimals,' Norman closed his eyes but Mason kept him awake.

'It exists anyway. That vibe's kinda sketchy. This your room, Cars?'

'Welcome to The Love Dungeon.' "

"Is that your room?"

"You know it. 'Smells good in here. You showered this week, huh. What's the other?'

'Thelizabeth Graveyard. Open their door, you'll notice the handle comes off. That's its best feature.'

'You still have this calendar? I'd rather not know what year it is.' Underneath it were Jacobinia plants, in case the room runs out of oxygen. 'Where'd you get that clock?'

'I had to fix my watch and I got really drunk.' "

"Sponges make oxygen." Amie Lynn turned the radio back on, static is better than my voice. She's been riding since she was nine or eight, at sixteen she placed third at the California Youth Championships, her feet are always tan. If her new board weren't broken she would have brought it down to hit up Cardiff or Black's or somewhere, though she's used to going up at Mavs where it's glassy.

"Sounds like a fun thing to make. 'I feel like finishing the rest of my forty right now but I'll just have it in the morning.' You know how you take a glass of water with you when you go to bed? Carson keeps a handle of vodka by his pillow. Or three."

"He got it from you. What's up with your watch, anyway?"

"It tells time. I told him, 'Don't eat the banana muffin, you won't be able to sleep!'

'Dude it's cool. Elephants have bananas to jump? When I woke up this afternoon my liver hurt, so I just started drinking, then it smelled like morning.'

'I see you also have a twenty two, to slow the rate of degradation.' He said I could sleep there on the floor if I didn't want to leave. 'Yeah lemme put my shoes on first. I can't see anything.' I didn't even remember taking them off.

'You put shoes on to go to bed?' Then you texted." Looked over to see us pass the mini golf place. She didn't say anything, in case you're wondering.

Alameda

And it was all your fault not mine ~ Marcus Mumford

"I noticed there wasn't a chair, besides Professor Klurton's, so I sat on the tiled floor. Klurton graduated from Chicago, not the musical, back in the eighties with her doctorate and made a couple books about literarily instigated social revolutions. Said she went there before it was hard to get in. The reason I went to Santa Barbara is I applied to make Antonio's application look better." They only took one of us. "She also writes for *Johns Hopkins Press* every then and now." Carson's class was Ephemera: 1601 - 1902. "Klurton introduced the fourteenth Dalai Lama when he spoke with us our first year, his fourth visit in a century of dialogue. She and her husband went to the same prom with different dates, her first love was teaching. That's what she told us, anyway. Next to me on the floor was an answer key scribbled on the back of a mustard stained napkin, the one Andera was on about. Through the window reflected on her computer screen I saw students out on the grass field bordering South Hall and sleeping someones on the balcony of Career Services, which also adjuncts the field. All this fun in the afternoon, so there I was inside because professors make their office hours during Friday soccer games and wonder why no one shows up. I'd been to office hours twice in my life, once when I was six. It's very beneficial to go a hundred times a week, but if you're conscious when you're in class. They asked how great it is to skip class. 'It's only great to *say* you do. In no particular order, one, you only go twenty times. And two, when you miss something, there's no making it up, so I'm unaware of the origins of the misconception. Costs thousands, for another thing, when you used to go for free. Paying for things is awesome. It's like when you hear, The professor is the class. That definitely may be, but it was even more true before. All these majors to choose from, so you'll also here, What're you gonna do with it? Everyone wanted me to do something empiric, seeing as math is natural. I didn't want any reasons to not like it, so I later inclined to the humanities, where there are more variables. I'm not in to restrictive calculative thinking, although its counter is on same side of the brain.

Like Michael J,' the J stands for Andrew, 'Fox said, Two plus two will always be four whether I do it, or you do it, or anybody else does it. I have to be careful about quoting people and things. I posted, Look for the girl with the sun in her eyes. All that happened was is a girl walked by our window, I didn't know who. Then Brad asked if I had broken up with someone, so I haven't posted a status update since. Anywhich, I entered here ready for Film, first quarter took a seminar where every week industry people talked about how they became all successful and weird.' They all told us, Step one: Don't major in Film."

"Who's they? And what's with the lie that it's better when you wait for something? You know what's awesome? Getting shit right now." The car had satellite radio so Palmer couldn't drown me out with static, but he still wished his burner was able to connect. He turned the volume up for Africa even though he doesn't know the song.

"Some were casting directors. Class always got out early. My main takeaway was they have same approach as you do for assignments - Do I have a script due tomorrow? Oh, it's due to*day*. I'll get started on it. 'Klurton got her first degree in Microbiology,' Mason got his in Track, 'but enough of my naiveté. I'm young for my age, I attended kindergarten a year early.'

'That's illegal now, right?'

'I didn't even know what grade Carson got. The best feedback I've gotten is from Biomedical Ethics, Thompson's strange concept of abortion: A. Nuff said.

'The rest of the times there are just check marks and smiley faces with dimples at the end of each paragraph and then at the end it says *B*. If that makes sense, I don't know what doesn't. It's challenging to excel subjectively, like how many ways you can answer a question that has only one answer. Everyone has the, I don't give grades you earn them speech; a few ace it, a few fail, everyone else is elsewhere. Doesn't make sense. To me, anyway. If on the first day your professor says, Everyone should get an A, you know she's smart. We just like to hear ourselves talk. Some talk a lot and say nothing. A la me. Andera made sure to, even when it had nothing to do with our discussion, like penguin sleeping patterns. Day of our final, falling out of her booty shorts and half a shirt, more than usual, she got up to hand it in, "Thank you *so* much." All wenchy. So she got an A.' Just for profound opinions on studying romances."

"Dude, diatribe. Think we can make it the whole way without stopping for gas? I shoulda told you, I can only go in a two hundred mile radius in this. Which is alright, I have to come back down and pay for all these drugs anyway. It's stupid though, I don't even get to use them."

"What kinda drugs?"

"Dumb shit. It's the group I went to Coachella with. They're so dumb, the last day we had to try and finish everything, there was so much. That's why you don't pace yourself."

"The way you drive we'll have to stop for the hospital. 'Just lazy, purely Socratic. You'll like teachers who tell you things, unless tuition is for peer to peer about something no one read. Honors Program last winter said I had to get my grade point up. Important to stay in, you get to register early and they send you a piece of paper when you graduate that says you're smart. Also you're eligible for more grants. Program makes you take honors units each year, I had no idea how many, by way of an extra class once a week, or however often Thursdays are. If your schedule doesn't allow, you can make a contract with your favorite professor. My schedule always had an unavoidable conflict, like snack time, so I did a contract almost most of the time. Don't know where Klurton went, maybe she was taken away by a tornado. I'm not even supposed to be here, at the beginning of the year I had my first experience crashing classes, like Madonna. More risky than parties, less simple than cars. Dropped two and added three. On the first day fifty unenrolled showed up, double the capacity, with room for only five. All of them except me and one other guy were on the Wait For It list. I didn't know there was a such thing, so I emailed Klurton saying I would like to attend until I either got in or there was officially no more room. "I appreciate your commitment. You're welcome to attend class as long as you want, enrolled or not, but I have to be honest, the chances of a spot opening up for you are vanishingly small." Second day, less than five of the originally fifty showed, so I got in, that's called being tenacious, then there were concerns the course would be cancelled cause we mightn't be enough. First midterm, on the board: Nothing will ever be attempted if all possible objections must first be overcome. Class averaged seventy two. She switched up the motivation for our second: If you do well on this test, Prof Klurton will make you cookies. Class averaged a hundred. Peanut butter chocolate chip. Back to the paper, "Carson, I admire the spunkiness of this argument. You've been able to see past surfaces - something one would admire - into the real complexities of the sister and father dynamics. But, what do you gain by showing that Kate is more favored than we might suppose? How does it illuminate gender and marriage themes? Does it enhance Kate's subversion of Elizabethan roles? Draw a conclusion from your excellent observations." Seemed like A minus maybe, but he referred to him as Will I am. A solid B. Weird thing to quantify, and much easier to go from a C to a B.' "

"How would you know?"

"He needs to think inside the box more. Better, create his own box. When class got them back she made a list of everything they did wrong, and he didn't do any. He invents new ways of getting it wrong." Should've submitted an errata. "Klurton came back with her Semicolons Rock shirt and almost stepped on me. 'Sorry about that, Mister Palona. Halkirk needed an extra chair, let me bring it back.' She did. 'S'asseoir, please. How are you doing? Who were you talking to?' Such a slouch, I stood up to sit down. She has sharp chairs so you don't stay long.

'What? I'm doing good - well. Uh, goodly. Anyway, I'm just wondering if you would look over my paper and if you'd grade it differently, or at least give some feedback so I can produce a good essay for the final.' Worth forty percentury, so a little change would be a lot."

"What if she downgraded it?"

"Wildly consistent in her grading, a just ruler. First day of class: Don't ever start an essay the day before it's due, you won't have enough time. Day of the final: Okay, you have two hours to write all these essays, go! 'Why do you care? *You* know how well you wrote it.'

Skims through all when they are first turned in, so she was at least familiar with what he wrote. Has you put your name on the back, but his was recognizable because I stuck a picture of Dorian Gray right in the middle. 'Photographer must be earned rather than arbitrarily bestowed.' Great start. 'And don't lead with The. Once you force yourself to use another word your work will become stronger and more interesting.' A la Kelly Clarkson. 'Here. When you begin, The unconscious mind became a point of interest no doubt inciting curiosity and previously taboo topics were explored and even encouraged so as to advance common knowledge about what makes people act the way they do - You need to do a better job of framing your topic. Why is this called The Benefits of Global Climate Change?'

'The question is the reason. Shot?' She was looking at the sticker on the flask."

"Kley, I got one for you: *Damn* girl, whoever doesn't believe them scientists has never seen you before, you make the whole earth more hotter."

"So stupid."

"It worked."

"That's the stupid part. 'Take your sunglasses off, please.' Those were half crooked, by half I mean completely, on account of only paying five bucks for them, so I've stopped doing everything on the cheap and stole a nice pair but not the free way. 'If your argument is from analogy, you have a weak argument.'

Very contrived, knew he should have auto tuned it. Intro paragraphs, the point of the rest when you already explained everything is a mystery. 'Yeah, I guess I spread things out instead of saying them all at once.'

No latency, 'How do you mean?' And at that she arrived at her door, the group moved aside. 'Hey Coral. And friends. Let me get your letter, Halkirk wanted to copy it.'

I sat down. 'That's okay, I didn't mean to be late. "I don't know."

"Carson." Looked up from the vegan paper. "Don't you think you should try to *an*swer things?"

"I don't even question things." After a brief perusal, more scrutiny. "What I'd really like to know is why, after I took the time to grade it, now there's a different grade on it."

"Excuse me? Thesis not clear in opening version, eventually emerges. Be careful, a couple points were asserted as fact when they were hypotheses or interpretations that needed to be supported." Cleared her throat. "In some cases you did offer that, using the text effectively." Only six pages, and couldn't be any longer than five, so it didn't take her long to finish. "Your summary is a little telegraphic." Whatever the steampunk that means. "That's not how you spell salute."

"Actually that is how I spell it."

"You don't go into enough detail. Have other professors told you that? You also don't need to answer every question from the prompt, I'd rather see depth than breadth." That whole spiel. He only put in details that were too specific or subtle, so he didn't get any credit. Adding detail makes as much sense as a talking mime when there's a page limit. Like a curve that doesn't add up - math professors always do that.

"So you want a little more editorializing?"

"Some argue commentary is more important than concrete details." '

'With what?'

'Who knows what she was talking about. "Statements presented as facts are tricky, anyone can dispute them. If you ever become an academic, you'll know how true that is. It's hard to have freedom of thought and expression." I kept staring at her wall clock. Everyone knows in the end.

Better to be an academic than become one. "Is that what the good grades did?"

"There are subtleties, but the reason this is not A level is you don't take the next step and say why your argument is important. And your vocabulary is better than what you use here." Everyone is wordier than Carson, except me. "You'd have an A with better language." Then he won't have an A. "Your efforts are too clumsy and obvious. Although you make intriguing points, it's not enough to observe Kate and Whitman share an affinity toward nature. Your argument wanders and is ununified. This is a shame because you bring up insightful - well, observations, anyway. When you discuss Kate positing dominion over nature, where Whitman sees himself as part and parcel, you bring up a point that merits a long essay. Your discussion of animal imagery is also intriguing. Next time use the critical vocabulary you have developed to focus your essay on a point that is supported by specific close reading of the passages you cite."

If you can figure out what his paper was about then that's better than anything I could do. "I see I should have spent more time on analyses." '

'Nature's happy. Is that what it's about?'

'More professing, "It's mostly mechanical. Admired professors don't understand what we're reading, so you're in good company. Unfortunately, again, some statements are too vague and your essay spends too much time on summary." Easy to overlook how bad your posture is until you are right next to someone who has perfected it. "Also, many of your points are too close to restatements of conversations in lecture to constitute valid original claims. Use section as a starting point out of which you extend an original point, this will become your specific thesis and enable you to write a more concise, interesting essay."

"What's the key to staying on topic when there're so many works were talking about?"

"That's a good question." Translation: I don't know, so I'll talk about something irrelevant. "You could improve your transitions - hold on. Hello? This is she." I ignored the rest. 'Good feedback for Carson, but instead I thought about animals, how humans are the only ones to have no awareness."

"You mean that backwards." La Jolla and its affluence shone through the dark.

" 'She has a fishy tank on her desk, hanging above is a picture of an elephant sneezing from a safari near Kanye, Botswana. Meant to ask if she sent it in to *Nat Geo*.' Though we did enjoy looking at your picture, unfortunately it is not a good match for us. 'Elephants have crazy good photographic memories so they always know where to find good friends and recognize long lost food. They also suffer psychological flashbacks and the equivalent of post traumatic stress.'

'We can see that. Do they enjoy swimming that way or would they rather forget things?'

'Take zoology courses. Other animals have no choice. Goldfish, I imagine, always forget their kids. Klurton finished phone talking and asked if I wanted to rewrite, like I would have gone there in the first place otherwise. "I consider that a very good grade, too." How reassuring. When admissions counselors question a B: Don't worry about it, my professor says that's a *very* good grade. We act as there's a contest over who has the most midterms and papers, when the winner is whoever has the least. Everyone thinks they have more work to do than everyone else, and we're all confused.

'I remember what Halkirk said after I finally found her Astrono class, thanks to the model. She was explaining her curves, you only ever hear of a sciencey class curved, and everything, and to not care about raw scores. "One time, on a graduate physics exam, I got a *nine* percent. At first, I was dismayed. But then I realized, not only was it an A, but it was the *high*est grade."

'What's the point of making a test that hard?'

'The story. I and Andera set the curve on her midterm with a ninety nine. Cool gal. Should have gone to her office hours just to talk, but I didn't know any better - they were listed as Whenever and I didn't know what that meant. By then I wanted to expedite our convo, say I was late for golf with the chancellor. How am I supposed to pretend? It's hard to leave. "Well it's almost cinco, and I told friends I'd meet them at Segundos when it opens."

She saw where I was looking. "That's right zero times a day, it's eighty two minutes fast. Remember to edit what's *not* there, then revise. Your grader's right, don't approach it as science where you just list observations. This class is not looking for regurgitation, it's looking for synthesis."

"Right, this helped a lot, even though it seems a bit aloof."

"I don't think that word means what you think it means." Right, *abstract*. "But sometimes really simple concepts are given strange names."

"I know." I didn't, it was just the easiest thing to say. "Thanks for letting me do this, I'll return it in before the month is out."

"You have a couple days, do what you want with it. Just don't take advantage of my generosity." A sign on her wall opposite the elephant: Take every advantage. "Have a nice three day weekend." They're all nice, some are just nicer than others. Klurton gave me a chocolate bar - nothing ventured, something gained. Two servings, which is fitting, those who sink and those who dive.'

She returned again I almost tripped over the chair getting up from the floor. 'Well, here you go, Kleytjen. To get an A in my class may be due to hard work, to get two is just plain lucky.' "

When the conversation stops well be facing our defeat ~ Rivers Cuomo

All year falling asleep I would think about how you meet someone after they've already lived a life. "I don't think you remember my question. I'll ask Sterling about Mason, he's a good judge of character." Sterling's funny, talented, some other third thing, and genuine, but I liked him anyway. I don't think Amie remembered my answer.

"No way, judging is always bad."

"Shut your slandering mouth. What's Stir been up to lately?"

"He cut his hair today."

"He *did*? How short is it?"

"I dunno. Shorter than mine."

"You're such a guy. He doesn't have a girlfriend, does he?"

"Not anymore. Not yet."

His best was better than everyone else's. "What happened to Andera?" Sterling always said Hello to everyone, you know, trail etiquette. Then he started to be nice.

"He felt like he wasn't giving her the proper amount of time. Kind of like Jordyn." He never liked Ms. Butterfield as much as his team.

"He'll never have as much time as he does now. And that wasn't her reason."

She went back to singing. "Why won't you tell me what she said?"

"Oh, you know. She loves em and leaves em." On account of her short attention span. "Mason's, you think you're indecisive, he doubled in Undeclared. He's like licking - clicking Random Article. Brilliant academically. Useless. Don't tell him I told you not to tell him I told you. He thinks he's the best."

"What's wrong with that?"

"He's not. What exactly made you want to ride down here with me?" She's born suspicious.

"Funny thing for me to try to explain. Although when you don't get it it's not funny either. Okay, our house was way up in North County, the one who doesn't mind me showing up unannounced is my sister."

"What's she like?"

What can you say about Grace? "She's half cat. Favorite play is *Fiddler on the Roof*. In January her Drama Club field tripped to see it and she made Ravi and me watch the movie during our spring break. She did that On the Other Hand monologue as part of her audition."

"Also how come you never mentioned why you didn't want a ride back last time?"

How could I forget. "Grace used to get Frank Lloyd Wright and Andrew Lloyd Webber up mixed. She and my parents lived on Stargaze, off of Rotherham and Galaxy, a cul de sac. I don't know how they afford things, must be good at amortization. Except they were renting. When I walked there Sunday in the afternoon, only one car was in the drive way, so either or both or just one - I didn't know who was home. Stucco everywhere. The hound dog next door, Husker, always chasing tail, heard my feet as they touched the ground and barked like crazy. Hadn't been around enough for her to get used to me. She's twelve, only admits to seven. An amicable canine companion."

"I heard the dog days were over. Your street names are so fluffy."

"Soon as I walked inside I knew my parents weren't home. I'm lucky to have them. Still, the next time they see my island view apartment will be the first time, to help move out. Forgot Grace's shirt, again, it was still in my backpack. There were a bunch of open notebooks on her desk upstairs and her binder was all ornate. Her finals are the same week as ours."

"I don't even remember having finals in seventh grade."

"Notes scribbled down. 'Why is Ponyboy's hair so important to him? Cuz it's tuff.' I didn't know that until eighth. 'What are two ways in which we can help save animals? Scientific approach, legal approach.' And an essay, with feedback. 'You made the same mistake as many: you based all three conclusions on one text detail.' Grace walked out of the bathroom all startled.

'Yo, meow. What are you doing in my room?'

'Yo, yo, yo. It's a free house, I can go where I want. You're the reason why I'm here.'

'Fine, it's a free house so I'll go in *your* room.' Already used it as a second closet.

'This house isn't *free*, we have to pay for it. What's your shirt?'

'It says See Ya Latte.' Minty breath wafted over.

'Did you find it?'

'Yeah, who else?'

'Will Smith. How bout your pants?'

'Gauchos, yo.'

'Why is your hair curler on your desk? When are you gonna get your ears pierced?'

'That's not a hair curler, silly head!'

'Hair straightener. Same thing. I'll mail you your shirt so you have it for the last day of school.' Let her keep my sunglasses, she really liked the frames. 'I think they're already bent though.'

'They're fine, your head's just crooked.'

'Well that's a relief, I paid for those.'

'Like, today, Hannah wanted me to ask Lunch Line Guy out for her.' She said, 'I said, Lunch Line Guy, Hannah wants to know if you like her. And he was like, Oh you mean Lunch Line Girl? Then after school we were hanging out in the band room.'

'What does he play? Did you go over to Hannah's on Friday or whenever?'

'Tuba. No, she lives in Park Village.'

'Where's that?'

'A lot of people live there.'

'Oh, that's where it is. Who kept talking to her and then asked her to marry him? That guy sounds awesome.'

'No Kleytjen, don't be like him! You wouldn't understand cause you're not a girl.'

I don't know, you don't have to get lost in Siberia to appreciate warmth. 'What the heck's the difference between -

whatever.' I kept reading her notes.' What's the difference between a geek and a nerd?'

'One is an expert and one's an enthusiast. But it doesn't really matter, sir.'

Her bed skirt hid tons of junk underneath. 'No wonder you lose everything. If I didn't know any better I'd say you came from a messy family.'

She says Language Arts is her worst subject, everything else is a higher A. 'Everyone who does their work is too dumb to write their name on it, and everyone who doesn't do their work is smart enough to go over to the No Name basket before grades are due, take whatever looks good, put their name on it, and turn it in.' Just like Mynor. A class takes on the personality of its best students. 'Friday after school my Spanish Dos teacher saw me and said, Hola Gracie! I said, Hi! Was I supposed to say Hola Profe?' Spanish in middle school, what a concept.

'He's probably gonna expel you now.' She sat down on the corner of her bed.

'He was my teacher the first half of last year too, then he was offered to be a counselor and did that because it paid more or something, but came back to teaching cause he likes it a lot more.' Like the track coach I had, Escanola.

But speaking of Spanish: 'Well we learned a lot in Tres this year. We're practically fluent now. I'll see you next year in Gov or Stats I'm sure,' Antonio Feather signed. We spoke less than two words of Spanish all year. I wish we did have those classes together. After our first test, Psychology, he put all those extra bar code stickers on his shoes. Everyone in a real class asked him which test he took, everyone else asked him where he stole his shoes from."

"How in the world do you remember your yearbooks? All your stories are about friends."

"It's like three directions away from cool, I know. Grace painted, 'He says stuff like, You only do what I tell you to, when I tell you to, and, most importantly, how I tell you to. He's obnoxious like that, but in a good way. He's pretty funny. Today he was like - Hannah, since you're not *in* the hood, would you please re*move* your hood? And whenever he hands out a test he says, This must be old hat for you all. Remember to buy low and sell high.' She works at their student store during lunch. 'Kleytjen, the student store has like *ev*erything.'

Erasers and candy. 'You'll never have to go to the mall again?'

'Probably. Oh and it also started thundering and lightninging on my walk home!'

'Wait when was this? Stop eating your shirt.'

'Monday. So last year, there was this girl in my class - '

'For really real?'

'Kleytjen. Let me finish. There was this girl in my class who ate my eraser and I said, Wow, you're lame. Well, I didn't really say that. I was like, I hope you'll lend me yours. That was in sixth grade camp. Which was in sixth grade.'

They went to the Laguna Mountains for a week, I sent her a card. 'This year is she the one who had her birthday party on stage?'

'No that was - oh, you mean this year?'

'That's why I started my sentence with it.'

'Yep, it was weird but it was cool. The cast and crew party is Thursday.' "

"That's cute but there's no way I could only shop at one place. I actually would stop right now at the Outlets if they were open." She drove down to Camarillo every month to do just that.

"What do you do with your old clothes? 'Sweet sauce.' Grace had to get ready for the eighth and last *Pirates* showing. Our parents went to see it opening night. Her room is at the front of the house so I kept looking out the window just to get a glimpse if they were driving down the street. 'So when are Mom and Dad gonna be back?'

'Ah dunno.'

'Well where are they, the opera? Enzymology convention?'

'Shh. They went to the store.' How fortuitous. They buy nothing, making sure to only get things for the lowest price and use all their time. In their thirst for bargains, their trademark is to get things no one uses just because they are on some clearance sale or they have coupons.

'Oh, okay.' Hadn't talked with them that week. 'How are they anyway?' I started to relax once I knew I had all day.

'They're good. Mommy had to go to the dentist on like Tuesday. Not for a filling, for something big - '

'Like a root canal?'

'Yeah, that's it. So I guess it's good now. She just talked about how expensive it was.' Drives me crazy when they need something for their health and all they talk about is how much it costs. Who the hell cares, it's important. 'Oh yeah. Daddy wants to be sure you talked to Grandpa, not just left a message, but actually talked with him.' He had hip surgery, on his birthday.

'Yep. I did. What about Ravi? Have you heard from him this week?'

'Yeah, kind of.'

'What do you mean *kind* of?'

'Okay, yeah, we did. But it was just for a minute.'

'Probably cause of that new girlfriend. Where's my Rubik's cube?'

She looked all around on her desk. 'Do you need it right this second?'

Judging by my antsyness. 'Yep.'

'Are you *sure* it's in my room?'

'First of all, I don't know where else it would be, and second of all, there's no where else it would be that I know of.'

'Well it isn't easy for me to find. It's so squarular,' her voice trailed off as she peaked under the bed skirt.

'In the world? You could just clean your room one of these years.'

It's very much Chase's side of the room. Times two. 'Stawp it. Here. Circles are better.' I shook my head so she kept the hula hoop to herself. She's terrific at it, with all her muscle memory."

I am 100 percent certain our waitress last year is Anthony's sister. I'm sure of it

It wasn't. I texted Palmer back asking what party he was at and then put it in my pocket. "Is a similar skill in you, like whistling?"

"Those are similar? Confused about how, too. 'Grace, how do you hula hoop so well?'

'What do you mean *how*? You just do! Use your hips.'

One of the shirts on her floor was for All Star Weekend or Super Nacho or Transit of Venus. Whoever they are, they're super good. 'If they're *that* good, how come nobody's heard of them?'

'I've heard of them.'

'There're way more who have not heard of them.' "

"That's true of everything."

"Yeah, so it's true. 'And Hannah went to their show here a few months ago. Their music just keeps getting better.'

'Don't they only have one album?'

'It gets better every time I listen to it.'

'Coolisterevenaroony.' First time I heard the clock on her wall ticking. We went down to the kitchen, fun picture of her at Sea World on the fridge. 'Apple sauce!'

'You an apple - you want an apple?'

'Think I'll just have some juice,' pulled the handle and out poured lukecold air.

'Hey, Chuck, wanna go to Bunny Park? Come along, child.' Then giggled like crazy. She knows when she's funny."

"Who does she get it from?"

"My grandpa says he'd be a comedian if I were his audience. Every time I tell him I'm going somewhere he makes me report back about all the girls I met. So we didn't see them that Connecticut winter and we moved over summer. Despite the distance, the offer from the G units still stands: If there's anything we can do for you, let us know." All the time. "Last time I was at their house they and my cousin Motley had me watch *The Seven Year Itch*. I was given a play by play, which I enjoyed, but our grandma: 'It's kinda nice when Motley's here, you don't even have to watch the movie.' Motley's in that picture Mynor likes, with champagne hair. Had to wait for her before we started. 'She said she wanted to stop by so she can see Kleytjen.'

'Why would she wanna do that?' That's what I mean. Once we were able to find the disc we also watched *My Week With Marilyn*, one that passes the Bechdel Test. 'Where did we put it?'

'It might still be out the car.' No extra words, they always go down the basement or out the lake. And they keep movies in their car. Antonio purportedly didn't cry during *The Notebook* so an usher berated him." She elbowed me to get back on track. "Just so you know, Bunny Park is a dog park on Sand Canyon where we see bunnies hanging around, eating, minding their own business, hiding in really obvious places next to pine cones. There's a garden of chrysanthemums too. Like a meadow, if you need to picture yourself in it. Wanted to go to *Penzance*, or England, again. I at least wanted to pay for a ticket. Had nothing else to do and my feet told me they were tired. We're soothed by perpetual motion. 'Those are your shoes? That's hamsta!' Grace only notices contrast. 'You are a dolphin after all, remember.' "

"Like Alameda Park?"

"Precisely the opposite, there's no sand. 'Oh yeah, look at this, Grace.' Held out my phone.

'Duckies! Teehee! Or are those goslings? Did you see that picture of the Valentine Bunny?'

'Yep, it's a good one.'

'Let's call Ravi.' Speed dial two, twelve seconds of ringing.

'Hey what's up!'

'Howdy. It's both of us. Are you gonna show us what Central Park looks like?'

'I will. I like the ones you sent, Kleytjen, I showed them to my director. He said photography isn't about finding something amazing and capturing it, it's about taking anything and making it look amazing.' Wonder if he would have told me that any day or if we happened to call at the right time."

"I haven't used the bathroom in a long time."

"Same. 'So what were you telling me about your classes, Grace? Can't you get all As?'

'Oh I'm sure I can, I just haven't done it yet.'

'You should get a card for Motley. Or else I could do it.'

'Mom and Dad have one sitting on the counter. Remember when I always thought Grandpa was in the mob? As a cover for his real job.' So much for being secretive, like your best friend's password. 'I still think that. When are we gonna see you next?'

'Couple weeks. When I get paid I'll come down. I'll talk to both of you when you're done with finals.'

'Hasta later.' I asked Grace when she had to walk to schoolio.

'Soon.' Whenever that is. 'Oh, oh, oh. Daddy says we might move again.' It's funny because it's true. 'But he doesn't want me to tell - '

'Are you kidding? They didn't think it would be worth mentioning?' So remiss."

"No one said a living situation is fixity."

"I just don't want her to switch schools and end up like everyone's favorite, Torrey. Didn't know about her graduation party, conspicuously absent from her own awards ceremony, too occupied being awesome. She was just afraid of not winning and being stuck as a duck sitting there, like when the biggest moment of your life doesn't happen. I had to remind Grace. 'She did a hundred ninety two hours of community service a week, played eleven sports, captained three of them, invented another, had a six point oh, and taught piano lessons on the side.' Arguably the fifth best Tenaya.

'Todos nuevo to me.' She picked up a pinecone. 'That's like, crazy. By *like* I mean is.'

'What do you mean by *is*, yo? I want you to stay where you are here unless you're forced out. That's all.' Should be familiar with the concept. 'Don't let Mom and Dad tell you they don't have a choice. Do you have enough hours now after you helped at Wellness Day or whatever the world?'

'Yes. But not because of that.' Oh, check this:

I just signed up Amie to get called by Associated Students about her interest in hunger, oceans, and textbooks. Also she posted a new pic. You can tell it's her because you can't tell who it is.

"Funny part is Mynor wasn't joking. I do like the picture you have now."

"Because you took it?"

"I like how the dude studied this quarter too, didn't make it past any first lecture. Second one: Wait, I've been here before. Ups and leaves. At least that's what you told me."

"Wasn't me. Jordy had my phone."

"I see. So Grace wasn't worried about moving and asked about school, something she never does when I call. 'Are you going to the beach tomorrow? *I* wanna go to a school with a beach.' She in her infinite wisdom imagines I go to the beach everyday and hang out with surfing dogs. 'We went to Del Mar last weekend but there was so much too much seaweed everywhere.'

'Was it gnarly?'

'Was it *what*?'

'How was it?'

'Pretty good. I didn't see any sea turtles or sea stars or sea horses or sea monkeys or sea bears or conch shells, but we might go to a beach that has them. We did go to the one that has different kinds of fishies. Also the one that has coral and clams and crabs! It'll be better over summer when I go with my friends and look for elephant seals.'

'Sounds bueno.'

'So! Last week me and Hannah prank called everyone on her phone. Twice. That was a little excessive.' Not excessive enough. 'When we called her parents it didn't work out, but it was a great idea.'

'Did you think it would? Isn't that the definition of a bad idea? Ideas need to be good in reality.'

'It was still the best idea at the time.'

'Sounds like it was the only idea you had.'

'Why does it matter what word I used? It's like when Daddy says, Don't break it if you can't fix it, or, I didn't say you were, I said you were acting like one,' in that voice and everything. 'Wait is Daddy a physician or a physicist?'

'Why do you ask what you already know the answer to?'

'To make sure. You ask too many questions.' It's funny cause it's not true. The way our dad got his job is *The Enzyme Factor*. Made him like books again even though it's a shot for shot remake of *That Other One*, like a new used car.

'Are you sure?' She is in every way, then asked my favorite question. 'I don't know what I wanna do when I grow up.' "

"That's why you haven't."

" 'Grandma always asks me if I know what I wanna do. She's seventy five,' acts like eighty is really young, 'and I don't know if *she*'s figured out what she wants to do.' Didn't look like this was satisfactory. 'I won't give one of those change the world answers, only geology does that. What we can do is picture the world differently, so I'll go for that. I just don't care about the difference between well intended amateurs and professionals.' "

"One follows a line of conduct and ethical standards, the other is a professional."

" 'Intering - interesting. But what are your plans? Take pictures for surfers?'

'I dunno Grace, retire in Hawaii maybe. Then you could road trip whenever you wanna visit!'

'There's just one problem with that idea. You have to be good enough to retire. *You* might just quit. Your nose!' It runs like a river.

'It's a free country and I'm allowed to have my nose bleed whenever I don't want it to.'

'Stop laughing. It's not even funny.' It really started to flow and I don't mind bleeding. No tissues in my pockets, money from my wallet sufficed.

'I don't know, it just is. It's not like it's a big deal. Besides, as Alan Alda said, When - '

'I don't even know who that *is*. You think everything's funny.' I've broken it five times." Second was while moving our new couch so we had to get another new one thanks to the blood stains. First time a bee landed on my nose, Ravi smacked it, crunch, knocked out a tooth, the bee fell and stung me on the tongue. "Sometimes breathing through my nose is complicated.

'Yeah right, *ev*erything?'

'Okay, what's one thing you don't think is funny at all?'

We were walking by the oak tree on the outskirt of the park. 'Okay, sí. Bark. Bark isn't funny.'

I know. It is. 'No, for real.' So bark is fake. 'Come on, something that's not funny to you.'

'Well what do you want me to do? Talk about broken bones and people who go to war and don't come back? You're gonna scare away all the bunnies.' She was quiet for a minute, her second nature. It's a Coral thing. 'Besides, it's not like I make funny things up. They happen.' Before she agreed or disagreed I all of a sudden got this from a creatively inspiring teacher:

Alrighty... It's 1:01. ¿Donde esta? I promised my gal smoothies... :)

"Sent her, Mrs. Kabiting, an email on Friday explaining I'd be in the area and if she wanted to meet up for something or smoothies on Sunday just after one. Didn't know where in the world I would be at that time."

Patricia slowed down as we started up Conejo Grade. "Where do smoothies rank on Palmer's scale?"

"Oh yeah, I'll get to that. Girls just wanna have lunch. I knew if I told her anything less exact she would flake with a convenient excuse, but with an exact time, even three in the mañana, she says yes. I wasn't able to check my email since."

"You still didn't have a smart phone or any of those dumb things. How close are we?"

"We're almost a quarter of the way there. It's always funny when people say something like, I'll be the last one to ever get a new phone. No you won't. My parents said when I upgraded it costs them more until they upgrade, which will in turn cost more."

"That's not even true."

"Exactly. I said I'd pay for it too. Anywhere, I frightfully forgot that we might meet up with everything that had happened between and within the days. Friday felt like months ago. As Antonio always says, I spent a month in Brooklyn one night."

"If you remember everything, how do you determine what matters?"

"It all matters. In my haste I began to run back to the house. After ten inches Grace stopped holding the pinecone and started hollering that she couldn't keep up, she's not the fastest person in the world. 'What are you, eleven?' I slowed down." Now when I fall asleep I think about how many lives are yet to happen to someone.

Alameda

With every double she sank ~ Florence Welch

"You know what I tripped out to last night? How loud it is. I was in Julian. That place is quiet." Without even using. Palmer turned up the volume more, "Check this shit out, dude doesn't even have an album yet. And he takes a whole bunch of drugs that take away all emotion."

"I gotta start again. 'We don't understand what others go through, we only say we do to show empathy, so I wondered if it were right to cut my visit short while walking my feet down the hall.' Weird definition of down. 'Right from my brain. I just wanted to get out of Klurton's office before our conversation devolved into what porous plans the weekend had for me and what my favorite type of tree is.' Douglas fir. 'We dined at six, or sometime between noon and midnight. Jordyn texted the game was over so I biked to the other side of the lagoon, Village de Zeigarn, same place as sophomore year. Upperclasswomen and upperclassmen predominantly, freshies get the other other side. When you look at aerial pictures on the eighth floor, by the model, you'll see it was a parking lot until three years ago when a sister school discovered the more persons, the more housing you need. Soon as I pedaled Westminster Quarters did its thing, I often hear them when I'm nowhere near campus.' Like, Utah."

"I put the good in Carlsbad." Still tripping out, it seemed. He'd've stopped to enjoy Legoland if he saw the sign. "What is that thing?"

"Those things? Power plant. The thing next to it's the ocean. As I rode by the Thunderdome a few were too smart to look for oncoming traffic before crossing the path and a few others forgot smoking is banned, so I had to maneuver around." Not guilty by reason of forgetting. "Every time I pass by the arena, instead of basketball and double overtime with Nevada, I think of last June when a girl was playing Do You Remember on her acoustic while skateboarding by. Rainy days are the most memorable." I always have a song stuck in my head, I lapse to lyrics without even realizing. " 'Music Theory I should have taken, rumor has it the instructor knows karate and gave more lessons on that than anything. Anyway, Segundos is one of the two best places to ever eat. A lot like to suggest the food isn't perfect because there's a new head chef so now it's just super awesome and then reduce their meal plan to starve half the week since they don't cook. And a lot like it more than I do, you get as much as you want - you get pizza every meal if you want. Most importantly, you get a salad every meal. More importantly, you get ice cream every meal. Family dinners are the best.' You could have every meal for free."

"Can you explain that a little more?" He opened the passenger window.

"Sure, it's the one with the colorful chairs, where Jack Johnson actually wrote that Bubble song, but it doesn't rhyme, so he changed it. I told them, 'I lived right over there, honors building, makes you smarter. Bathrooms are nice, one for every room. Now I live on the street where he wrote Taylor. Parked my bike and walked upstairs, basking in the sun, third floor, top shelf. Whenever anyone saw our room they told us how special it is, that it's the only time we're ever going to live with an ocean view. The halls are like spice and sugar, seeing coeds when you walk down the stairs, even when they're just taking out their trash or filling up their water bottle or sleeping on the floor.' The alternative is a private school where when you're caught thinking about one you get put on probation, remember? 'Likewise, a double major is much better than one, even if you have to squeeze it all into your last three quarters. Too sedentary to have your own room.' I would sign up for a triple. 'One of the reasons to stay on campus another year, a lot of friends have been out there all year and still don't even know their neighbors. No one understands that. Our Ballroom Dance instructor tells everyone the way to have a successful life is to meet people.' Andera took that class every quarter. 'In the dorms, as long as you're awake and alive you get to know all your neighbors. But if you really want to, most fit twenty into their lease for six, so at least that's fun.' "

"That's illegal for sure."

“That’s how you know it happens. ‘You all made an excellent choice. I’ll be around if you ever have more questions.’ ”

“I was so happy when Torrey told me she wanted to move in. And I’m much happier now that I don’t need that.”

“You don't even like her. You just don't like losing. Double or nothing, I say we make it there by sunrise.”

“Talk for hours, just go ahead now.” He does quotes now.

“If you say so. Don’t always like the skin I’m in, like at parties. After I got back from the worst one I can remember, ‘You were gone? No I noticed, I was just in your room. Where you been?’ Where else would Mynor Pritts be?

‘Norman’s birthday, like I told everyone.’

‘You *par*tied?’

‘Yes I was there too. Might not look like it, but I pre partied, I middle partied, I after - ’

‘Smells like it, thanks for letting me keep my money. I went to the free bowling thing with the soc club.’ The beer club. ‘They weren’t sociable. You want me to tell you how I did? Okay, I’m gonna tell you anyway.’ Probably better than three hundred. ‘I met someone. You know.’

‘Huh? You don’t just *meet* someone when you - ’

‘You should’ve seen her. Trust.’ Always looking. ‘You gonna do the homework tonight?’

‘Do you think I’m that dumb? Don’t answer that.’

‘Movie date with the roommate?’

‘Nope, Sandy Eggo. I’d like to do our assignment before it’s due.’

‘Weird. You’re leaving now? It’s *late*, man.’

‘Amie just found out she’s able to.’ This made him more animated.

‘Wait. What. Who? Oh, I see. She’s your type, huh? Crack that egg.’

No one ever dates their type. ‘You’re my type.’ ”

“My type is *hot*, so obviously you’re wrong.”

"Sure, everything about her is cute, her slightly crooked nose and all that brown eyed girl stuff. 'Aw yeah, I see.'

Well, sort of midnight blue for one. 'Here, this's what she just sent: Happy text. What's that supposed to mean?'

'Dude, I don't speak girl. I'll find the book when I see it.' Right next to Chase's collection of postcards, only thing he's ever collected aside from girls' numbers. Should have bought my own book, I thought."

"You have a very intricate thought process."

"Obviously. 'Here ya go. I still don't know what inspires you to get your work done.' It's easy to mistake motivation for inspiration. Anyone can watch *Rocky*. 'Thanks a lot, really appreciate it. I'll try not to sell it or anything.' Another door opened to our powwow. 'Andera, you're just in time for our crisis!' She walked out holding a pen that records your lectures and does your homework.

'Crisis? What Crisis?'

'Mynor's in a good mood. Also we have some questions for you.' Turned back. 'She thinks it's weird that we have questions. I find that questionable.'

'Whatever, Kleytjen, you're always drunk. I'm excited I might sleep today. Even at night.'

'What you mean?'

Second floor bagpipe practice. 'The past few nights they were really going at it. It was pretty pedestrian.'

'I'd cheer em on. Kley was wondering what's up with the dude in your class who keeps talking to you.'

'Oh, it's a long story. Okay, let me tell you all of it. He's *lit*erally forty. He's thirty nine!' Her hands do the talking.

'He's living the dream. You ready to graduate?'

'God, thank God. You guys have like every class together, right?'

'Yeah it's always either me and this guy or me and Amie. You should go with.'

'Amie's kinda weird, though.'

'She means she doesn't like her,' Mynor explained.

'If you gave her any thought you probably would.' Highest cognition of everyone I know. For our Development final last December, her study guide: Know your shit. Best grade."

"When intellect is dominant, it's easy to miss beauty."

"Not if you're a sapio."

"Nah. Beauty's objective."

" 'Forget about it.' Forgetting disguised as remembering. They're the complete opposite of each other, if not more. Amie insinuated Andera's dumb."

"I tell people that outright all the time."

"Which is way better. 'Well that was a waste of time.' Like a good show.

'Any way, we're about to hit up the parties. Me and Chase. Andera, what say you?'

'Ici, vous allez.'

We pardoned her as she went back to her room. Mynor all ready to roll, 'Let's go, baby.' "

"He the one who organized Relay for Life?"

"Last year, not this year. 'Aw, he's still sleeping. Chase is my rock.' Also one of Marie down the hall's spring flings.

Chase woke up like he was never asleep, popped the question, 'You take your medicine yet?'

'Pass me that bottle of big whiskey and I will. Well, looks like I'm going and you're going. I'm gonna text you tomorrow,' Mynor assured me. 'It's gonna be good. Or next year.' He and Chase turned around halfway out the door. 'Oh, Kleytjen. Jordyn's friend asked for your number. We told her you're a great bowler. Apparently she really wants to see you.'

'So we gave her Sterling's.' Yep. These are my friends. Knew I didn't need to bring the assignment: Read the whole history of the world in one night. It only reminded me what I needed to do. I was mainly deciding if I should get back for Andera's biggest show of the year that Monday, Polynesian Dance Club. Tika tonu. Brandon Baker started it. Should have just brought a coloring book."

"Wasn't that tonight?"

"Yeah, they wanted a better turnout than last year."

"I thought it was sold out."

"It was. Written on our door in girl handwriting was, You are so fly, I assumed in reference to Sterling, also assumed Mynor wrote it when he left the second time. Lot of handwritten typos underneath it too, asking to write a song about him. Good thing I packed everything up earlier.

"When did he leave the first time?"

"Ah, Mynor got to the room after I did to officially start Memorial weekend. 'Ay wassup homie?' We're like homies or something."

"When in the *hell* is Memorial Day?"

"Are you serious? Let me finish, I haven't even started. 'Where's the culmination of a series of virtues?' Instead of just saying his name.

Try to walk away and I mumble ~ Macy Gray

"As it happened, I took my dad's car for my juicy journey. Didn't move the mirrors. First I changed shirts so as to not be running around with red stains anymore. He drives a twelve year old silvery Accord, too monochromatic. No choice in all my rapidity. Kabiting stayed up late to help me, and Ravi before me, with personal statements when we applied to Califragilistic schools. I dallied until midnight like an idiot, then emailed her my rough draft, embarrassing as it was."

"No choice whatsoever. What's her girl's name?"

"Jane. 'Start out stronger. Draw me in. Be willing to let your Kleytjen show. Risk more. You're getting all rigid because it's an essay, but you should be creative. I'm imagining you as the voice over on *The Sandlot* or something: "You'd think after attending nine schools across three states before finishing eighth grade, a kid would give up on getting involved. Mesa, with miniature golf courses the only outlet for teens, is a rather uneventful place." But *you* have to come up with this. I know you can do this with wit because I've seen it before. Take it as fun. Reveal how your world has shaped your aspirations, but do not compromise your voice.' "

"Interesting Mickey Evans reference. How did you break your nose?"

"Sneezing attack, hit by pitch, trying to surf - slipped and fell onto a shark." After the fifth I stopped getting mad. After the fourth I stopped putting it back into place. "Now it only hurts when I sneeze laugh when it's raining. All I know is that to me she's a huge help, although I didn't give myself enough time to photoshop it and make it something august or even save the thing from being terrible. Ended on a tangent. I'm blah at aggrandizement, so she also had to tell me, 'It's okay to be proud of your accomplishments. Actually, you should be.' "

"You're not?"

"No, I am. The first thing I wrote for her class I did very poorly. 'Change everything. You're good at disputing other people's arguments, but how about making one of your own? It's easy, and if you don't know how, you'll learn.' Teacher contributions defy quantification. My favorite thing Kabiting said to our class: Don't ask me how I discovered this because I really can't remember, but I'm pretty good at clucking like a chicken. Best thing she said to me: Kleytjen, it has been rewarding reviewing your work, which has consistently improved with each assignment.

"That's back when I wanted to be a teacher. Not even Escanola inspired that: I was a bad student, and I'm not gonna support anyone else who is."

"So you ditched your sis for her."

"Like Ashton Kutcher said, It's easy to talk about the right thing to do when it's not your life. I felt weird leaving, no one would be home to tell our parents anything about taken without owner's consent. Since she really didn't want me to take the car, I left a sticky note on the garage door explaining everything: Grace said it's cool to take the car."

"Could have sent them an elaborate text." Moved her pony tail from left shoulder to right.

"Their phones are even dumber than mine, they're holding out to sell them to a museum. They wait until every last atom of cereal is gone before they even consider buying more, always acting as if their income is two dollars. Since it's not, it comes across as plain greedy. That's the weird thing, their new jobs haven't changed anything. Haven't changed the way they think about things. Haven't changed the way they do things. Haven't changed one single thing, so they might as well go back to - "

"Isn't it crazy how small phones used to be? Your parents care a lot, they're just not good communicators."

"That's a bad thing to be bad at." I paused to hydrate from the water bottle in my backpack and enjoyed the silence for a minute.

Amie waited another minute and then participated. "On my sixth birthday, my mom and brother were out getting a cake. My dad and I missed the ice cream truck when it stopped near our house because he was cleaning the pool or whatever, so he decided to drive me around and we found it a dozen streets over. Those are the things I choose to remember."

"Well. What's obviously true is they thought the same things about their parents. Also true that they were awesome when they were kids. As long as Grace don't pay no mind she won't internalize any of their nonsense, she had plans to waltz to school with Hannah. I walked to the front door and she just stood there standing by the stairs, shoelaces untied. 'You have to get going too, right?'

'Yeah I'm going right now.' She has a weird definition of *now*. Broad constructionist. 'Don't walk on the grass. Happy Sunday!'

'You know it! Happy Put A Pillow On Your Fridge Day! I'll see you in a couple weeks. Unbreak a leg.' " Amie takes an annual Disneyland trip to celebrate acing finals and the year before the person in front of her on Splash Mountain broke their leg getting out of the ride. "Are you and Jordyn leaving on Thursday or Friday?" Then I saw the time.

Half a Happy Birthday, go hug a cake!

"Yes. Who are you texting?"

"It's Jordy's other birthday now. I still say we make it there by sunrise. Which one?"

"Thursdee. Why?"

"I'm going with." Thought maybe I'd go there to study for my Friday final.

"Wait do you really want to go? I'll have to check with everyone but it's probably fine." Whoever that is. "It's super expensive, though."

"Not spending money is small consolation for not living."

Thanks, I think I'll have another! Congrats on the first thing you've sent that woke me up and did not send me into a flying rage!!

"Oh, that reminds me. Can you hand me my wallet from my purse? Don't look at my license picture, it was windy that day."

"No worries, I've already put copies out on the black market. Wanna go on a run when we get back? Or is your wrist still injured? Is that a - fine. How was that Gary Small lecture last Tuesday?"

"I went to the gym instead."

"Why did you do that? You talked about going all month."

"So now you're mad? Why do you always do the same run if all you care about is variety?"

"What are you talking about? The beach is always different. We're still going to see Bill Nye, right? You promised. There's gonna be free food." Every meal for free, it's a real thing.

"More of a casual agreement." Feels Like We Only Go Backwards now finished. Then it clicked. I removed my phone from my pocket again.

"I just want you to go, it'll be fun. Plus, Mynor is famously fickle about these things."

She cut this girl in a Tesla off as we rounded Thousand Oaks and were told how far away Santa Monica was. "Oh noes!" She'll do it again. "Why are there so many Santas in California? I don't think we're that holy."

"Because the more the más. And there's a law of the universe that says everything is connected."

"And what law is that?"

"What d'you mean? It doesn't need a name, it's a fact." She just laughed at me. "Really, what do you want me to say?" Apparently nothing, except for Cheesebro Road in Agoura Hills, and Topanga Canyon, those always attract comments, so I just thought about how long it took to pave the whole highway. "Your backpack's ringing. I think it's your phone."

"Can you hand it to me? Oh, it's my dad."

It stopped ringing so she took to typing. "Are you really? I'll do it."

"It's okay, I just can't use it as a floatation device."

"Seriously, let me take it."

"Calm down." Tossed it at my lap. "Just say I'm only halfway there."

"That's all? When's your final final?"

"Wednesday. Did Marie tell you she already had one and doesn't have any next week?" I figured the only reason not to send it was because there might not be a response, and that wasn't a good enough reason.

It's Surf's Up.

At that point I noticed the shaking of the body when moving at that velocity. "Who when? I feel like you're trying to talk with me, but I don't know what you're saying."

"I didn't know what to say to that either! Was it worth it, visiting your teacher?" I was still staring at my phone so she pressed ahead. "What's the best thing about our house?"

"It has a revolving door. Also you and the roomies have full conversations without words."

"I'm gonna need to get your key back."

"I thought it was an extra one. When do you implement your grad school plan exactly?"

"How bout you go first? You never tell me about your life." My bad.

"I'm getting there. So as I said, I took my dad's car. Ignition has a key instead of a button."

"Very intimate." Those who have phones that save every single text and us who had ones with only enough memory to keep the best.

Alameda

You dont know how lucky you are ~ Chris Martin

"No one can put you in a good mood like Sterling. 'I dunno. Probably down at the beach or something.' Mynor put the book I was staring at back on my desk.

'With some girl. He's a *player*.' Always asks Sterling for advice on how to get girly action. He was single and Mynor's the one with a girlfriend. 'Once he had four Emilys at once, took em all to the same movie.' "

"Yeah, why would you ask *him*?"

"He's objective."

"Doesn't mean he gives good advice. It's so weird, you're nostalgic for the recent."

Palmer always makes eye contact when he speaks, so the Corvette took up two lanes. "Ignore me, pay attention. 'He's not like that.'

Mynor was barely listening, so I stopped looking at him, hearing myself talk and him smell things on Sterling's desk. Always the same, smelling shoes. 'Oh that's right, not a movie, he took em golfing or something. Trust, dude, trust.' Then he unclosed one of the drawers and saw a condom mixed in with pens and pencils. 'See!' Incontrovertible.

'That's been there all year. See?'

'He has a kid? Damn.' Opened up Sterling's snowy leopard laptop, presumably to leave him a letter or a note or a message or all three. 'I don't see a question mark on this keyboard. I guess Sterling knows everything.' He did see a photo of him and his sister when she graduated. She's a year younger. 'What the hell? Sterling doesn't look happy in this picture. The girl does. She's poppin, huh? Dude, even his laptop case is gold. What an alchemist.' A compliment to alchemists. 'How come you didn't call me back last night?'

'I didn't know you had a phone. Hey, you wanna open his printer? It'll remind him he needs to get more ink, like an octopus, he bought the wrong kind yesterday. Might as well do nothing while you're doing something.'

'I'm just gonna chill in your chair.' In the middle of the room, Sterling used a yoga ball instead of the chair that came with the room and I did too, he told me to. We put his in Mynor's room and then they got fined for having too many chairs. Only our RA cared we took the screens out the windows.

'You gonna go to the alumni game Sunday?'

'Are you kidding? It's gonna *pour*. Who won today? Us? I'm trying hard as possible not to spoil anything.'

Mynor knew I hadn't missed a game in three years. 'There are more important things than going to every game. When I figure out what they are, I'll let you know.' Blank stare. 'I don't know, office hours. It was tied at half.'

'What the hell? You *ser*ious? Will you ever win?' Chair done, he walked over to me, as routine. 'Dude, how come your desk is so clean?'

'It's much easier to find things.'

'Easier than what? You don't like the spirit of adventure.' All intrepid. Picked up a picture of me with my cousins. You can tell there were two photographers, half of us were looking away. 'Daamn. How old's she again?'

'Same as us. You already know though. You also know she has a boyfriend.' Motley, in every picture of her she's wearing a cast, left arm for that one. Last year she injured her knee while brushing her shoulder length hair. Trestles looks so clear," but not enough red moon for a picture.

"Could be worse. She could be single. Y'all have the same last name? Where'd you say she's from, Alabama?"

"Rhode Island."

"Maryland? Close enough. Too bad for you looks aren't genetic."

"Weird definition of *close*. 'Damn right she does. In all her gimpiness.' Mynor exchanged the picture for my sunglasses. 'You just get these? How much?'

'Five even.' Still had money from Christmas. I don't like buying things."

"You like buying things, you just don't like paying for them." He glanced down at the dashboard but not the speedometer. "Dude I like how you don't have your seatbelt on."

"I do. That light just means the airbags won't work or something. 'Damn, you're loaded.' Checked himself out in the mirror on the inside of our closet door. 'Why don't you get some nice ones? Have your parents pay for em.'

'They'll never pay that.'

'Of course they will, you just gotta explain it correctly: Save so you'll be rich forever, spend so you'll be rich today.' You're only rich forever once. He went back to the laptop. 'Here, check these ones out. Oh, is there a more expensive one? Ah, these would look good on a dog. I look fresh, huh?' He did, then grabbed the book. 'You're still not finished with this? Learn how to *read*, man. Or get the club remix. Dude, I might go the whole day without napping.' Never have time to take naps in school, never have any need to when not."

"That ain't no good. Sleep solves everything."

"We who are awake take care of everything and then it looks like that to you."

"As I said, sleep solves everything."

" 'Crazy. You might go to bed before tomorrow, too.'

'Yeah, that three.' His phone started moving then fell off my desk.

'You gonna answer that?'

'That's just the bank, they keep calling for the same thing, so I ignore it.'

'Which is what?'

'They say I owe em money. Let's improve the environment.' Mynor started up Sterling's speakers, same ones I bought last month, with Everyone's Gotta Learn Sometime. After a few listens you realize it only has five words. He lets you use everything, like the smartwatch he was borrowing from his great grandmother. She remarried that spring. Is it eavesdropping when Sterling puts everyone on speaker? She makes a terrific enchilada. Anyway, I sent a textual message to Marie since she's a friend of ours."

"*Now* it starts to get interesting."

"Nope. I said, That song you were asking about is by The September Sessions Band. Speaking of which, wanna go to the store today? Or at least get married?

Not today. I thought I'd be a good student except I don't think that entails leaving ten more pages of my paper to the literal last minute.

"The week before we were gonna see *One Day*, until the grocer told us she didn't like the ending, leaving our plans up in the air. Marie decided not to transfer to Lost Angeles cause she didn't wanna go to a place where nothing happens some weekends, whatever that means. Her favorite thing there would've been Paleontology, Greg Graffin teaches it. 'Should I go to that lecture next week?' "

"It means everyone here sits in traffic all day so once they get home they don't go back out. For you everything is two seconds away."

"Some science guy visited the Wednesday after. 'You made that decision a week ago, I don't know why you're still thinking about it. There's gonna be free food.' You could have every meal for free. Do I know who you saw tonight?"

"She took the best picture ever. You do know her, but you don't know who it is."

"She. You want me to guess?"

"No, you're unusually bad at guessing. That's why you still haven't figured out that movie." Turned away from the ocean and at the exit for Dana Point we sidetracked, Palmer said he didn't eat anything all day.

"But I did. 'You know I have no life.'

'Your life is school, that's so much better than anything else. What are you doing over summer?'

'That's what I'm saying, it's gonna be boring. It's just gonna be me and boo hanging out. She's the only one I got. Sick huh?' Weird definition of *sick*. 'She's got a job this summer, now we can afford water. What did you get last quarter again?'

'Two A minuses, two B pluses. How boring is that? I need a three seven five to stay in Honors, or graduate with it or whatever.'

'You're in the program and you don't know the difference? They *bet*ter drop you. Don't worry about it, I still want you to be my editor. Or Valentine, either one.'

'You did better than that, yes?'

'Yeah, I had my best quarter, three As and one minus. I'll get you tacos again or something and you can put it on your resumeh.' Most important thing of all time, his simply includes the parties he's thrown. 'You know what I mean?' I knew what he meant. Gobbled some sponge candy sitting on the ball. 'That was yours, right?' My head shook. 'Oh, snap crackle!'

'Tell him I took it.' Palmer, hey. Check us in when we get there." Instead of just coasting down the ramp, we hit the intersection still going 90 and eased into a left turn toward the Marine Institute.

"Why would I do that?"

"This new phone doesn't do what I want it to. You already know that. Did you get the extra insurance on this thing?"

"No I mean *why*. We're just going to a drive thru, it's not like we can go in anywhere. I'm on the mediterranean diet anyway."

"That sign literally says Always Open."

"Fuck Denny's. Remember how I went there after prom? I don't know. I just want to do a drive thru. Everything is smarter than you."

"Well that's good. I got a pick up line for you: Let's go shopping."

"That one actually works. When's your picture? Newspapers aren't declining due to digitization, they're declining cause there's no more news. I was up for thirty hours yesterday."

"I've missed your time lapses. It was published yesterday."

"I miss me too. You notice how everyone has an Uncle Mike? I have two and I don't even have an uncle." We stopped at the first place he saw, ordered four tacos, three burritos, two chicken sandwiches, one hot sauce box from a half asleep employee who wasn't sure the diameter of the tacos. I wasn't sure why Palmer asked. "Why is this shit taking so long?"

"You have six uncles. How are you alive?"

"I survive on pure rage." Whatever that is. Our steamy food and an orange bowl was handed though Palmer's window.

"You confuse hunger with anger."

"I can survive off either one. Let's post up here." In the drive thru, no one was behind us. I wanted to stretch my legs but the child locks were on or something. "This is a lot of sour cream. I like that she didn't ask me how I am today cause that's always, like it's okay but it's like, you know they don't *want* to know how you fucking are and then I feel bad just saying, Good good can I have a burrito? But then I'm always like, How are you, and you know they don't give a fuck about me asking them and then they have to say, Thank you, and I say, You're welcome now can I have burritos? You know, it's like a fake thing, a social interaction created by corporate America, it's awkward." And with that the tacos were gone. "You confuse frame rate with speed. And you're still thinking about goldfish all wrong. Don't get any crumbs in the seat. The bigger the pond, the bigger the memory. You know who would give anything to be human? Elephants. So who's your crush?" Goldfish are people too, but elephants laugh.

"You do know her but you don't - you trivialize everything."

"Hell yeah I do. Are you friends? That's always tricky."

"There are no tricks, I always thought you're supposed to marry your best friend."

"I don't wanna break your heart, but I'm not interested." A la Demi Lovato.

"I'll keep that in mind. I know what girls - "

"Clearly you don't know. My advice: Don't waste your time. You'd hate to hate her. Being a boyfriend is hard work. Hell, it's probably harder to be a good one. Actually, why not go for it?" He's remarkably clear. "Could be the last chance. Or you could wait for the reunion. You have massive insecurities just like everybody else but if you want her - she's a girl, right? Go for it before she passes by, like the Doppler effect."

"She has a boyfriend." Palmer turned the engine back on after the first burrito and started back toward the 5.

"And it'll be like that until it's not like that anymore. Dude, your grandma was engaged before your grandpa met her. Whatever you don't wanna do is the right thing to do. You should work in Admissions and write the rejection letters for all the idiots."

"Of course I should. How did you get Torrey to care for you?"

"Poked her in the eye! I let her. It can't be taught but it must be learned, sorry I'm not a karate sensei. She obviously didn't care. Why you asking me? I don't know shit, man. Ask your parents."

"No apologies, I'm the one who messed up."

"You asked her for lunch?"

"I asked you for second dinner, should've made it for dessert."

"No, I asked you. You're so deferential."

"Agreed. I just don't like when there's no reply."

"I don't like speed limits." Spits the truth.

"It only takes a few seconds. It's deflating."

"Let me say something. Let me say one goddam thing in the middle of all your bullshit. You're the rudest son of a bitch alive if you don't answer someone. I'm serious. That's indefensible. If something's going on, then say that. What is your life that you don't have an extra second and a half to answer? That's exactly what communicating is for. There's literally no excuse. I don't care if you're on fire. Just say, Hey I'm on fucking fire let's talk later. I don't give a fuck, dude. Get this person out of your life."

"You didn't answer me yesterday."

"I didn't know you had a phone." Catalina was just sitting out there, but so hard to see. "Do you think you're special? Better than someone saying Yes and not meaning it. You can't get offended just because you're not the most important person in her life. Your problem is you have to stop trying so hard. But let's hear some more peeves, you're not a person until you hate something with every fiber of your being."

"I reject your premise."

"You'll arrive at the same conclusion."

"I'm not trying at all."

"Pessimism is just inaction. I totally recognized the drive thru chick, dude. Okay, this is what you're gonna do. You're gonna dye your hair deep blue because that's what you're supposed to do in life." Again. "I don't know if anyone's ever told you that. Well anyway, good freaking luck, let's talk about something real, the good ones move on. Did you see how that fan inside the kitchen was going counterclockwise? Made me think of how I lost my car in a garage."

"It was going clockwise."

"What? It was counterclockwise."

"It's clockwise. Want to turn back? Then you can ask where you know her from."

"We don't need to deconstruct this." Whatever the powderpuff that means. Some Lennon cover arrived through the speakers. "Why would anybody want to hurt somebody? Karma's a bitch."

"Only if you are. Do you need more beer? Are you choking?"

"I'm okay. I don't think you know what karma means." After two minutes the cough receded. "So, I'm gonna get an internship on The Hill this summer. Leave the country. Yeah. Or I'll go to Costa Rica."

"Gonna run for mayor?"

"Hell no. I hate politics."

"What do you think about Gary?"

"The actor? Oh, for the Clippers."

"For president."

"They won't win next year. Their general manager offered to trade their best two players, first draft pick the next three years, plus his wife, and it was denied."

"What are you gonna do when you're out there?"

"I wanna get involved with solar energy, we act like it's new and revolutionary when really it's old, like a young turtle, actually the oldest thing to exist. Politics is nerdy, it's only academic, politicians don't study it. It appeals cause everyone at the top cheated their way in, and whenever that's exposed we think it'll be the end of a career but it ends up as one of those things they all get away with."

"And then we get angry when kids cheat on tests."

"President should have a six year term, minimum. We live in a country where people get mad when they have to wait at the drive thru. Do you know how many countries don't have enough food for its population? Education is absent from the constitution, so we wonder whether it's a right or a privilege." Whoever that is. "There needs to be more reward for smart and less for mediocrity. Less billboards, less accidents. Credit cards should not exist. Education, it's definitely a privilege. It makes sense if you don't think about it." That doesn't even make sense. "Let's be real for two seconds, check this out. America has the lowest tax rate out of any country that I'm interested in. They go to make and maintain things you use everyday." Says everything like it's a fact. "Holy shit my grandma's calling." Dropped his sandwich. "Hey! I'm eating. Say what? You can't hear them, they're invisible. I'll call you back, I'm driving."

"You answer your phone to say you can't talk, you wake up to cancel your alarm."

"Every weekend she sees if I wanna to go to the casino."

"She needs money?"

"She doesn't know what to do with it all and doesn't know where else to go. Whoever invented casinos was a great person." Liz agrees. "It's why this is the most popular tourist destination in the world. I'm too poor to travel."

"To where there's a real poor. You have two laptops."

"I only had fruit by the inches growing up." Also couldn't afford lined paper, drew his own. "There gonna be fireworks for the parade whenever that is? How loud do you think the sun used to be?'

"There's always fireworks. When will you go back?" He chose the 405 and Costa Mesa and it opened up to six lanes. One open lane at this time seems more empty. Highest daily average number of cars.

"Whenever everyone least expects it. Thinking of going to Mexico for breakfast. What makes Sterling so good?"

"He's self aware without ever being self conscious, does everything on his list. Dropped out of eleventh grade, up in San Mateo, also had to repeat kindergarten. Professors ask to write him letters of rec. Whenever you need something done, take it to Sterling, he'll find a friend to do it."

"Dude's got it all."

"Nothing more. Puts his socks on five toes at a - actually, Sterling, born happy, has an improper allocation of toes on his right foot, but that's irrelevant."

"Not irrelevant enough. What does that mean, he didn't cry when he was born? I saw his fan page has thousands of likes, what's he gonna do with all them?"

"You know how you think of the soundtrack for your life? He thinks of the songs that haven't been recorded yet. I always wondered what it would be like to have a roommate who becomes famous, like if you could tell they would, you know like Tim Herlihy. 'This is one of the top ten rooms in the world, right?' Always high fived me and thanked me for getting good grades so then the best room. Don't know if Housing even has accesses to that, but I reminded him he did better. A straight A sophomore slump, all sixteen. Exceptional at everything except bowling. Bowls a thirty three. I did better than that after two frames with basement tequila in both hands. Also, first one was *Pulp Fiction*, Sterling's seen two movies in his life at most, so I don't get quotey around him. When I told him I watched *Benjamin Button* with Brad Pitt, 'You went to the movies with Brad *Pitt*?' "

"No pin action, huh? Cate Blanchett was better. Think I figured out your movie, anyway. *Hot Tub Time Machine*."

"Nah. Another song started and I checked on the hummingbird Isabelle and her nest right outside the window. Sometimes the birds would just fly right in the room. When he actually grows his hair out, a la mop, it's beachy, everyone thinks he surfs. When we met I told him he looked like that guy from *Blade Runner*, and he had no idea who I was talking about. Mynor was still eating sponge candy when he appeared on cue. 'What's up? Guess what! Susan's gone. Would I be able to borrow yours later today and tomorrow? You need to go anywhere?' "

"You like him so much cause he always asks you to do things for him. Makes you important."

"Yeah, of course. 'Yeah, of course. Whatever ever happened to Susie?'

'Got stolen! Can you believe it?' Absolutely. Sixth net loss of the year, highlighted by the time he was reverse robbed. Sterling, all smart and sociable, didn't lock his bike to anything, just to its frame, and left it in the middle of wherever, and then got surprised when it was gone, like when a magician's trick works." Bradshaw style. "That's the only way bikes get stolen, all you have to do is care about it a little and it'll be fine. Always told him he should skateboard, like he did before."

"That's not stealing, that's owner's indifference."

" 'You know where the key is. Just don't make it magical number seven, you know I don't like waiting.' Only because we were running out of names. Natasha, Lillian, Alexandra, Gabriella, Melanie, Susan. 'So the good news is since bikes stolen per four years here is one and a half and you account for six, four extra students will have zero bikes stolen.' I noticed the error too.

He found Susie a couple weeks later, whomever took her gave her back. 'Right on, Levon.' Has an arsenal of phrases and resorts to, 'No prob, Bob.' Very corn ball."

"I like it."

"Mynor's turn, 'Hey Sterling, where were you?'

'This lecture by Tim Wise. He's fantastic, let's go together next time.'

'That was to*day*? Aw, I fucked up.' And left. He's never dramatic.

'Huh. Weird kid,' is all Sterling offered.

'Singaling, where you going tonight?' I knew he had plans, seeing the moon rising.

'I see you're wearing matching socks today, Kleytjen.'

'Thought I'd mix it up.'

'I'm gonna go outside by the stairs for this.' Didn't even need to look in the mirror. Hair half an inch long, cut it every other week with my clippers. Went back for his speakers and Porch walked out.

'Let's do this, Brutus.' Previous time he went over to Liz's so she would cut it for him. Liz Ellwood was crazy about him, so I lent it under the condition he tell her it's mine. She was already impressed with him so she should know I'm at least good for something, I told him. I was joking, but the thing about Sterling is, he did tell her it's mine."

Alameda

All I do is maybe dream of you ~ Dan Auerbach

Abandon all doubts - they're useless here.

That's the sign on her classroom door. Kabiting comes from a town in eastern California, one where its population is lower than its elevation. A ditzy cheerleading punk skater. Every ditzy cheerleader I know is super smart. She always knew she would be a teacher; didn't like school, loves teaching. "First day, first thing Kabiting did, she stood on her desk and recited Jabberwocky. No one knew the hell what was going on, not even the principal. She handed out What Did I Miss, so we had impeccable attendance. Also tripped on her way to the front of the room because she's not clumsy. Kabiting increases your potential. Everyone did well, we had quizzes everyday, even Saturdays, for fun. She learns your learning style. Right before we started, remember how Santa Barbara asks you to nominate a teacher? First time I came back for a visit the award was on her wall. I hadn't eaten anything all day aside from everything I ate, there's outside seating between a real estate place, a barber shop, and Happy Wings. And the smoothie place across the way. Them two were already at a table. Kabiting, wearing sunglasses that cover your whole face, looked like she was twenty nine. I apologized for being late. 'Next time I'll leave yesterday.'

'Sit down. You're making me nervous.' Jane almost remembered me, exquisite curly hair. Smarter than a seventeenth grader. Anywhat, they were both reading five thousand pages of *Harry Potter*. Always thought I went to good schools, but when I was in third grade, we read the alphabet, and that's it. She told Jane to scoochy.

'It's hard to believe it's been a year since a year ago.' Time passes slowly but goes by fast.

'Yeyeah. You're looking pretty beachy.' Whatever that means. Life is too cool to wear white socks. 'You don't have class tomorrow?'

Leaned in close with a secret. 'No one does. It's a holiday, remember?'

You might think a teacher knows when there's school, when really anyone over the age of five never knows what day it is. 'Oh, right!' I mentioned a prank we pulled on her best teacher friend. 'I remember that day often. That was a wonderful Wednesday. When was that? February thirtieth?' And vintages, *Midsummer Night's*, *Separate Peace*. 'I still remember that group project you and Antonio did.' "

"That day actually existed."

"Sure did. 'I kept that one.' I kept it all, even Blight and things that didn't understand me at all at the time, We Real Cool.

'You miss it?'

'I don't want to repeat your class, I just wanna ace it again. How'd everyone like *Algernon*?' We got up to order food, wings so hot you need to show identification. Happy's offers a contest where when you eat six of their spiciest you get your picture on the wall. No one'd ever done it. Not even that one guy. If you think Jane ordered two dozen wings, then you're absolutely correct."

"I don't think she did."

"All I had was a little bite of rice. 'That got moved down to the freshies. Good times.' Her favorite saying behind 'Ramble carefully.' Wouldn't have to say it so much if I abided. 'Have you memorized The Horizon Has Been Defeated yet?'

'Only all his other songs.' My favorite assignment was when she had future us write a letter to our past selves. It involved building a time machine from scratch. My new favorite assignment: Take a picture of a thousand dollars. 'Grace is in *Pirates*.'

'Yay! Jane's signing up for community theatre next month. So what's going on with you? Girls and school?' Kabiting knows what's up. 'What's the scoop?'

Less important one first, you remember. 'I need straight As this quarter.' False ultimatum.

'What are you taking? I know you emailed, your desire to keep in touch has made me so happy.'

'E S One Six B. That means basketball. Show up twenty times out of sixteen to pass.' "

"Boating and Sailing was better!"

"And yet here we are in car. 'Irish Lit. Just for fun. Heaney, Yeats. Our professor is from Ballysimon or Belfast so his accent makes the lectures. Second day of class: "Those of you who left unexcused during last session were, I trust, not planning to return. The technical difficulties in the lecture hall are trying enough. It's simple, but there's a lot to it. If, developmentally, you have yet to graduate from middle school, please drop the class. You are disrupting the rest of us who like to focus." On the girls sitting next to us.' He changed the final the day of, we had to structure our own course."

"Weird non sequitur."

"Cool guy, much more so than that impressed. 'Social and Cultural Environment. *Germs and Steel* and *Taking Sides*. British and American Language. Anthologies of Swift, Adams. Similarities and differences of two concurrent cultures. We got to make our own poem parody. Outro to Leadership Development. Talk successful components and walk them with our groups. Our project is to share ways of keeping the beach healthy. Once a week all the recyclables we collect are cashed in and go toward meals at a shelter downtown, which is run by a group on campus. In preparation for our final presentation, we five each took a hundred pictures documenting our progress.' "

"Jordyn likes Taylor Swift now. It's Facebook official. You know, the - "

"The thing about the Taylor Swift hypothesis is it's false. No one has that option. Norman lead us to an A. 'Great class, everyone should take it. The other groups call us overachievers, but we haven't achieved anything yet.' I emailed Halkirk about the textbook and she responded: My own experiences lead me to believe we are too quick to call managers short sighted, or at least to assume their goals are straight forward. I'm dealing with complex organizational issues now and here's what I see. Our manager, though less concerned with the long view, has a more complex understanding of the issues than I do. If I acted in a leadership role without her advice, I would be overlooking important perspectives from her constituents. In terms of the Covey example, I might say, Sure we could leave the forest, but what about all the neighbors, colleagues, and inhabitants we would leave behind? So there.

Best leaders share, there's no monopoly. If only class were more than thrice a week. 'What else. Exercise Psychology. We take personality inventories. I know you're not big on sports, you'd really like it. Our professor's great, he tries out his stand up in class.' You can tell, he takes notes on what students say. 'I'm doing an Honors contract with him, I just have to read *The Inner Game of Tennis* and write a twelve page paper. It's easy.'

'You must have had an awesome teacher years ago.'

'True. I can't think of who, though.' I don't classify things as easy or hard anymore, just a matter of time you spend."

"You're not a big spender."

"Wing Ninja was still hungry, no napkins necessary. 'Can I come to school with you? I want to take the Lit class, Seamus is one of my *fav*orites. I adore that man.' She's infectious. I studied for that final. Memorized Stations. 'Did I do the sonnet about folding sheets with your class? I did a project on him in my poetry class, let me know what you think about him.' Decided to get her Masters after teaching for about however long it's been, the program only met on weekends so it didn't interfere.

'I don't remember you doing *Clearances*, so I don't think so, but we did last week. With a full demonstration, it was good. It was good. But yeah, you can definitely come to school with me. Anytime!'

'That's a lot of classes for one quarter, isn't it?'

'It's only four days a week. I have uno more accounting requirement, Annual Returns, so I signed up for Shakespeare's Sister for the fall, and I'll take more electives or add minors or something.'

'I always loved *Macbeth*, used to teach it, and *The Tempest*, almost taught that one this year. The *Henrys* get me mixed up. I'll have to go back into my hugantic anthology and see which ones I read. *As You Like It* is fun! Sounds like you're a full time student, anyway.' "

"You talk a lot for a shy guy."

"Those aren't related in any way. 'Yeah, I've been been applying for work study to appease the parents, but I suppose I'll find something that's fun to donate my time to. I won't have to take as many classes per quarter after this.'

'Get a second major, eh?'

'I don't care about majors. They're only a quarter of your classes.'

'That's all you care about, Kleytjen. If you like it, study it. If you're concerned about being generalized, rethink your priorities. Have you had any interviews?'

'One, to be a lower division accounting section leader. I would run one of the discussions that complement lecture, and work with the professor on material.'

'That would be awesome! How did it go?'

'I dunno. It was okay. It's just, afterward, like now, all I'm thinking about is how dumb I am cause all they asked was: What's the worst class you took? What's a time you had to work with someone you didn't get along with? What's a time you received negative feedback?'

'Shouldn't you be able to talk about that?'

'No I know. I agree. It's just that shouldn't be all. Ask only one of those things, maybe. If I wanted someone to work with me, I'd be far more interested in the best class they took, a time they worked really well with someone, and a time they received positive feedback.' Also I had no idea how to answer the only good question, What is your proudest accomplishment? You know, since I'm goal obsessed, ultra concerned with grades, and played sports only when they got serious. There are big picture things I could have said but they want a specific moment, like making it to the top of the Empire State Building. All those questions focus on the past, yet recruiting is about the future. 'I was not asked anything that led me to believe they want educators. They did ask whether I've had any problems with authority. It was confusing.'

'It would be a fallacy to think they don't have a reason for asking.'

'It's a fallacy to think someone did something wrong because you don't understand them.'

'Kleytjen. I know you like to criticize critical people, that does no good. We're not here to criticize, we're here to encourage.' Jane smiled. 'Have you ever actually experienced negative criticism, or do you just anticipate it? Seems like a weird thing for an optimist to do.' "

"You're not an optimist. You're optimistic."

"You just defined optimist."

"One is everyday, the other is day to day."

" 'You're overlooking the kindness in criticism. If you want a hundred percent chance of acceptance, go work in fast food. And if you want that rate for teaching, make yourself qualified. Get the requisite number of units in math, physics, whatever, to meet actual needs of schools. I know it's more competitive now, I probably wouldn't have made it if it were this tough when I graduated. I never took chemistry.'

'So I've been doing it all wrong?'

'Most def, man. If you consider what you've been doing as wrong, just imagine how everything'll be when you get it right. Think back where were you four years ago.'

'I made it on to the next round. There will be another interview.'

All the wings were gone. 'Sombreros off to you! Are you nervous?'

'No. I will be.'

'Just be outgoing and you'll be fine. Keep in mind you're not only learning how to teach, you're learning how to be a teacher.' Jane got antsy just sitting there, wasn't her flavor of conversation. Mine neither. 'I told her we'd get ice cream or smoothies.' Got up for The Drip on the other side of the plaza.

'Sounds delicious.'

'I have coupons!' She asked Jane to go get them from her car and she sprinted away. 'You run like the wind.'

'The wind doesn't have legs.'

'Yeah, but it's fast.' You're only allowed to use one coupon per transaction, price you pay. I ordered a magnificent mango mania mash and asked for extra everything. Drank the whole thing in one bite. We resumed our conversation and got into grad school."

"What flavor did she have?"

"Red orange."

"Katy Perry's favorite."

"Well, yeah. We sat down at another table, with chairs that don't move. 'It sounds like you are way into your major classes. Are you a senior already?' International Finance, Econometrics, Managerial, Auditing, and Antitrust were all wrapped up that winter.

'Sorry it took so long.'

'You are? I may fall off the couch.' I looked around for any hint of a couch. 'Because of your placement classes, right?' Nope.

'Yes, that's right, I've had senior standing, but I don't really know what that means. I plan to be a senior for as long as I have money.'

'Enjoy it to the fullest, squeeze everything out of it. It is so much fun, I just loved it. My mom always told me, It's not a race, you have afterward to work.'

'I don't know how to approach what follows. It depends on whether I have something lined up by next summer.'

'So you don't want school to end and you don't want to go to more school?'

Everyone except me is getting older. 'I'm really looking forward to an income of negative thirty thousand and getting the same grades as everyone else.'

'School takes more thought and more time than a job, but you're doing it for yourself. You'll have the freedom to go broke. It's a good dilemma.' Like the difference between twelve and twelve and a half million dollars. 'I think I know what you'll do, you love learning. You have an insatiable curiosity.'

'I just don't wanna go to another school after finally staying, everything is going so well.'

'Stay. Apply to Santa Barbara. First you need to figure our what career you want.'

'One that pays.'

'Really. What's your dream job?'

'If I ever dream about a job I'll have failed.' Any salary is worth less than your time.

'You need one anyway so you may as well like it.'

'Why should I have to plan my second step before my first?'

'Everything is an opportunity, it makes sense to know where you're going when you start to cross the street. You still interested in photography, a la Peter Parker?' "

"Or Edie Brock."

"You latched onto the wrong detail. A photographer shows what others don't see, and spends hours preparing for seconds of action, which I like a lot, but I blurted, 'I'm not sure I want all my problems to be pictures.'

'Maybe you don't *want* to be sure. You could find out everything you don't like, or, you could accept what you do like. If you're really not sure what to do, ask your mom what you enjoyed most as a kid. Being dynamic is great until you don't dedicate yourself to one thing one hundred percent. Does that make sense? You have to be obsessive to get what you want.'

'Especially if you're not good at it at first. I like most liquor.'

'Right, but besides Meryl Streep, should you expect to have no critiques? In my first year of student teaching, my class had twenty six kids. Collectively, they spoke seventeen languages.' They all asked her to prom.

'I can't even list seventeen languages.'

'I cried every day for the first month, just what I needed. It humbles you. They will end up teaching you way more than everything you thought you didn't know. You can pay it back any time, it's well worth your investment. It's fun when you get good at something.'

'Would you rather not know exactly what you want or know exactly what you want and not get it?'

'Is there something you're not able to do?'

Free thinking and slow walking. 'Sure. I lack talent.' "

"I see why everyone says you're too general."

"Not general enough. 'Everyone does, we are good at one percent of what we try.' We're in disagreement on that. 'So find that and stick with it, and know that most others aren't good at what you're good at. Apply for scholarships and fellowships.'

'Those are for smart people. I'm just not dumb enough to keep going to school.'

'Maybe if you stop your self deprecation for one minute. If you think you're good enough, you are.' I asked about the proverbial gap year, as it were. 'Be careful, it's harder to go back. Lots of my students say they will, and five years later they still have yet to do anything. I know being an educator isn't simple, people used to just read. Now it's very industrial and formal. The whole idea of schools is a construct that - the whole idea of educating people through schools, I don't know why we think that idea *has* to work. Education is lifelong, not something that ends when you throw your cap in the air. Or tortillas. School's whole reason for existence is to make you better. It makes you take criticism better. Take a creative studies program if you want. You need the real deal.' Whatever the caramba that is. 'Frame your research as a question. At least be professional about what you do.'

'I don't want to end up like that aeronautics dude with nine doctorates who couldn't figure out that the reason the spaceship wouldn't launch is he forget to put gas in it. What do you do when you get everything you want?'

'Celebrate! Even if you fulfill all your present day desires, and I hope you do, I promise you you will always find something else to strive for. Peaking is nothing to be afraid of. Once you've done everything you wanted to do, like Polk, go to bed. Just remember that you have coasted through school and there are so many who have to work much harder at what you take for granted. Counselors will offer more value to what we're talking about, if only because they will tell you all this better than I just have.'

'I suppose I can go see an advisor one of these days.'

'Wishy washy.'

'I guess.'

She smiled. 'Kley. Don't you think it's important to be precise?'

Too colloquial, too. Jane's melting ice cream dripped into the shape of a spade. 'I guess.' She liked that one. 'Of course it is! I don't think it's good to have an opinion if you're truly uninformed, that's all. Why pretend to know what you're talking about when you can learn about it instead?'

'There comes a point when you have to be sure of yourself.'

'Well like Oscar Wilde said, I don't understand a single word of what I am saying.' She's crazy about him.

'Yes, that's good.' Actually, it's Walt Whitman she likes. 'Quoting people is great when they've said it the best, but there's something to being original. You were my least creative student the beginning of that year.'

'Your class encourages creativity. For novelty to exist, you must know what preexists.'

'Don't let your craft exceed your wisdom. It's not creative if you think the same as everyone else, by definition.'

'What about turning in the same answer? When more than one gets it right, we're all cheating? Isn't it possible, if not probable, for different people to think the same thing?'

'You don't have to purposely conform, that's all.'

'Everyone does all the time! Songs are covered constantly. Movies are always being remade.' How do you know if you can do something better than someone else?

She steered a different direction. 'Are you going to travel again?' I'll go to Italy if Elizabeth goes, or Saskatoon. 'I love those Lisbon pictures you posted, you caught so many great details! How do you get the clouds to pose like that? I saw Torrey in Washington over spring break.' Torrey's bestie is Kabiting's niece, they go way forward."

Right around Calabasas I felt my hand shake:

You always say twice as much as necessary

I knew exactly what she meant. "They're best friends because they hang out everyday or they hang out everyday because they're best friends?"

"Neither. 'She's interning at Nat Geo and she loves it. Now I'm all about that traveling life! I'm planning a trip back there for once Jane is in middle school. American History is fifth grade, she will love it. I want to spend more time at Vernon, and explore the Smithsonians at my leisure.' Exploring the one house someone lived in is unrelatable to me."

"That's not even close to the only place he lived."

It wasn't a wasted guess

"Right. 'Oh and the Library of Congress. I could take a tour of Heaven and it would look a lot like that building." Jane rolled her eyes at that, but in a wholesome way. "Ahh, Torrey's little sister - do you know her? Well, she just signed her letter of intent. She was accepted to New York, but their aid package was deplorable. She's excited about Santa Barbara, as she should be.'

'Isn't that funny?' Yes. 'She'll be glad to know when she gets to her second choice it should have been her first all along.' Is it like that with pursing girls? 'I just remembered a couple books Grace enjoyed when she was in third grade. They're good for anyone, *Frindle* and *The Report Card*, both by the same guy.'

'Oh, bangarang! We'll have to check them out.' "

I bet you're wondering where I am

I wasn't, but Amie could tell I was distracted. "How about you get on with the more important part?"

Alameda

You were only waiting for this moment to arrive ~ Paul McCartney

"You're full of shit, dude."

"I probably am. Sterling plugged in the buzzer and put on the three clip. He used it more than I did, to be honest. At first his speakers wouldn't work outside, faulty outlet or something, and Sterling is one who talks to electronics. 'You could turn on, that's always an option. Oh, there we go!' "

"Electronics is the root of all stress. Anthony told me about a fridge that requires an internet connection to operate. What happens if the cable goes out? Whoever invented that should be thrown in jail."

"Prison. He stopped trimming to reach in his pocket, 'I got a new phone. Visualized it into my life! It's gonna change me, I can tell.' We used to have super old phones, with buttons. I didn't even want a new one, but it is a lot lot better. 'I skipped lunch, as you know, then there was Tim Wise.' That lecture Mynor missed, he went to that instead of Contemporary Techniques. Who wouldn't enjoy class?"

"Anyone who takes it seriously. Sorry, that was my stomach. I haven't eaten anything." For a second I almost believed Palmer when he sighed.

"Or smart students don't need to go. Now it was Hallelujah, one iteration. 'Want me to skip this? This is the song I would listen to in Seattle before I climb to the top of the Needle and jump.' Mynor gave me twenty dollars to say that.

'There are no sad songs. You turned something into music? That's amazing, melodically and rhythmically.' That's fair. With my still beating heart sliced open I wouldn't be able to write two words. 'This is the song I would play to talk you off the ledge.' Up next on the shuffle was Game Called Life. 'This is their best song!' He meant it's his favorite.

I tried to make a campus map out of his fallen hair before it all blew away. It's good to be crazy, helps you stay sane. 'I'm only asking, so take this the right way. You still like Andera?' Every few whiles, he's into a new Andera. Like how every girl I like, her name starts with an A. It's true. Every single one. Even Lex. More fluff plopped to the ground and a miss mononymous started singing. 'You have this song?'

'Am I supposed to say no?'

'She sings about taking drugs and shooting people, and she doesn't do either.'

'It's nothing personal. It's just a song.' He knew she didn't write it. 'This song makes me want to have sex with her.'

'A girl's name makes me wanna have sex with her.' Mynor gave me ten to say that. Next was Dancing In The Moonlight, Sterling's jelly. '*What*?' The way he laughs is he kind of leans his entire body forward, so it knocked the trimmer off the makeshift counter and out from the outlet. I plugged it back in after a second.

'All you do is stare at your phone. Even when it's off. Whoever I marry, they have to like this song.' The only thing he doesn't know about music is what's originally from a movie, like Unchained Melody. Primarily plays tenor sax, even though Pearl Jam doesn't, and whether it was because of his inclinations or something else, never pays attention to lyrics. I went to an ensemble performance of his, remarkable depth and arrangement. He had a solo for Slinky and Hunting Wabbits. Need to learn to actually play the guitar, that's how Sterling attracts the ladies. Music is other people.

I understand the finished piece but I'm ignorant of all the component parts. 'I want Amie to take Enviro with me.' This was before she slammed my single lens into the sand."

"You don't need her, you just need a better camera." Switched to the right lane and I thought he was gonna get off again to find more hot sauce, but he went right back to the left while Costa Mesa's lights disappeared from the sideview mirror.

" 'She's smart and you don't want her to wrack her brain out over a class that doesn't matter.'

'They all matter.'

'Except for econ. Micro and Macro are the same. You just wanna get rich.' I just wanna deserve to. Sterling asked for another favor so I had to remind him. 'Oh yeah, when you get back then.

Sounds fun! It's gonna be weird not having you here. When are you taking off?'

'Whenever the time's right. I could experiment with planning. But I think I'm just gonna get drunk.'

'Stay salty. Kleytjen, what's your favorite word?'

'I don't know.'

'Mine's balance. I saw a pod of dolphins from the window, I was gonna wake you up but you were asleep."

"What's your favorite word?"

"Poise. Always level, like a palindrome. 'Yeah you were telling me to look for them last night. Or it was a dream, I don't know how to tell the difference. You gonna skip dinner too?'

'*Your* dinner, if that's what you mean. I'm going over to Liz's early to get homework done.'

'She said she would go to dinner with *us*. What's on the menu for tomorrow? No time for homework means you're doing things right. You get Deanslisted all the time.'

'Yeah, that one time I got Dean's List all the time. So yeah dude, just if you could look at that grant proposal at your leisure, that'll be great. If you're here at all during summer, it's always home for you.'

'No problema Jenna. Give me twenty dollars if you win.' "

"Did you get your money?"

"I told him to keep it. 'Would you rather be a good brother or a good son?'

'Dude, that's like asking me to pick between my mom and my dad. I put some mail on your desk.' Should have opened it right then but I figured it was a, Thank you so much for sharing your photos, they're wonderful but they aren't the right fit for us at this time. Oops. Scary to think what they'd say if they weren't wonderful.

'No's not.' His parents send care packages for us both. Sterling unplugged everything and went back inside to put on a clean shirt.

We do like to live beside the seaside. 'Hey, Kershaw. Never leave any place that's super awesome. You're in whispering distance from your prime time.' Turned to the open door head first, followed by the rest of his body. 'Later, skater.' Whenever anyone leaves the room feels extra empty, so I descended to the second floor lounge. No television in our room, thank God. On the couch were Mynor, asleep, pants tucked in and collar popped now, and Carson, nodded Hello. First time I was there since the last time I was there."

"You're ridiculous. I still can't - imagine how you'd feel when you realize you're *born* happy. You were born confused, and that's about it."

"You'd feel guilty. You've never taken the truth well. 'What's the score?' "

"Do I ever lie to you?"

"Almost exclusively. 'One to one, Bruins are winning.' Mynor is a voracious fan, wears it on his forearm. The whole family's from Boston. Even the in laws.

Carson's unconcerned. 'I'm from hockey town, don't care for all the fighting. But in the playoffs, they don't fight much.' They have a form of that conversation everyday while listening to Jim Rome or - "

"They're clones? I thought Carson was from Cali."

"He's from lots of places. 'How late you stay out?' Had to decline his invite to a garage party, already went to nine others. Thursday's neighborhood citations: four for public urination, eight for carrying open containers, and a couple dozen for public intoxication. Low key. 'Huh?'

'I dunno,' Carson laughed.

'Doing anything tonight?'

'Can't say man where I'll be tonight. Conducting a survey, Kley? Don't cry yourself to sleep over how much shenanigans you missed out on, just join us next time. We'll give you a shout.' Marie, right from her study tree, walked in via balcony to fill up her canteen. Bountiful bangs. 'Oh, hey Marie. We weren't talking about you.'

'What're you guys doing? Watchin the game? Boring.' If you don't understand it. 'I don't know what all the hype about professional athletes is. Last night I heard the best player made forty two percent of his shots. If you're a professional musician and you hit less than a hundred percent of your notes, you're not a professional anymore.'

'Defense gets paid too. We're watching hockey.'

'Oh.' Sat down on the floor. 'Am I in your way?'

'The back of your head is real pretty.' She started to turn around to Carson. 'You ain't in the way.'

'Well I hope you guys aren't going out, I'm not drinking today.'

'Shut up, Kleytjen. I'll give you four hundred dollars if that's true.' Mynor pays cash, too.

'Is it easy for you guys to follow the puck?' She was trying so hard to.

'That's what we need!' Boston earned a power play. 'Dude doesn't play a beautiful game, but he sure is effective.' Two scoreless minutes later Mynor slammed the remote on the super soft cushion, inflicting grave damage. 'We can't make anything today!'

'Nothing to get mad about. They're gonna win.' Carson walked out on the veranda, I sat by Andera, doing homework over at the corner table. 'How're the hydrogen bonds going?'

Looked up, 'How did you know these are *hy*drogen bonds?'

Andera, student by day, hair stylist by night, vegetarian by diet, doesn't like tomatoes. 'My stomach told me. What else'd you be doing?'

'Radioactive nuclear isotopes. Or working with gap acidosis, usually non anionic.' "

"So, ionic."

"That's so. 'Hey Andera. You mad? Your hair looks angry.' She always falls asleep during movies. We thought it was we never started until after midnight, then we watched one at high noon and she was out for the count before the second act. She fell asleep during a drag show."

"I feel like Andera reminds me of what's her name. Anthony was like, 'She fell asleep when we went to see *Wedding Crashers* and I pushed her to wake her up but she just fell on the ground and I left.' So fresh."

"Movie is a weird thing to do for a date. 'Where's Chases's girlfriend?' She's more than that.

'In the room,' Mynor said still looking straight ahead.

'Chick flick?'

'*Midnight in Paris*.' Carson's dad's friend's cousin's brother's cousin's friend's son got it."

"He doesn't strike me as a person who would have a cousin."

"I said, 'Oh nice, I heard it's good. Should I join them?'

'Naw, right *now* it's a chick flick. If he watched it by himself it'd be different.' First floor freshmen walked in and dragged one of the couches outside, the one we were using, thirteen beer cans fell out. Next time I saw it was on the beach. 'Hey Carson, how the Seahawks gonna do?'

'I only answer football questions during football season.' Mynor indicated time, Marie obviously asleep on the floor. 'Wake up, it's Saturday. In more than half the world.'

'Dude, let her be.'

'She'll miss dinner. She's snoring, too.'

'At least she doesn't drool. You wanna barbecue on the patio tonight, Chase?' Mynor yelled, literally woke up Marie."

"Figuratively, stupid."

" 'Yeah, ask Cars if he's down to barbecue a pizza with us. Actually, just tell him he's down.'

'What? Are we ready?'

'Meow? It's already six?' Our dinner schedule was clockwork.

'It's only six? Let's do this thing. Marie, you joining us?' Looked over to Mynor. 'Silence means yes, right?' Didn't say anything.

'May as well, time to take a break from taking a break.' Andera decided she was in the zone. 'You gonna get an A on Tuesday?'

'I'm getting an A right now.' Studying is fine as long as it works. She prepares for tests like a chef."

"How do you prepare a chef?"

"Watch out dude. 'Go have fun without me.' That's what we did, and."

You think Im funny without any makeup on ~ Katy Perry

"How bout that. Your Song was Kabiting's wedding song, she and her first date ever reconnected. Married before she graduated, though that was a different millennium."

"First dance or a different one?"

"How many are there?"

"Cutting the cake, walking down the aisle, introducing the wedding party, like tres million. I like Unchained Melody."

"Tracy? 'What's a good movie to watch for an engagement party? My friend bet I wouldn't guess what she picked out for us all to watch, so if I do she makes me a batch of cookies. I have eighty ideas but only five guesses.'

'That's uber. This sounds like a spicy kind of friend! This is difficult, there are so many. Is she talking about new releases, classics, every movie *ever*? Also, realize she is in a different age bracket from me, so she may have completely different choices.' Drum roll. '*Say Anything*, the ultimate John Cusack movie. *When Harry Met Sally*, Meg Ryan and Billy Crystal, love it! *Pride and Prejudice*. Duh. *You've Got Mail*, another Meg Ryan and Billy Crystal, but it's so good. She owns my dream bookstore.' Tom Hanks. '*Shakespeare in Love*, duh again. Now, we have big problems here because we are leaving out way too many.' Should have taken notes, instead I thought about *Five Hundred Days of Summer* and how short that is. 'If we're going bratty, we've left out *Sixteen Candles*, *Pretty in Pink*, *Valley Girl*, *Reality Bites*. Ahh. What about the classics? Some would recommend *Casablanca* or *Gone with the Wind*. Impersonally, I would say *Roman Holiday*. With Audrey Hepburn. For after we got married, there's *Sabah* and *Medicine for Melancholy*.' Whatever those are."

"*Casablanca*'s great. I can't speak for the rest. Gwyneth all the way though."

" 'And you've got the good, solid Drew Barrymore flicks: *Never Been Kissed*, *Fifty First Dates*, and the *Wedding Singer*. These are fine,

fine films, worthy of Oscars in the romance department.' Until then I wondered why the Academy doesn't have such a category, like for *Annie Hall*. 'Then there is *Serendipity* and *Sliding Doors*. That idea of fate and relationships, gotta love that. And *Just Like Heaven*, very good, plus Mark Ruffalo is in it.' Duh. 'Dude! What about *The Princess Bride*? *Family Man*? *Sweet Home Alabama*?' "

"If there were a Best Romantic then *Annie Hall* wouldn't have won, just like *A New Hope* is the better all time movie, but not the better - oh who cares?"

"I do like Reese Witherspoon. 'There is a wonderful Christian Slater movie called *Untamed Heart*. It is a sad one, though, very sweet. And there is a violently wonderful, romantic movie, another Christian Slater, called *True Romance*. Loved that one, the heroine's name is Alabama. What about *Jerry Maguire*? The kwan! *Hitch*? *Time Traveler's Wife*? I've only read the book. It's so awesome, though, I just ate it up.' Yummy. 'Whew. I'm glad you didn't ask about scary movies. I always watched them in school, I can't handle them anymore. I would say,' she did, 'that *you* know this girl, so you've got to know what she's into. If you lose, I say *you* make her cookies.' Just then we felt a small earthquake, lower than my GPA, so Jane got excited. 'And if you *real*ly wanted to make an impression, make your own movie. Here - People become really quite remarkable when they start thinking that they can do things. Keep the faith.' John Wooden said it better.

'I have faith in credit.'

'Why don't you grow up and start believing in something? Do you have feelings for this someone?' She waited. 'That's for you to answer.'

'I have feelings for everyone I've met, as far as I know.' You think girls don't make sense, try talking with guys."

"It doesn't work."

" 'Okay mister Secret Pants.' Used to be Sassy Pants. 'But do you know her well?' It's no secret until it's shared."

"Secrets are unhealthy."

"That's why you go to the gym so often. 'I know what makes her happy, and I feel that that counts for something.'

'It's really taxing to love someone who doesn't love you.'

'It's really hard to convince yourself you don't like someone when your whole conviction relies on that premise.'

'Where did you learn to be a contrarian? There's only one way to get hurt here. It won't be because she likes someone else more, it will be you finding out she's not as infallible as you think she is.' Nothing's obvious to me.

'I think this is becoming over analytic.' Ran my fingers through my hair.

'Whatever you may be thinking, you're too young to get serious. Do I know or care where any of my boyfriends are or what they're doing? No. Did I think I was going to marry them at the time? Yes.'

'I'll let you know what movie it is whenever I know.' I'll text her in the morning."

"You know what it is? *Amélie*? Tell me!"

"Think about it. 'One word more about grad school, in a way that will mean something to you. Just think of all the people you'll meet.' Good use of math. 'You have time to make these decisions, just beware of inaction making them for you.' Obviously there's a reason why everyone has to repeat things to me. 'Just live it. Life takes you to the people you need to meet.'

'I know.' I really do, but I was getting a call. Wouldn't have answered it since I was already conversing, yet I knew Jen needed to know when to take me.

Kabiting took no offense. 'What's happening?'

'Nothing, I'm getting a ride to the train station later. I have to drive back now, actually.' Stood up and straightened my back. 'Thanks for coming down here. And for the smoothie.'

'Enjoy the joy of Santa Barbara.'

'Always. Hey, quick question.'

'Quick answer.'

'Is it Younger than I, or Younger than me?'

'The first one. The verb *am* is understood, therefore making the pronoun subject case. You'll hear the other way more often, however. So it's your choice on the level of stuffiness you want.'

'Coolio. Thanks for meeting up. It was, educational. Have fun in third grade!' Jane was back to Hogwarts.

'Will do.' She has what joy looks like. She and my aunt." We reached the edge of La La Land and Amie stayed on the 101 to the 5, didn't know any better, so we drove right *through* the crazy city where nobody cares to know. Too late to stop at City Walk too. Meant to tell her ahead of time, like when Obi Wan warns about scum and villainy. "When I'm in San Fran I'll have to remember to ask you which way to go." At least we didn't go the other way up through the Grapevine. We made it past Glendale into Hollywood, and the exit for Union Station, all passed in silence. "This city has the most *bor*ing skyline."

"That seems pretty superficial. I heard its tallest building is not its highest building. That seems more interesting."

"Well, we could get off at Santa Monica to check out the scene, see the hookers on parade."

"I'm gonna steer clear. Who's more objectionable, the prostitute or the trick?"

"The one more afraid of being caught. What are you afraid of?"

"Nothing." If there's nothing, how could anything go right? "And spiders."

"I was too when I was two. Let's go to the Grand Canyon."

"Dude it is one of my life goals to see the Grand Canyon! And a beluga whale, which my family did without me a couple weeks ago. Jerks."

"This song played at Sweet Alley tonight." Blue Orchid.

"I was singing it the other day. I have last album, actually."

"Is it good?"

"It's decent. I just wanna, do some sleeping tomorrow. Wow, that sounded smart, I gotta stop saying like."

"I didn't even notice."

"I might need to stop before we get there." We were right by the Citadel.

"There's a rest stop just before Oceanside." It was weird to have my feet off the ground while awake for this long.

"Dunno where Oceanside is, but that might work."

"It's right next to Carlsbad, where your roommate is from." Where Route 101 Diner is, and Flying Elephant Pub, heard it costs forty dollars to look at the menu. I've spent that on worse things.

"Hmm, yes I see. Wait that's where she's from?" You know you're tired when you stop talking. We counted the headlights for what seemed like ten minutes but was just two. "Oh my gosh, you know what we should do?" Her arm was around my neck but she wasn't strangling.

"Yes! No, not really."

"We should go to Segundos! I miss it. We'll go for brunch or something. And eat food." Began to open my mouth. "You be quiet. Ooh, the Be Fifty Twos!" She's into alphanumerics. Montebello's station was then a commercial, I changed it, and Fourplay was playing.

"You tryin to smooth jazz me, Coral?"

"Um. No? Do you want me to?"

"Maybe later, but you can change it back to The Judds so I can sing along."

"I don't care what anyone else says, it sounds really nice when you sing."

Looked away from the road. "Thank you." Her blue suede eye shows off her brown eye, and she switched stations again. "This The Kinks?"

"The Who," Can't Explain.

"The Kinks?"

"I meant it's The Who."

"Oh. So that happened. You know what *this* is?"

"Two Chains?"

"So close."

"Are you gonna tell me?"

"I did. It's called So Close. Why don't you tell Sterling to form a band and I'll take care of the vocals. You know he sounds flat, right?"

"I don't know what that means."

"It means his octave is a half lower that it should be."

"Yeah I'll tell him. I'll text him right now." I did. "When do you wanna get married?"

"We're getting married?"

"Lots of girls have an age picked."

"I guess that's true. That's crazy. How could they know? I do know I don't want to have kids." She kept anticipating me looking over in judgment. "You have a problem with that too?"

"I just don't want you in twenty two years to end up with thirty cats and dogs."

"I prefer snakes. One time, me and all my friends were - "

"All two of them?"

"Har har. If you wish you heard the story, don't blame me. It's about signal transduction, if that interests you. It should."

"It does. Want to stop at Wildwood Bakery so I can buy you mint chocolate chip cookies, your favorite?"

"You're crazy." I probably am. Kept forgetting everything was closed. "Let me see your wallet." She wanted my wallet but I offered my money.

"How much we talking? I'm willing to pay twenty five. I might be willing to pay ten."

"We'll go halfsies on it, it's fine. I just want to see if yours is sewn like mine."

"Train would've cost more."

"Don't worry about it." If you're too nice when she doesn't really like you, like a lot, it's insecure. When she's crazy about you no matter how much of a loser you are she don't care how you act. Whenever any girl is really nice, which is all the time, I take it too personally. "Who are you meeting up with? You can tell me, you did last year. Don't you remember?" I already did tell her.

"I begin each day anew. Hold on." Right under the 34th parallel or wherever we were my ring tone song played.

"Hiya, Papaya."

"You're awake?"

"I'm just really coherent when I sleep talk and text. I've been thinking about what I said. You're not repeating any situation, you're still in the same one."

"What do you mean?"

"Kleytjen. You already know. I'll see you." And that was it.

"Who do you know who's awake right now? And who cares about last year? Tell me what you did today."

"I, ah, went to baseball, it was the best comeback we've ever had."

"What a happy coincidence you've been to the two best games ever."

"It's true. I left early both times. Turned in a paper and went to my study group. And then it was game time again, with Jordyn. We went out to dessert after my last tour. Saw Sterling. Then you texted. How was tennis?"

"Sounds like you didn't watch a movie with anyone. We decided not to play, the courts actually had a wait list."

"There's always room by Alameda."

"Dude, what have you been talking about? The park by the beach? Alameda's downtown. You mean Haskell's."

Alameda

Its hidden all over your face ~ Beyonce Knowles

Palmer's car collided with a footstool the way the Milky Way will collide with Andromeda - without consequence. He didn't say anything other than noting it already had some dents on the front. The bumper sticker on the truck it fell from asked what the definition of cool is.

"As per usual, we walked down to Segundos, a hundred ten meter trek. Mynor started with a caesar salad, tortilla chips and salsa, and sticky rice. Liz came through for pita chips and hummus, vegetable sir fry, and noodles. When we first met I wasn't wearing any pants and it wasn't even No Pants Day. Marie had stir fry noodles, corn on the cob, and pork loin roast with garlic and ginger. Also ate roasted potato wedges, chili and noodles, with a side plate of steamed carrots. And tried the far east vegetable soup, garden marinara, and housemade whole wheat pasta using only her hands, utensils are barbaric. Mynor also went for fettuccini, a baked potato, and jasmine rice, Carson took white wine garlic sauce with chicken, plain pepperoni pizza, and artichoke pesto on wheat. And lemon cake with raspberry filling since the apple pie was out. He eats Dutch apple everyday, twelfth generation American that he is. That and crusty French bread, comfort foods. The rest I don't recall, I had a lot of everything, plus two glasses of assai berry. Sterling says it helps you live forever, like vinegar."

"When my conditional matter professor started talking about the internal energy of a potato I laughed. No one else."

"Went outside to eat since twilight hadn't set yet, Carson was the last to the round table. We chose the one without enough chairs just to see if he'd stand the whole time. 'Hey gentle snowflakes. Where is everyone?' He wasn't used to Marie's newest color for her tresses, she changes it every month. 'Heads up, Victoria's Secret doesn't let you try on clothes if you're a guy.' "

"Whatever that biologically communicates."

"Would you believe she got lost in a stairwell one time? 'There's an upstairs? Where?' Takes her nine weeks to find her classes."

"There's no way it only happened once."

" 'Hey Palona. We're all here. Liz, give your opening statement.' Carson lived where I do, the sixty seven block of Trigonometry, bought a meal plan anyway, like Liz. Says it's the best thing anyone ever purchased, including Louisiana."

"That's the name of the street?"

"It should be. 'Ah, right. I met Marie in the beginning when I didn't know anyone. On the second day, she and Andera asked me to eat lunch with them. They are still my best friends today.'

'We haven't figured out how to get rid of you either.' They're opposites."

"Other than that there are no differences between them. Would a guy like you ever go along with a girl like Liza?"

"Absolutely. I, specifically, have no interest."

"Jackass. How is it you're picky about nothing else?"

" 'Beth, go to Laughology with us.' Marie participates in everything, won the annual Staff Cookie Contest while unemployed.

'Hell no. Tonight or tomorrow? Want a tangerine?'

'For what? Let's get pitted.' "

"Kley, check this out. All the guys I know are six five, but you're plainly taller at six even or whatever you are." It's true. I like to eat twenty five hundred calories each meal, with a smallish appetite, haven't gained a pound four in years. Even when I'm at my grandparents' house, just back from dinner, You want something to eat? I still don't put on any weight. Or mass. "That's how you were born. You need the Herschel Walker workout."

"Mynor rapidly ate to his fifth plate, silver spork in hand. Applause worthy, we told him to slow down. 'No way, this might be the only thing I eat all day.' Filled up a non spill bowl with soup where if you hang it upside down nothing pours out.

'You said that at lunch.' Fridays he lunched early due to his physics lab.

'Dude, Kley - you brought your flask? Dude, Mystery Girl is a mystery no more.' Mystery Girl is a mythical being who only shows her true face once every twelve thousand years. He constantly talked about her except around his girlfriend, on track to be a registered dietician, we always had to sneak him cookies.

'Oh yeah? What's her name?'

'I sat with her at lunch!'

'Well is she everything you wanted to find?'

'She's cool. Yeah, she's from where you're from, I think. If she were dropped off in the middle of Brazil, which is Goiás, she'd speak perfectly perfect Portuguese by the end of the hour. Doesn't subscribe to the authority that you can't be great at everything, or that axial tilt is the sole reason we exist. She has a rich tan, a real Cali girl, from Arizona. You can tell by the lack of vowel shift. Born in Arizona, raised in the desert, now a Santa Barbaran. Tell me what I'm forgetting. Don't tell anyone.'

'That would be taking all the fun, I'll let you. How was physics? Have any good dreams?'

'It's called Nonlinear Phenomena, of course I did. We talked about how Brayton borrowed and developed equations, got off topic and learned about pedagogical propulsion techniques.'

'Is he the one who invented lightning?' Carson, gulping water. 'Torrey was telling me about that class.'

'Who's she?'

'I told you, the girl I've been chasing since freshman year.' Tell me if you want me to stop."

"No it's fine. She's a good ex."

"Whatever that means. Mynor looked back with a greasy grin. 'And she's been running away ever since.'

'I keep telling you this, but I'm not sure if you know what I mean. She's the one.' No one knows what that means. 'She's the other bowling girl. It's an inside joke.' Which is why he said it in a public space.

'That's like me and Chase,' Liz indulged.

'I thought we didn't like Chase,' Marie divulged.

'We like Chase, he just has to decide if he likes me or his girlfriend more. You think he's my phenotype?' "

"What in the *hell* does that mean? Girls always make it sound so easy."

"Right? 'Carson, you owe me ten.'

'For what? You actually went?'

'Course. You have to turn it in Monday. You might want to ask for extra credit.'

'If I do she'll beat me up. I still don't get it. It takes half a year to read a few assignments and give them back like next quarter. She doesn't let anyone rewrite anything, how'd you do it?'

'Well I didn't know what she was talking about, so I just agreed with it all.'

'I'll improve it by a letter.' In the rewrite he discussed how small minds discuss people couldn't be less true. 'Who has the most magnificent mascot? Anteaters are subtly intimidating.' Best one is a smiley face, Motley's middle school.

'What about Arthur? Everyone thought Arthur was an anteater,' Lizmeister said. 'I thought that, anyway.' Carson got a call, up and left. 'Who's he talking to? Girlfriend?'

'One of them,' Marie specified.

'What person needs to talk with their girlfriend at dinner?'

'A boyfriend.'

'Good call, Kleytjen,' then she left my side of the table.

'Bye Blondie.' The only color she hasn't tried. Marie saw Jordyn on the way to the bathroom and asked if there was a reason she wasn't eating with us or if it was a big accident. Reason was Carson, accidents happen on purpose."

"From the swim team? That Jordyn?"

"And diving. As soon as he stood by the table again, 'Cars, what are you two doing this weekend? Pool party?'

'I have no idea. She's not mine.'

'You do everything together.'

When you're accused of it you may as well go ahead and be it. 'It'd be like marrying my sister, dude.' He doesn't have a sister.

'And?' He left to come back balancing more food and dropped his phone into his drink. 'Not my tea!' Used the rice to soak it up. The table made my arm wet. 'Nah, your arm made the table dry.' Used nine napkins to make it more dry. 'Capillary action! So anyway, for lab quiz I got seventy nine and a half.' "

"You could at least *try* to do an accent."

"Yessir. 'And it's out of eighty.' My vocal cords are getting tired.

'Who do you hang out with?' Carson got glasses three years after he needed to so he never saw anything or knew what to do. Got straight As. We should eat more salmon.

'It's cause our professor saw Flava Flav over the weekend and on Tuesday showed us a video of him telling us to study hard.'

'I still wish I had your brain power.'

'You could just read the same chapter I read.'

'Well that's pretty good, dude. I got a sixty nine and a half on Vertebrae Morphology. Out of a hundred. Average: forty nine. That's almost as good as Sterling, right? I heard he really turned his life around.' Absence has Mynor talking.

'Yeah he used to be lazy and uninformed. Now he's uninformed and lazy. I've had a change of leaf, too.'

'If he's not smarter, he works smarter. Kley you should know, what did he do?'

'Cleaned up, found Weezer. He just works every five minute gap.'

'Cool story, Kley. No I know, Sterling makes me feel slothful.' I tell myself a story to fall asleep."

"I still don't get it. You can consume what he does, study who he admires, listen to his music, eat his food, and ride his bike, but you'll never be anything like him."

" 'He would want you to realize your untapped potential.'

'Yeah dude, tap that.' Carson's buttoned shirt tucked in for the feast finale. 'What are we talking about? My Friday class is too boring, I have to chew gum.' What a thrill. Replaced it with chicken.

'I thought you were vegetarian.' Liz thinks everyone is, wants her cat to be too.

'I'm just not good at it.' Smiled wide.,'I just thought of something really funny.'

'Are you gonna share it with us?'

'No, it's cool. Anyone wanna go on a hike next weekend?'

'I'm not gonna be here.' Liz went to her brother's graduation.

'That a yes?' Mynor went to grab more grub."

"Damn, he's skinnier than you. If y'all fell off a unicycle it wouldn't hurt."

"It would. 'Hey, look. Bread goes in, toast comes out. You can't explain that!'

'What's the plural of toast? Is that what I think it is?' Liz ate a whole apple, core and everything.

'If you thought it was peanut butter and honey. And secret sauce.'

'Ew. Whatever, Thin Lizzie, that's hot. Whoa. So was that lime juice that went straight in my retina."

'Good use of retina.'

'If by *good* you mean Cars meant cornea, then yes, good.'

Carson heard my silent laugh from inside by the pizza line and yelled, 'Just think of the stupidest thing you could say and that's what Kleytjen says. I love it.' Carson, if you didn't know, matriculated to biological sciences, switched to communication, then to computer science, then to earth science, then to history, then to geography, before sticking with economics because he heard, 'If you don't get an education in finance, it'll be worthless.' If I had *Fooled By Randomness*, I would have given it to him. Then he would've made a major switch again. 'What can I say? You bring out a really good part of me.' I reminded him about the undie run on Wednesday."

"Whenever I'd do an econ experiment at school they'd say, Your decisions are in no way linked to you. I couldn't think of anything more opposite from real life. You always have to remind everyone of things."

"Gotta give everyone enough time to plan and not enough time to forget. 'I don't know if I'll go though, I have a final and a paper due the next day.'

'Everyone did it last quarter, anyway,' Lizzette's defense.

'I didn't.'

'Did I say you did?'

'Be*cause* I have a paper due and a final the next day, I'm going. When are we doing our sunrise walk?'

Carson spoke up, 'I don't know if I'll make it this year. Just a matter of time.'

'You go clubbing twice a week. Everyone has the same amount, it's not like you have plans for five in the morning.'

'Some of us don't have the luxury of time.'

'If everyone has it it's no luxury.'

'It's timing. Mornings are club meetings and practice. Afternoons I tutor at the elementary school to help with they homework. At night I stay up to work out. You don't even know, man.'

'I do now. You'll go to bed later but you won't get up earlier?'

'Dude, I already get up before my first class ends. Alright, let's go at five thirty after we go to the gym.'

'How did I know you would go to the gym?'

'How does Kleytjen know anything? Like that time we saw the chancellor there because it was way early.' Apparently there's room in Mynor's brain for that."

"This is a cool ass song." Me Gusta Tú.

"Muy bien. 'I,' Carson licking his fingers, 'remember cause I wasn't there.' Quite the breath of recall. 'Have you heard of baby carrots? One time I hurt my ankle on one of those ellipticals. Sure, I'll go with you guys. Or Jordyn, whoever texts me first. Like a litmus test.'

'That's not a test. You're gonna go with her anyway. Whatever, we'll go during summer when it's less crowded.'

'You're staying?' Carson took summer classes every year.

'You think this is camp where your parents pick you up at the end of the day?' I then was invited, via text, to a movie by Brad - the texter, not the director. Opposite of Sterling, seen more movies than I've heard of."

"And is his life any better for it?"

"Better than what? Only told me he was going to *The Hangover Part Two* and was gonna chill so hard. The first took them six years to write, the second they wrote in six months, so you could tell it had no chance of being as good. Or any good at all."

"Is part two the second one? It was written by different people. Do you have any idea how good you have to be to get a bad review? Also you told me this, it's cause you watched *Princess and the Frog* for the second time, like a moron. Who the hell is Rosecrans anyway and what do they have to do with this area?"

"First time with Amie, dude, it was on The List. And that was the week before. We did everything together, like bike races, beach studying, baking pi day brownie cupcakes. Before Casey's:

You still have my brownie dish to bring back

"We talk all the time, most of the time. Anyway, after Brad, Norman told me about a party up in what is now his former wasi:

We're playing beer pong and other drinking games at my apartment for my birthday if you want to come over. It's not gonna be anything huge.

"Depends on your definition of *huge*. Didn't say when, like he's on Hawaii time. Held up my phone, 'Anyone wanna go?' Carson never invites anyone to anything."

"Depends on if you have higher standards than the stupidest game ever invented."

"It doesn't hurt anyone."

"Again, higher standards. Games exist that are both harmless *and* enjoyable. Wanna stop by this club here? Long Beach is nice now, dude. They fixed it."

"Dude. 'What kinda fiestaing?'

'I dunno.'

'Then the answer's yes. But I haven't showered yet.' No one knows what time frame Mynor was referring to. After Norman, Jordyn said she was getting ice cream, so I asked the occasion.

My half bday!!! Only the third most important day ever!

"Every sentence for her is! I did want to go, but I told her I needed to pack and homework.

Get that shit doneee then go to sweet alley with Cars and mahself

"The next day they had the real fun, with cookies, with flowers, reservations at a romantic restaurant on State Street, Snack Shack, a place that serves spumoni. He paid for half."

"No one should have to tell you what an honor it is to be invited to a celebration. No new friends for you?"

"Yeah, big birthday weekend, definitely Antonio's. Parties that no one ever knows what they're for, like, hey, it's Thirsty Wednesday, are the way to do it, so I only went to those. 'Aight alright. I'm probly gonna get goin soonly.' Ellie's always first.

'When we gonna ball it up?'

'Prolly tonight or tomorrow.' Mynor sat down as she stood up, we stopped stuffing spoons in his backpack, he'd brought it to sneak food back into his room. And ours. 'You don't have to finish the rest of your food, we already did that for you.' He was done regardless, he said, just in a different vernacular. Irregardless.

'You're done eating? It looks like you dissected your pizza. That's a sin, and I ain't even religious.'

'Eh, it had too many toppings.' Can't not eat pizza cause the cheese might fall off.

'You don't like olives?' Marie took it as an insult.

'I don't really like onions either,' I confessed. 'Or dubstep.'

'You're too picky, Kley.' Selective. 'What don't you like about a hundred twenty beats per minute?' We bussed our plates and heard a jolt of cheering, Pizza Guy broke a plate."

"Nah, cause you all were leaving. Let me get this straight. You think you're cool since you always have lunch with other people? The guy who goes in, sits by himself, and doesn't give a shit about anyone else - that's the definition of cool."

The heart is button to button ~ Jack White

"Here's the thing - let me go back to Grace. The day before. It wasn't yet two, the play started at two thirty. Since I showed up early I got in free." Forgot to tell Sterling that. "I had the wherewithal, it's just no one was at the ticket booth and the doors were open for the crew and cast. All you have to do to go to anything freely is get there before anyone else."

"Or show up after it ends." Amie always on point.

"A few kilometers after the hotel, a couple miles, I was at Cabrillo Bridge when it got a little brighter. Right by Balboa Park since I took the 163 down north, so I stopped for a minute to take in the view and there was a group walking through the fields planting seeds. Smelled like honey."

"What whimsy. Life is what doesn't happen when you don't make plans."

"Plan is a nice word for procrastinate. Drove through Hillcrest by Urban Mo's and Squeaky Pickles and Shit, then - and La Pizzaria Arrivederci - then saw someone drive a red light at the intersection of Washington and Cleveland. From there I drove straight to Grace's school. Hey, that's the first time I've ever seen that Orange County sign."

"What sign? Wait, no turns?" No twists either.

"She goes to Maplewood, a very good school. We contend that for anyone to attempt progress without youth is like leaving grapes in the sun and not anticipating raisins. I first saw Hannah, running the permitted lemonade stand, and she described the Balboa museums to me when I asked, all sixteen. By the big fountain, there's Air and Space with an Apollo Nine module, the Model Railroad with the Tehachapi Pass, Natural History with a skeleton of a tiger, 'A dinosaur!' And the Museum of Art with collections from El Greco. I think, kids are people who find ways to make things happen. When you're older it takes a long time to change your way of thinking. People didn't think putting lead in paint or cooking with it was crazy. Anyway, the director told her they had to get ready. She asked if I would go watch the fireworks at night, I just shrugged, that was first I heard about them. 'Hey do, do you have a phone with you? I might get a phone when I'm a teenager. How old are you?'

'Nineteen for another day. When do you turn a year older?'

'On my birthday! Grace knows she better be there.' Let me set the stage. I enjoyed watching the crowd grow, like I knew I would, from the fifth row. After less than twenty minutes it was close to capacity. There are crazies out there: people who live in the middle of nowhere, people who have a heart attack for three days if the volume on the television is at an odd number, people who don't want to get wet when they go to the pool. Always inviting to listen to one side of a conversation, like when your roommate is on the phone. Except Sterling."

"Are you in love with him?"

"Everyone thinks they're the favorite. As you heard, I eavesdrop all the time, it's how I get most of my mental pictures, in all my vicariousness. Text from Jordyn gave me something to talk about with Carson, she finished first in the sixteen hundred fifty freestyle. What's impressive about this is she was still wasted.

Thanks for the words. Good use of scales lol. Have fun in sd this weekend and you better get twisted

"And from Norman.

I just saw the albino raccoon on Pasado. Yes I did. It was spiritual. Also we are going to ball at 6 outside if you are interested. Even Liz

"I'd something to say but right then the lights dimmed. All the shifters set up, just like at one of Ravi's plays, *Up the Down Staircase*, when a huge set piece fell over, spilled all over the stage."

"I'm not interested in imperfections. Are you guys twins?"

"I don't think you know what *twins* means. Texted Marie, meant to ask her at Norman's, a binary question about Liz before it started. Halfway through I felt my phone but didn't look, so for the next hour didn't know if it were a yes or a no. Or it was both, like Schrödinger would say, until you realize that doesn't make any sense at all because it's self centered. Marie already knew for certain whether she said yes or no. Conventionally enough, I told Grace about *Curtains* a few months before, but that's a higher production. The musical was piratey. It goes like this. Some dude turns twenty one so is no longer an indentured servant. They didn't modernize it. He meets someone's daughter who is at least seventeen and it's love at first sound. There are a couple unforgettable lines that I'll remember later. The thing is that the guy was born on February twenty ninth, a leapling, a la Bradshaw, so by law has to wait until he turns eighty four for his actual twenty first birthday and freedom. He dutifully obliges and at least has the promise of the lady girl that she will be true and hurry up and wait for him, like an ambush predator. And they're pirates, so you can figure what happens. All in two acts. They did really well, none of them got hiccups. When you're a kid you know how smart you are, your parents and teachers forget. Me too. Things they do seem irrational, except from their viewpoint. They're just a couple years away from being smarter than anyone. At least that's what the program said." When it was over I didn't see Marie's yes, but:

You crack me up obviously

I'd told Jen about all the food they were selling and that Twix was the only one for me. "I saw Lunch Line Guy's mom, dressed in red, dozen bracelets on her left arm. Her son played boss man Stanley."

"Do you think I haven't seen this play?"

"I don't know what to think anymore. 'Hello, Kleytjen. How are you?' Curiosity in her thin eyebrows.

'I'm doing fine. How about yourself?'

'Great, how are you? Ah, where are your parents?'

'They were here opening night.'

'I haven't seen you down here in a while. Is this your penultimate year? Do you know what's next?'

'I don't predict the future.' It's always funny when we try to.

'What do you want to be?'

'What do I want to do? Fill up my passport.'

'Some people travel a lot and go nowhere. Well that's okay. I didn't even start school by the time you'll graduate. Have you ever seen *Pirates*?' We moved outside where the stars were gathering.

'Yeah, a long time ago.'

'*I* saw it a long time ago. It was really good, you agree?'

'Yeah, that's a great way to describe it.' She asked me about still getting my degree in accounting, a most inevitable topic. 'That's the ship I'm on, yes. It's mentally changing every day.'

'You like it there, right? My daughter visited last year and thought it to be very nice but decided not to apply because the program she wants is chemical engineering, and they don't have it.' The craziest thing she ever could have said."

"By every measure, our top rated program."

"Honestly. I let her step away and Grace arrived, still in costume. She played one of the other daughters. 'Hup. Was it good?'

'Gracie! Yeah it was funny. I like the how beautifully blue the sky part. And when you switched your hats.'

'You noticed that! You are very observational.'

'Observant. Punk.'

'You're welcome. Our director said we did great.'

'That's a really good word.' Grace said she had to go home and wanted to walk with Hannah, who was Kate."

"What'd she have to do after the play?"

"A whole bunch of nothing, that's what. It's in our blood. 'Cool. I'll probably go see a movie or something if I find someone to go with.'

'What kind, a shootery?'

'Yeah I dunno. Whatever's good.' Forgot to give her her shirt, left it in Jen's car. Drove out of the parking lot before these streets crowded and went back to leave her car at the hotel." Glad she was back in my atmosphere. "First I stopped at a gas station, made sure to fill up at the Highland Ranch place that always sells winning lottery tickets." Now past La Mirada and Cypress, kept looking for the Disneyland fireworks even though I knew those were hours gone. Amie, when she was little, her parents said that the park closes right after the fireworks, like at eight, when really it closes at midnight. My parents said that too. "After Jen went back to work I left the Parsippany and walked around as the evening passed, slow as summer break, no movie. Besides, I only see movies I've already seen. Mynor called, hard to understand and harder to tame. 'Hey Freaky Fresh, you were really super drunk last night.'

'Did you figure this all out right now? Let me know when you get paid.'

'Our employment rate does keep going up, I just need a car. But I need money to buy a car, so I need a job before that. I'll need a car to drive to work though, so I need a car a priori.' A fire truck drove by so I didn't hear this the first time. 'Alright Kley, I'll let you know who wins tonight.' By then the streets were more crowded, with the Kensington parade on Malborough, between Palisades and Adams. Lots of marching and a lot of non marchers holding forget me nots. The parade was scheduled to set with the sun. Forgot to let you know, the whole reason it was moved up is there was a big storm on the loose in the forecast for Sunday into Monday, guaranteed precipitation. I didn't know what to believe, it's no Philadelphia, where it's always rainy. Or Zanzibar. May showers in San Diego are as common as the management of expectation, even on a cloudy day."

"Why would you expect anything? Preserve your anticipations."

I didn't expect her to do anything until she said she would. "Even more crowded toward the USS Midway, but I was going the other way by the Convention Center. I headed onward to my hunger, and all that presence got me thinking about *Things They Carried* and *Thousand Splendid Suns* and *Catch Viente Two*. Likely the best there is, like a Scorsese film done well. It's not funny on any intellectual level, so I must have read it wrong. No way around it with Yossarian. I like it when there isn't an overly romantic end where the i's are dotted with hearts accompanied by super dramatic music and all that that messes with you. Just have nothing happen. Credits roll." She didn't think about that enough to verbally object to it, and after Anaheim and Savanna we were in the city of Orange. "There should be a town called Apple so you could compare everyone from each."

"You're *so* random." How can you not be?

"In fairness, apples and oranges are the two most legitimate things to ever compare."

"I like *In The Lake of the Woods*. Side question, how come you don't value money anymore?"

"It costs too much. I got some food quickly at Cheap Charlie's, over between Dirty Mike's and Peggy's Lavender Pie Place. Where I wanted to go was an eatery this waiter Jessie Valdivia told me about. There's something about food that makes me hungry."

"You're always hungry, and never inclined to cook."

"Kept the menu closed, just ordered what the party next to me had, some funny rice burgers. 'These are delicious!' With unbridled joviality. Wasn't sure if they were being polite or if they just never tasted a good burger before, but delicious is a strong word. Turns out they were right.

'I hope you like this.' Served on a square plate.

'I hope I like it too.' While gobbling I rerealized I don't understand girls' boyfriends. They sneak up on you. You sit next to the same girl for ten weeks, then the night before the final you ask her if she wants to study, she says no, she's having a twelfth anniversary dinner with some guy she never mentioned. Nothing understandable about that. Finished my burger, bun, salad, licked my lips and fingertips. Don't know why I ate so quickly."

"Good at eating, not a good eater." It's true. Food falls out of my mouth.

"So then I took my time and ordered dessert, warm and melty, like you're drinking a cookie, and decided to stop making up conundrums. Just have to let it marinate."

"That's a lot to digest. Have you been to Deja Vu? My aunt says to check it out."

"That sounds familiar." As we cruised past the Ducks and Angels, my only thought was, Norman's party's probably just ending.

Youre the night kind of dreamer ~ Pat Benatar

I broke my nose when I bounced too high on our neighbor's trampoline during fifth grade. That's cooler to say now than it was at the time. "At the exit entrance this tall, like a short basketball player, girl walked in and slapped Carson. Marie postulated, 'What if we tried to name all of his past girlfriends? Well I'm out of meals, does anyone wanna join me for brunch tomorrow at nine?' We thought that was called breakfast, but no one likes turning her down. 'I'll be going to Periwinkle's probably. Even though I always imagined it was on State.'

'You don't have to imagine it. Just look at a map.'

I have never seen Pizza Guy that talkative and excited in my life haha

Even though Mynor was walking right beside me. 'Garlic curlicue fries at Zodo's, anyone? Hit me up if you're down. It's free since our club is paying for it.' When we go out to dinner he has to stop and get food on the way. I asked Sterling about Norman's.

Hahahahaha if I didn't have plans I totally would be down just because of that

"He *would* totally would be," Palmer observed.

"Like Lady Gaga said, Da da doo doo mm."

"You're so diva'd out."

"My phone saved received ones until it filled up, deleted sent ones automatically, so I don't know how I phrased my invitation, just that I said Norman would fight a bear." Except when I sent a picture, those were saved.

"Weird, most keep asking until they get a yes." Right around Torrance or whatever's right next to it Palmer kept looking at the lanes like he was wondering how long it took to paint all the lines. We were nearing the airport now and Santa Monica. I think Palm would have fun being a pilot.

"So we all went back to the dorms, I was told to slow down twenty times. Think it's more having a long stride, but if everyone else says I walk fast, then obviously I do."

"Finally you understand that it ain't no good to walk faster than the rest of your group."

"I asked Amie about Chase before deciding what lease to sign and she said, 'Don't worry, I have a leg up on him.' Later I understood how she meant. Most went back to the lounge to watch nothing, I packed all I thought of for the weekend. I brought a toothbrush, some toothpaste, and clothes. I'm a light traveller, not because I eat less. Grace, when she was younger, whenever we went anywhere, even just out to lunch or something, like down the street, or to check the mail, or to a lemonade stand, she brought her whole room with her. A pillow, minimum of seven coloring books, and extra shoes, even though we were just going a minute away. That makes all kinds of no sense. To everyone. Had a few minutes to work on Sterling's grant project. Wasn't zoned in, thought instead about who I would see in San Diego. A joie de todos, who you really like spending time with, someone you make time for by saying no to other things. Jen's so funny, when I did something dumb like wear mismatching shoes, the next day she did the same thing. Without warning. Or different colored sleeves. Even wore tie dye socks to Winter Formal junior year. Or, when I set my phone to Spanish, she did too. English interface looks weird to me now. She also has all her contacts saved as nicknames. I left on his desk: I won't. Forcing myself to work on your project now would be doing you a disservice. Give it the attention and passion it deserves.

"Jen never took notes in pen. Always in pencil, always. I thought to ask her if she still used pencils, but it seemed like such a silly topic to bring up. I think what you're knowing, but she makes me want to be - "

"She's not here right now."

"I'm gonna call her."

What started it all is when I first saw her at the Parsippany. "Morning, sunshine! Actually it's kinda foggy." Jen's a great hugger, if you're wondering. Spun around in a circle, moved my spine. Took so long to get my first from her, I never understood. Everyone else it's right after the first second they meet her, or before, so I don't know what the rules are. Last one was the summer before, she was out of town, in Los Lagos, Chile, taking classes that started before spring ended. Eight hours before was so different, though it didn't seem like any halfway point. Eight hours before *that* was when Mason and I'd went for ice cream. It's nonlinear, learned that in Astro, and I can offer no information in mitigation. Actually, it was the voicemail before that, "Hey Kleytjen! It's Jen, giving you a call. I'm changing - we have work clothes, so I'm changing and then I will be ready! Give me a call back so I know you got this, that way I know you haven't passed out or something. Yeah, give me a call when you get this and we can meet up, okay?" All others are disposable.

"Don't do that." He glanced at the cupholder holding a phone, either his or the one he stole.

I didn't because my phone showed another notification. Played it on speaker, "Kley your mailbox has been full. For five years. Go with me to the zoo, Paul was going to go but he has to get a haircut so we can't go, not tomorrow. Tuesday not tomorrow, tomorrow I'm going to the beach so yeah go with me, I got my money next to me. Palm was gonna go but he has to get a haircut, I guess it's really bad."

"I don't know what he's talking about. San Diego doesn't even *have* a zoo."

"It's so weird, he left three voicemails all at the same time but they don't show up until like an hour after each other. Anyway, you never know how dark it is until you turn on the lights. So I put on a Sterling shirt, a little less yellow, turned the lights back off and left the dorms to Sweet Alley. I talked with Mason, he called to tell me he was going to Norman's too. Mason'd planned on going for months, goes to less than three parties a year, two of them are in the library, so he was looking forward to it, even though it goes against his personality. He won the Oregon State Chess Scholastic Champions tournament when he was twelve and thought of himself as a perfectionist until twenty." My dad went to Oregon on a summer camping trip. "When he got his first cavity he acted like it was a big deal. We saw each other crossing the bike path and hung up to continue our - "

"Your life is a series of unfinished conversations. Go back to Mynor."

It's more than that.

We saw the sun go down in your eyes ~ Paul Hewson

"How am I supposed to get around this?"

"What do you mean?"

"I always think something big won't see me and then they'll turn straight in and it'll be all over."

"Well I hope not. Just think of all the people on that bus who would be late." There was some art on the side I would have taken a picture of if there were daylight. "Punch it." And just like that Patricia made it past. "I did feel bad for leaving Grace the way I did, especially since she didn't have a phone. Only way my dad would know anything is if they came back before I did. Doesn't check the odometer or anything crazy and it wouldn't take too much gas. Or maybe they hired the neighbors as spies, that was the only other way I thought of. Or if they happened to see bus driver at the wherever they were. Took a few minutes to say bye to her, she was worried about them getting home and freaking out. You know how height, simple or polygenic, skips a generation? That's the only thing I can liken it to. 'Grace, the car's gonna be fine. They won't care anyway.'

'Yeah, except that one time. Do you have to go see her *now*?'

'Course, otherwise it would be rude. It'll be a good time. Hey, we have a hall light here. Who knew?'

'You think everything's a good time.'

Nodded my head. 'Aren't they?'

'Maybe for some people.'

'That's right, yo. What if I didn't go and she'd went there to tell me something important?'

'I don't know why you'd worry about that. It seems like such a selfish thing to do.'

'If they get back before I do, tell them everything that's happening.'

'I don't wanna feel pressured to do that.' She sat down on the kitchen floor in protest.

'That's not pressure. That's what people do.'

'Besides! I'll be at school anyway and won't be able to. What o'clock is it?'

'Time for you to eat an avocado.'

'*You're* an avocado.' She tossed it back.

Grace wanted to heat up a quick burrito, but the house had no microwave, one of the good things about it, and she was already late. 'It's one oh eight.'

'Don't put that piece of hair on me!'

'I'm giving it back. I haven't worn this shirt in a while, does it look okay?'

'Yes, but yeah, they,' whoever that is, 'say you're supposed to wash clothes like once a month even if you don't wear them. Whoa. There's a big bug I've never seen before. And I'm not sure I'm okay with that.' It did have immense girth."

"Bigger than a breadbox?"

"Gargantuan, yea big. 'Actually, no one said anything when I bought it.'

'So what about Mommy and Daddy? Can't you call em maybe?' She didn't see my urgency.

'Tell them I needed a ride somewhere. That's a reasonable reason.'

'Yeah, but it's not true. Since when do you tell random stories?' Hang on." In Santa Ana I felt a buzz.

She says summer's started sizzling, Saturday's still smooth sailing somehow, since supreme sedulous shenanigans seized seven seas' smelly sandy shores, seeing several symmetrically synchronized scarlet shanghaied swimmers skedaddle, sans sincere savvy school spirit, so summarily speaking such silly sizable sentence sounds.

Not when he said he would, but who's counting? "Look. Mynor tried to be sage." We passed Irvine where we could have stopped in for Science of Superheroes if it were class time before Amie finished reading it one glance at a time. Ferris wheel lights at Spectrum were off.

"Successfully. That's the worst sentence of the year."

"His or mine?" Amie accidentally exited instead of joining the carpool lane; my fault, left exit. "Wow, now we're lost. I still say we'll make it there by midnight."

"We're not lost, just temporarily displaced."

"We can reenter in this lane. 'It seems nice here. Mom and Dad make any friends yet?'

'I think so.'

'Good. Alright, I really gotta go.' Backed out of the driveway. I drive like a koala bear when I'm in a hurry. Didn't even know Kabiting would be able to meet up and I was already late before I left. Does it make a difference if you're late on purpose or late on accident? Left the Seven Hills neighborhood toward Ted Williams Parkway and drove past the Welcome Inn up to Vista via the fifteen, our designated equidistant. Only once I had to slow down real quickly because some dude didn't know how to merge. Don't have to change your speed when you're doing it right. Took twenty six minutes in all. Three hundred eighty if I walked it. Did I tell you how I wasn't allowed to sell back my astronomy textbook?" If you have the opportunity, don't. The sequel course uses the same book. "I know where I was going with that, but I'm getting a call." Those who tell the truth and those who give a complete story.

"Okie dokie karaoke. How are you so popular at this hour?"

"To make up for the rest of the day. Ah it's just Palmer, we'll talk later."

"Does he still have energy drinks to calm down?"

"On parade night when I met up with him, I didn't know where I to walk to after Charlie's until he gave me a ring. Palmer, he's nocturnal, like a gargoyle. I originally called just to hear if he wanted to hang out in the daylight. He didn't answer but he answered,

This is the thing I was telling you about when I was telling you about that thing.

'Yo. You called twice so I hope this is trivial.'

'Shut up Kley, are you coming here sometime?'

'As we speak.'

'Oh. Don't go in the room. I'm serious, don't go in the bedroom. Don't. The angel's in my bed.' His bed was disgusting, like a really good beer. 'Let's go to the place where you have that gift card.' Broken Yolk on Sixth, fancier than usual, we didn't know what else to do. Jen had said she was going to Elephant Bar over on B Street.

'The who? I'm not going to your place, just gonna post up outside La Puerta. On Market.'

'Well hold on I'll be there sooner than you know.' When I asked where he was he said, 'Yalready know where I'm at.' Always, 'Yalready know what it is,' except I don't. Why else would I ask? 'Watch a movie and before it's over I'll be there. Yeah, do that. You seen that vampire one? See it. Best fuckin scene I've seen in my life.' Ignored the imperative to know who. It takes Palmer an hour and a half to say goodbye, had to tell me how his supervisor asked him if he wanted to get drinks with their marketing team right after she fired him. He learned to talk before he learned to walk. 'Shit's about to go down.' Like a toilet. 'Alright I'm gonna let you go. First let me tell something to you. If you ask to get drinks it means you just wanna have sex that night and don't care if you see her again.'

No particular plans other than to loiter inside. Bartender looked over. 'How you doin? Came here for preflection, huh? Gonna get blasted? I can tell just by looking at you that you're in a relationship.' His voice's raspy, like a berry. Or Brad's.

'I can tell just by looking at you that you have a beard.' Even though he couldn't tell I was underage, I ordered a strawberry lemonade, and then a second one. Only one flying solo. Gay couples, straight couples, somewhere in between couples, couples who aren't even really couples, where there's like six of them, or four of them, like Fleetwood Mac. Feeling part of the scenery.

'Here ya go, big boy.' Condescendingly, it seemed; it wasn't. 'That's three for the lemonade.'

'For each?'

'No, for each of them. Actually I'll let it go. Just don't take advantage of my niceness.' Got up from the barstool to see Palmer, lolled in in a brown blazer, fancied himself early.

'This your foreign energy drink? You only had half.'

'Nah, I bought eight. I had to hide my car, I don't want anyone to know what's in there, there's a lot of private info like my medical records.' At least twelve people heard him say that.

'It's easier to just pay and park here.'

'That's how you know it's not right. You're wearing shorts. Kley, can you keep a secret?'

'Most of the time. What is it?'

'Nothing. Just wondering. You see that movie?'

'Is it that good?'

'No idea. Never seen it.' Now the good news: in spite of having no script, no cast, and no director, the second sequel has a release date. 'What day is it? June? So does Anthony know she's there?'

'I don't even know who's there.'

'Yeah you do. Well you can think whatever you want. Unless you're wrong.'

'Aren't you still with - '

'Don't worry about it, Kley. If I had any type of currency every time a girl was faithful to me, I'd be in debt.'

'You *are* in debt.'

Then we took a seat, 'Hey kids, I'm Natasha. Can I startcha off with some drinks?'

'I'll take your best IPA.' A mad ale. 'And do you have any graveyard specials? Kley here wants to know.'

'I just want water, please.'

'Do we have any what? We have what we call the No Name. Give us eleven ninety five, get it for free. Plus tax.'

He thought it was a trick. 'Hold on.' She drew a picture. 'Man this shit's expensive. I was gonna offer to split it, good thing you have that card.'

'Just enjoy crowd watching.'

'I watch chicks, I don't know about this *pe*ople watching. Man, where are these girls during the *week*?'

'Getting ready. What's their table protesting?'

'Sundays. Sorry, we're ready now. We were gonna share an appetizer but he's in the mood for breakfast and rage recently removed itself from that category.'

'Monte Cristo for me, por favor,' I ordered.

'I'll have the same thing, except I'll have the Santee Chili Burger, whiz, with. That's all.' Natasha said that's her favorite. 'Torrey makes a mean breakfast, but breakfast is cheaper than a wife and shit.'

'More inexpensive.'

'Less expensive. There are two kinds of people. Those who order the same thing from the same place and those who never order the same thing twice.'

'I think there are way more than that.'

'Kley, we possess neither the expertise nor the prerogative to make judgments.' All sheltered in our own way. 'Don't counter with crap about I should be happy to have someone to spend money on.' "

"Kleytjen, let me ask you, what do you think about digital currency?"

"Same as any other. It's as good as what it's used it for. I'm two feet away from Palmer when he says:

Dude our waitress is that stripper from last month

It actually was, although he meant last year. Then he says out loud, 'I'll take care of the tip.'

'Antonio's calling.' I answered.

'What up Kley. I need someone to talk with about not having spending money."

'There's another kind?'

'It would be nice to afford to do fun stuff on the weekends.'

'It is nice. If it's cause you owe me mini golf money, don't worry about it. Get a job.'

'I already have one. Money listens.'

'Compliment your income.'

'Supplement. Then I won't have time to do fun stuff on the weekends.'

'You have a mental budget, not a real budget.'

Palmer grabbed the phone, 'Dude, we gotta go, I'll see you later.' He did.

'I heard this last night from Mason: I hope you're a utilitarian because if you say yes to me, the happiness of the world will increase by much more than if you say yes to someone else.'

'What's that supposed to be, a pick up line? I don't think it's gonna work, it sounds like she's hot. That was like a disastrophe.'

'Weird definition of *like*. What are you up to though? You still with Torrey?'

'Torrey is with me these days.' "

Parties were meant to last ~ Prince Nelson

Everybody remembers where they were when they first heard their favorite song, and this is mine: our plain room. Walked into the Dragon Tavern and Mister Birkenbuel wasn't there. Found Ravi's acoustic close to the ceiling. I always left it in exactly the same spot next to my dresser and plastic sandals; Sterling always put it back in a slightly different position, like the bathroom. I'm glad, us who don't play the guitar have no advantage over those who can't tocar la guitar. His sophomore roommate played, way better than I but not nearly as good as Sterling, and didn't let him use his capo. Why would you get mad at someone who's better than you? Enough vanity was too much, I took my sunglasses off to be productive. Took a shot of corn whiskey and charged my phone, it only needed juice once a week instead of ten times a day. "My other contract was for *Outliers*. Felt like I should stop, thought I wasn't going to be honorificable anymore anyway, but I sat in bed and followed the words. It's good for your life, like *Treasure Island* or *Twenty Thousand Leagues*."

"But does it make you a better person? I prefer Verne to Nabokov, narrowly by a lot." Since when does being a better person matter?

"And I doubt any of them ever wrote anything as good as Bach did. I'm unbookish, I know Twain's stuff but not Nin's, so I'm aware there is nothing that cannot happen today, and that's it."

"Interesting. You're influenced by people you have never met. How do you know he's the one who said that?"

"People I've never met have memories of hanging out in our room. Our neighbors below sounded like monkeys again, same time everyday. They do that and then they go to this place, I don't even know what it's called, but they go there. Footsteps echoed down the hall and Mynor, self described as bad, walked in, rocking a new polo. Most times he was already there, always unlocked. Door was actually always wide open, even when we weren't there. If you don't lock your door, you won't get a thing stolen, not one. Only times we closed it were to use our mini basketball hoop and dart board. And sleep. So, ocean view and all, we had the corner with an extra window. My parents always think my friends are gonna steal stuff from my room."

"That's fucked up. Who do they think you hang out with?"

"You, mostly. I miss it everyday, now that is an understatement. Sterling put up a sign by the toilet, Who's got it better than us? Everything else he hung up on the cork wall above my bed." Met back up with the 101. "Dude, you already know the Mynor part. Member that guy we met last week of Mesa?"

"Yeah what was his name? Aaron? Trevor?"

"Mel. He was at the party Mynor went to after me."

"What'd you do?"

"Nothing. After Mason bounced off his bike we met Jordyn at Sweet Alley, no Carson. Enough belligerence in the streets we call home to be a typical Friday night, or Tuesday afternoon."

"It's Halloween somewhere. Wait which party is this? What kind of rich spoiled asshole rents out a rooftop for their birthday?"

"This isn't that one."

"Oh. Whatever, talk about whoever you wanna fuck and fuck whoever you wanna talk about, I don't care."

"Alright then. Post ice cream, I paid for Mason since he didn't have his money he said and then felt bad not paying for Jordyn but she was meeting up with someone after anyway, we walked to Trigo but didn't know the address, only'd been there thirty six times before, so we were off by one. Door open, Mason walked right in, no need to knock. 'Hey, is this the party?' Sweaty and scandalous, everyone waiting around for the weekend. Bloody sugar strewn over the floor.

'Holy shit what party? Oh. Naw man, this is the pre party. Slide on through if ya want! Gotta get you a drink to get.' Mel stood at the top of the stairs with a couple girls, noticed we were by ourselves. 'Hey, these girls are single.'

Mason put his arm around me. 'We're not.' We walked a few feet to the right, only slightly more sleazy second story symposium. No one below made any plans to sleep, they had a subwoofer."

"How many stairs?"

"Fourteen. Carson greeted us at the door, he was boozing day, night, and whatever's in between. 'How come you guys don't have a doorbell? Your neighbors do.'

'I thought we did! Damn thieves. Y'all want anything? Vodka? Whiskey? Multivitamins? Guys, one rule: no drinking durning serious conversations. Two: no serious conversations. You want me to write it down? Here, I'll write it down.' Party favors.

Mason looked around at the tapestries. 'Nobody here but people?' We were early. 'Time to imbibe!' Really wanted to use that word.

'You bring your A game tonight?' Almost every night. Carson when he's not watching hockey says he's from the Yay Area. That's as specific as you can get. He means whatever's west of Fruitvale.

'When's what game?' Mason was still holding a spoon.

'I'll take that as a no. Where'd you get Sweet Alley from?' From Sweet Alley. 'Why'd you do that?'

'It was on the way.' I called Sterling since he knew everyone there.

'I'll stop by right now, Kley. What's their address? Six nine something? Pasado?'

'There is no six nine block. Six seven four nine. Trigo.'

Liz's palace was across the street, so he stopped by for a minute, no more, but Norman saw him. 'Sterling! What an honor it is.'

'No sweat, Brett.' He's really good with names. 'You're ready, man.' And Dirt Off Your Shoulders was on. 'The big two oh!' He's young for our class, like me but smart.

'It's the weekend! Ready to make mistakes?' They don't need a reason.

'Heck no, Techno. Kay Kleytjen, I gotta head back. Do you know you gave me the address to next door?'

'You gonna be asleep when I get back?' He just moved his head.

'Yo, we gonna sip Bicardi?' Carson wanted to shared a cup.

'Yes, that's way too slow, but you had me at yo. You had me at yo.'

Still sober I introduced Liz, dandy of the party, to Brad. Already knew him for a year and a twelfth. I always claimed matchmaker, 'Hey, have you met - '

'Why yes, eight times, we also have nineteen classes together.' I was anterograde about these things. They originally met at Marie's kickback.

She had just left Kappa Delta, said it's too fake. 'Shut up, dude.' No one was speaking. 'You need to talk louder.' Ubiquitous red cups hogging floor space, like my grandma's favorite country song. Only way you could identify the party is she'd brought a big cake and bigger balloons."

"Real live balloons?"

"Sí. If presents and confetti were involved, it happened elsewhere. 'We got you a cake!'

'Just one?'

'Now you can have your cake, and eat it, too!' I don't get it. What the hell else are you going to do with cake? 'For whoever's hungry, there's cake on the coffee table!' Norm was already under there and drinking.

'What food do you have for those who aren't hungry?' Mason cut a tiny slice. 'Anyone want to share this? Fine, I'll just eat the whole thing myself. Dude Kley, come on, have half.' I took it all and filled up another cup.

Liz loudly wore her belt over her shirt, some kind of fashion. 'What ya got in there?' Replaced my cup in all her charm. 'It's where the fun is.' Like a banana peel waiting to be slipped on. Nights like these I don't understand. Didn't even learn how to have a girl like me after a long time, presumably because of the whole lack of kindergarten.

She gave the same line to Mason, and I tried to reacquaint them with the benefits of hard liquor. 'I don't have time to drink beer. I'm getting hammered trying to get rid of my stomach virus before tomorrow's thing tomorrow.'

'You have like three eyes!' Liz looked intently at Carson. 'I didn't know you wore contacts.' Convex. 'I drank mine this morning. You wanna dance with them bitches?' She meant *ladies*."

"Dude, are you from a different century? It's like you're telling a story to the queen to spare your life. This one wouldn't work."

"To show you how it all began. 'Are you always sarcastic, or only when you're somewhere you don't fit in?' Like the fifth member in a string quartet, but that was a loaded question."

"Seriously, turn the bullshit filter on. Was Paraskevopoulos there?"

"Chase," Apastathopoulos, 'went later but his brother, looking even better than his picture, said, 'You're funny as shit, man. Consider the possibility people are talking serious.' I'd thought it was against the rules. He asked me what I thought about Liz, she's like a whisk.

'Thoughts rarely cross my mind.' Mason stood back in the corner trying to start his homework, not watching the girls dance. Living large. 'How come you're wearing so many watches?'

'I never want be late.'

'You don't talk much,' Torrey observed.

'I'm really smart so I like listening to myself think. I can't find my notebook.'

'Call it. What's your name? Chase? I really like that name.'

'*He*'s Chase. If you say Mason, I'll turn around. It's a big name in Italy. Even Montreal.'

'Is that a city?' Marie explained, 'I'm not drunk, I'm just stupid. We're all gonna have a study sesh tomorrow, wanna join us?'

'No thanks, I have to study.'

Refound the birthday boy and asked how everything was doing and going and everything. 'I'm doin de Loop tomorrow.' Where you take a shot from every place in walking distance so then you don't make it to the next day if all goes well. Or something. Said his older sister would be there to give him proper identification.

'Norm, you go downtown last night?'

'I'm not single.'

'What you coulda did was sneak in, stupid!' Carson, in sunglasses. Wherever he goes it's always sunny, like Sunnyvale. 'I know we're friends, but tonight I'm gonna hurt you with liquid.'

'Sweet, how many you invite to this thing?'

'Four thousand one hundred six hundred eighty two. You seen my main squeeze? Also, who's that girl? She's the drunkest one here.'

'The one jumping on the table?' No one was on the table.

Norman had normal amounts of Moscato cascading through his body. 'Thank you, Happy Birthday to you too,' to everyone. 'Remember gravity is irrelevant.'

'My birthday always seems to be during summer. You want a beer?' It's funny he was wearing red pants. Amie wears red pants too, but she's not who I got it from. Do you ever get the feeling someone's sleeping with everyone except you?"

"You don't think people can be friends?"

"It's not that. 'That's like asking a fish if it wants water. There is no magic in getting drunk.' Then he took twenty shots of jagger.

Mason attempted one. 'This tastes like it could run my car.'

'Good, isn't it?'

Carson wondered, 'If there's a party and everyone doesn't remember it, did it still happen?'

Norman completed the call and response by continuing it. 'Absolutely. If someone *does* remember it, was it really a party?' I prefer Lupe Fiasco's inquiry, What you drinking liquor for?

'You don't like reality? Don't let your euphoria interfere with your fun. I'm parched.'

'There's beer on the thing. Kleytjen, make sure to see if the girl friend you had come two weeks ago can come this week, but not this month.' Brad was talking about soccer. Amie's deft with her legs, sure knows how to make you prurient. When she turned sixteen her dad took her to see *Knocked Up*.

Carson stood up on a coffee table to give a toast and I took the drink out of his hand. 'Thanks dude. Great parties are all alike, every bad party is bad in its own way. I'm pretty sure it's a direct quote.' Carson makes terrible first impressions, was elected president of the Coastal Fund during the first meeting he accidentally attended. Here he was elected to play beer pong first. 'Wait, hold on. I'm really sure I gotta make a phone call.'

'Your mom?'

'Dude, really?' His mom. 'Fool, come on. This shot is dedicated to her.' Missed by fifty three feet. Think it hit Mel. 'Shit. Don't tell her. Anyone wanna finish my drink?'

'Me,' said I.

'What the hell's wrong with you?'

'My dentist says I have a big tongue.' Bite it when I'm sleeping. 'What do you have against it?' "

"What did you have for it?"

"Liz walked over and underneath to me. 'Kley, just calm down and have a cocktail. Drink your happiness away.' Took a ten out of ten effort."

"Whoa, wait a time out. I wasn't keeping track. You freely forfeited *four* hundred dollars?"

"I said I wouldn't drink that day, didn't say anything about night. But yes, yes indeed. When a girl made me a drink, I didn't wanna be rude."

"The best part about not drinking is drinks are free."

"Agreed to a little taste of a French martini. Liz gets everyone to do what they don't wanna. 'Wha'd'ou think this is, a bar? You'll have this.' I forgot to have it when Norman walked by, one girl in each arm. It works out that she and Marie were roommates. If he had three arms, well. Only there for two things. The Edge of Glory was on so I asked him if he heard it before, thought it was new.

'Dude, I've had sex to this song.' Norman also claims he's a standard deviation below average intelligence."

"Both sides of the curve. Do you think he's gay?"

"No, he's just awesome."

"Does he switch teams?" We were back around Calabasas.

"He was one question away from a perfect score on the SAT. Kaplan asked him to teach their prep courses, instead he retook it, gave himself a nineteen twenty, he likes the Jazz Age. I find no fault in him. Last year he had a dream he was taking twenty two units, fifty percent more than the median, more than we're allowed to. 'That's how much I'm gonna miss it.' Realized his agenda would be blank, so the next day he applied to Geffen School of Medicine. Due November first, did the whole app on Halloween, in costume. That's why I forgot my drink. At least I remembered it. 'Is this what they call a remix? You guys can join the circle.'

'Nah, I'm gonna keep it kosher and stay outside like a fiend. Hey yo baby.'

I thought Carson spotted one of the single girls but it was a sorority girl. She wasn't late we were just early. 'Hey Cowboy. I'm gonna stop you right there. I like girls.'

'Great, we have something in common. Can you do a huge favor for me?' He looked eager. 'Wanna hand me that beer?' Jordyn finally showed up like I knew she would. Cut tee shirt, toxic. The way that she learned how to swim is when she was three her parents took her to a lake and tried to drown her. If under water, blow bubbles and follow them. Same facial features as Hayden Panettiere. And a winsome set of teeth. She once told me she's a two drink girl."

"Two first names, too."

"She brings the Jordyn batting average up. 'Sup gurl.' Certified fresh. 'You ready for trials tomorrow?'

'Sunday. It's such a small part of what we do,' not interested in being one kind of person. Jordyn instantly had the best idea of the night. 'Do you know how good pineapple pizza sounds right now?' Tastes even better. 'On the scale of one to good, like, amazing!' She makes the laundromat exciting. Carson agreed and ordered from Pizza Bob's.

Jordyn left the room and he followed her with his hooded eyes. 'What a waist - Hi. Nothankyou. Yeah. We'll take two big pizzas. What? Oh. Um. Extra large. Pineapple and pepperoni. One pineapple one pepperoni. You guys want anything else on the pizza?' Weird definition of *guys*. 'The hell? Okay, yeah, just one with pineapple and one with pepperoni. Okay. Thank you.'

'Why'd you call *Bob*'s? I got a great pizza dealer,' back to Mason. 'I'm trying to go home but Norm wants to rally.' Sixteen minutos later, knocking on the door. 'There's nobody in here!'

Nobody but me heard. 'Carson, there's something alive at your door. Should just keep it open.'

'I have, two extra larges, correct? Is there a reason your pants are down?'

'Yes, thank you. Um, sorry there, we don't have any more for a tip.'

'You have twenty eight dollars and forty one cents exactly?'

'We can give you a bong hit, Pizza Girl.'

'No way? Alright.' "

"The more tipping is a part of a culture the more corrupt it is. I don't use my name when I don't tip." Palmer's very proud of that.

"I like how you see no grayscale. Carson walked away from the door, 'Man, I'm so fucking hungry.' We thought he bought it for decoration. 'We got any candles? Norm could get a wish.' Twenty four slices spread unequally amongst everyone. Jordyn had just one bite. 'I smell like cheese. That was only twenty eight bucks? We shoulda bought more beer.' Slipping away, 'I'ma be dipping early.'

'Why's that?'

'Gonna get up early. I gotta shower and get dressed and everything for my phone interview.'

Liz returned from wherever she was, screamed when she saw Jordyn. Hugged for five minutes, like where you haven't seen the person in years. They had lunch together at Hollister. 'Have you seen my phone?' She gives the best texts.

'What's it look like?' Mason took another cup, 'Yes I'd love one,' turned back. 'What were you asking me earlier? Never mind, beer is the answer.' They had used a bedroom door for pong. If you think about it, it's the best game ever invented, so don't think about it. Even with root beer. 'Okay, last shot, bitches! Yeehaw!'

'Man you won, Cars.' Braggadocious. 'What's your strategy?'

'Oh, I just - what the hell's - I just close my eyes. Who were they?'

'Two Emilys. I'll introduce them to you when they come back,' Norman promised.

'Noice, just tell them which bed is mine.'

'They're not *can*dy bars.' After that round it switched to King's Cup. Liz asked if I wanted in, told her I would with a bottle of rum, and the oldest was implored to get more kegs. They know all the right friends.

When Chase's brother got back, 'The cashier was all, What are you doing tonight? So I was, You know like, I'm studying. Anyway, you owe me a hundred bucks. It's cool I rounded up, right?' Talk about a discount. 'Norman, what's up?'

'Good! Where's Mason? Who's this? It's so fun to meet you.'

'Different shit, same toilet. Why you fancy, huh?'

'You use lots of nice language. I ran out of regular clothes so I had to look nice today.'

'Obviously. What kind of pants are those? And why are there two?'

'The good kind. Protection.'

'The shoes?'

'Norman's. The shirt? Brother's. Brad, you haven't left yet! Come for the food, stay for the booty. What'd you think of the physics take home?'

'Haven't started. It's not due - *ah*, shit.' Ran straight home. Well, not straight."

"What does this have to do with *an*ything?"

"Are you still listening? Brad had just signed the bathroom waitlist, so he turned around and asked Jordyn to save his spot, that's how they met."

"Whatever this is about, I can tell it's important because you're getting really into it telling someone who doesn't give a shit."

"Thanks. I'll accelerate."

"I will too. Just give away the ending."

"You think I know the ending? Fine, I'd just put my shoes on to pass out on the floor.

Actually I can take you

"To translate, I went there looking for a ride south, pending sobriety. First step is always the hardest, especially when it's the shortest. Amie was going in twenty three minutes if I still wanted to go instead of taking the train the next day. There was the after party over on Pasado with Immoral Justice, recently'd won battle of the bands, forget the new noise ordinance. She'd driven me before, always goes to bed before midnight. Didn't want to stay nor leave, never knew when to go and would end up staying longer than I should, so at least this time had a reason to."

"Only one? You should have asked Anthony, he's a carpooler. He finds girls who look for rides and says he's going there too. He gets paid to have chicks sit next to him."

"Yeah, that would have solved everything. 'You headin outta here?' No silent exit, Mason expected to leave first. 'I owe you money.'

'Yep, I got to. You owe me like a dollar, that barely even counts.'

'So we're even? Alright, take care. I'm gunna stick around for a little bit but I should leave soon myself. I'm startin to feel a bit tipsy.' After finding it, I squeezed out of the doorway into fresh air as a group of party people taking no collective notice walked in, like a gaggle of geese, and ran down the stairs." Tipsy. Whatever the hell that means.

What are you gonna do when everybody is sane ~ Ann Wilson

"I think you're full of shit." In Amie's half laugh sort of way, which seems to highlight the few freckles on her face. By the time we were approaching San Clemente I was getting nervous. Road opens up and at that hour five lanes seems excessive. A full rotation on the clock and five is helplessly inadequate. Laguna Niguel or San Juan Capistrano air would have freshened things up. Even though it was just empty space to the eyes the return to the coast had its effect. Past that the speed limit increases at the edge of nowhere in San Onofre.

"Palmer slings, smokes, and sleeps with lots of women. I'd be under the impression this would have gone differently had we talked elsewhere."

"Personality overcomes location."

"While on his way he said we should check out a strip club, Back Alley Girl. If he were serious he would have just gone there and then told me he was already - ah, he wouldn't tell. The last weekend of my summer he drove over so we could whatever and hang out. Of course he already started, every school in the country starts before us, lucky them. He decided we should check what they're all about, Torrey encouraged it. Went to one in Kearny Mesa. Some club. Cheap one where you don't have to be twenty one. Children go there. All there is is just a bunch of old guys sitting around doing nothing. Wearing suits too, cause they're in such a classy place. Palmer had some spangled shirt."

"Maybe they were gangsters."

"I kept feeling like when you know someone you can't see is looking at you, wondering what we were doing there, but what were they doing there? Sure hope I didn't see anyone's future wife at that place. Indicator species that he is, in negative five seconds Palmer's halfway into a lap dance. So I'm just sitting there by myself for four minutes, like a jerk, *then* he calls saying he's in his car and the only way he wouldn't spend all his money was to leave. 'You mean you already spent all your money.'

Seriously, without telling anyone. Gets up, next thing I know he's calling from the parking lot. 'That Natasha chick is Anthony's older sister. Seriously.' It wasn't. 'It's her stripper name.' The voice of reason has no shame, told me to take my time but I figured I should get out of there. I didn't have any singles, not that anyone believed that. That's the shirt he was wearing."

"Could have used twenties. How'd you meet?" He lived in Pleasonton, a small town physically, not politically, before moving down to the coast.

"An astonishingly dumb, like a smart criminal, conversation in the school parking lot. Deliberately arbitrary, like a peptide. He started and I continued out of politeness. Had a grizzly beard longer than his hair. 'It's okay, I'm a professional.'

'Professional what?'

'Now you're interested. Oh, such politesse.'

'Hey, do you mind if I ask a question?'

'That's Mister Hey to you.' Like a cat ready to pounce.

'Right, well anyway, I'm doing a survey. Would you rather be an elephant or a goldfish?'

He pivoted and cursed. He's really nice to talk with. 'That's gotta be the *stu*pidest question in the history of humans. What if I could be any utensil? A whisk so I could make whiskey.'

It made the top ten list. 'Like, wouldn't you want to forget this whole conversation?'

'You make the dumbest jokes ever.' But at least they're jokes. 'Look, no one thought the world was flat. No one should teach Freud.' All true, but the whole time I was afraid he would pull out a dozen knives or something. You know, because of my rationality. 'Goldfish memory isn't bad, they're not ants. What do you think it is, a few seconds? It's months. Get your facts straight.'

'That's why they're facts. For goldfish, a few months sounds nice, only they live for fifteen years.' We kept walking.

'Well, sure, they're not dolphins, but they always look content. They capture the moment. You gotta feed their vibe back to them. That's my theory.' He meant hypothesis. 'Ah, you only like people who agree with you - '

'I wouldn't say that.'

'I'm sorry, did the middle of my sentence interrupt the beginning of yours?' That's who we're dealing with. 'You just like contradicting.'

'No I don't. Didn't mean to make you mad.'

He was mad. 'I'm not mad. You just have to adjust your frame of reference.'

'What does that mean?'

'I don't have time for semantics. What you want to do is ask the right questions from now on.' Everyone knows what I want except me. 'It's all about moving forward.' It's all about telling people what it's all about. 'I think you're a well intentioned fool. But don't let me stop you. Cautious optimism is the easy way out. Be relentlessly optimistic, like a gambler. You know what time it is?'

'Three thirty, four?' When it's always darkest, although the midnight sky looks the same.

'Three thirty four it is. Nice talking with you.' Gave me his number, as he walked away I heard him say, 'Well that was screwy.' I thought it was good. Got back to his car, Camry or Corolla, don't know how to tell the difference from the outside. He just drove off, crisscrossing lanes. Best thing about that car: four doors, two seats.

Did you see the study showing that for a drive like this, whatever this is, the lane you're in makes zero difference? Anyway. Yeah, my twenties. Also, the dancers you could tell did some moonlighting. Natasha kept telling me when she started work and that I should wait around for her to get off. I'm always *al*most doing things. 'What's your name?' Rich hair, smooth skin. 'Well, come on Daf, there's an a tee em machine,' doesn't get any more redundant than that at all, 'right over there.' Only Natasha I know besides Sterling's old bike."

"What are you talking about, that bike was young."

" 'I don't even have a card.' I had two. I only feel bad about lying when it's not true. 'I'm sorry I'm so unprepared, I didn't know you'd be here tonight.'

'Well, wait up for me and I'll take ya to the bank.' She's crazy. Who goes to the bank at three in the morning?" Palmer does. "She was almost cute but it didn't seem like a great idea when I thought about it. Besides, I didn't want to end up in a situation like Groucho Marx described: I remember the first time I had sex - I kept the receipt."

"If you think it can't be that important since you can buy it, you're wrong." The custom plate on the car in front of us made Amie laugh. Like a cackle kind of laugh for a second.

I got a job for you, Palm.

"Anywho. Palmer campaigned for Hot for Teacher to be our graduation song. Didn't even make it onto the ballot. 'When did you get out of school?'

'It was, last Friday. No. Last Tuesday.'

'So, Monday's a holiday.'

'Yeah the internet told me.' Such googley people. 'But I also would have figured that out inferetically. Dude, shut up, everyone makes up words. Everything's a verb.'

'You're a verb. Spelling something wrong isn't ingenious, it's the opposite. Or is it like irregardless? Which way did you drive down here? Fifteen?'

'Yep. Took longer than I thought.'

'You need to think longer.'

'The freeway is like congress, only takes one asshole to slow it down. Thought I was gonna be able to make it to happy hour, shit outta luck.'

'You did everything right, but it don't always work out. Like the dinosaurs. I talked with Antonio about getting us all to Joshua Tree this summer. Last year he had three birthdays.'

'Anthony and I still think you're part of the Illuminati and the Mojave Mafia but we don't have enough evidence to confirm our suspicions. What'd you say? What do you wanna do today, Kley? You can do whatever the fuck you want.' He has a weird definition of that word."

"That's the same way everyone uses it."

" 'My problem is I am stone cold sober right now. Your problem is you forgot to drink. I'm gonna go get some drinks from Flux or somewhere and then I can stay up all night.'

'To do what?'

'Not sleep. I can catch you in a few hours, I don't know what your plans are.' Neither did I, but my phone did.

'Kleytjen!'

'What's up, Carson? Thanks for the call.'

'Are you awake? I'm just calling you back.' I don't know. 'You know where Mason is? Went rogue.' Before he ever had a girlfriend he proposed to someone and broke up with someone. Regular."

"Do you think he chose to be single? That's like asking if you choose not to be a millionaire."

"Those couldn't be any more different. 'I'm in San Diego, I'm sure Norman knows where he is.'

'Yeah? I went to SD one time, on accident.' Savior Duds? 'Drove down there.'

'You have a weird definition of *accident*.'

'The time I went I brought my friend back here. He was in a bag under the seat! I gave him drugs so he was sleeping almost the whole time. I don't know. My whole car was falling apart, I drove through too many walls. I pissed on it and left it in Newbury. Right near Oxnard.'

'Okay. Last I knew Mason went to sleep in your bed.' Least I had an alibi. Cars wants to be a lawyer and not only only charge the client when he wins, but pay the client when he loses."

"Law school?"

"Cause it's easy. 'But he didn't wake up there, Kley, that's the problem. And we checked downtown's.'

'Well, you were both in Goletaville, right? First thing you did, what did you do?'

'Um, well Mason took her car.'

'Who's her?'

'What? Oh, we don't have any electricity either. Maybe that's why I can't find him.' Freebirds was temporarily closed, wind knocked over some branches or something. 'Ask whoever you're with if we could borrow some of their power, the apartment is really dark and scary. We're not opening the fridge either.'

'The blackout's just in the fridge,' I noted.

'I need a nice suit for the second phone interview. But I can't afford one unless I get the job."

'You could get a horse.'

'Even more expensive. I'm gonna call around and see who knows about Tenaya's whereabouts, can you hear everyone in the background running down and up the streets in hysteria? Flipping cars over.'

'That's what happens when you're denied a monster burrito.' That's missing everything when not there."

"Yeah, but did anything happen to him?"

"This is what I woke up to the next day, from Antonio at three eleven in the manaña:

Cold chillin in the Mes. Mason called me tonite. From the SB. Said he was in the ocean. The phone went out. Lol... dude cant swim.

Always hoping for the song ~ Norah Jones

"The girls you know know how not to lie without ever telling the truth." Palmer was keeping track, "Mason ever pay you back?"

"More than that. He used all his money to take us out to dinner on Arbor Day. Now on ground level, I had to cross dark streets when I'd barely made it down the stairs. Missed the last two. Of course I couldn't see much in the way of peripherals so I asked some guy on the corner to tell me when to run across Cordoba. As I walked through the parking lot of Taco Towers, this girl started shouting from her balcony unbuttoning her shirt. 'Hey! You. Hey, you know where any dubstep parties are tonight?' Inside seemed so bright to my dull eyes, all I saw was hair put up and a pair of glasses.

'Tonight? No idea.' I still don't. Haven't been to party since."

"Get the fuck out."

"You think I'd lie to you?"

"You'd make it up. They in*vent*ed parties for you. And Norman."

"Doesn't matter who they were invented for, matters who uses them. Like watching music."

"Music is a dream. You went to Mason's with me."

"I drank lemonade and watched him play pool. And my professor's thing was to secure my grade."

"Gross. You already had an A. Anthony said you wanted to tutor or some shit." If you don't teach, tutor.

"I never told him that. He's right."

"Says I broke up our circle. *You* know that's crazy, just like a lot of people we know. Or knew. He keeps posting stuff about his dog."

"I didn't know he had a dog."

"He doesn't. He's living in his car. Man if I had a dog I wouldn't want people coming up to us and petting him all the time. Well, unless they're girls."

"His car has seen a lot. Hey, Andera said I'm dumb for thinking she or any grad student has a spring break. Is this true?"

"Yes, everyone knows that."

"Really? I would protest."

"True that you're dumb."

"Dumb with triangles. Whenever backhanded stuff happens, I get 'nothing's gonna change my world' stuck up in my head. I know it's not even remotely true, but I think it anyway."

"That's not backhanded, you're just a moron. Take what you want. Life is too short to ask for forgiveness."

"The rest is too long not too."

"You don't believe in that place."

"You don't because it's convenient not to. And it isn't a place, it's a time." Have an undeveloped sense of what makes us tick, too superficial to understand the buds of May. "Just like Freddy Mercury once said, Classy people can be whores as well. Things make so much more sense when I understand them. It's not nice to sleep with random people while the person who cares for you is left wondering what's going on."

"Yeah, you're the *one* person who cares about her. And that's not what that word means."

"I'm not the one who said it."

"You can start taking responsibility for your thoughts." Moved over into the shoulder for a second. "Dude why the hell are you braking? There's no one here!" As if his audience could hear him. "I swear, just one asshole, Kley. That's all it takes. I do like this car though. When you got in it didn't change the brake weight."

"Okay, let me switch back. 'Aw, damn. Well. You know where any parties are?' Don't know how she didn't hear straight. You could hear the music from here.

'Yeah,' just kept moving, 'six five five six Del Playa.' Must have been desperate. Sure she found what she was looking for, all dressed up in sweatpants."

"Easy access. That's where Aldous Huxley stayed." Stayed for what?

"It hurt to walk so I just ran. Didn't want to make Amie wait."

"Or leave without you. Where's she from?"

"True. El Cerrito. Bay Area when you ask Carson. Her mom was best friends with John Fogerty. As I passed Fortuna Park I thought of the same night sophomore year Jordyn and I saw the albino raccoon, Ricky, who's too elusive for anyone to get photographic evidence of. Except one picture of him that looks like Garfield. Saw a girl riding her unicycle and heard 'no hands, no brains' from the pirate who lives in the park riding his own. Further down Cervantes someone was painting a chiasmus on a fence, before I crossed El Greco. Ran slower by Picasso then past Embarcadero Hall, a bank until we burned it down."

"By *we* you mean, people whose kids are older than us."

"Beyond that there was a concert on the corner of Trigo and Embarcadero. 'Grab your favorite ho and enjoy the show.' I think it was The Calaveras but I didn't slow down.

Kleytjen! So good to see ya earlier, hope all is well

"Platonic, of course. Even at this time." Andera triple majored in three things, I wondered if she'd think about me more if I did or didn't reply, a wonderfully strange thought to have. "All our friends say she was a good girl, very voluptuous. "It was eleven, eleven thirty three as I got to the dorms, when everyone else goes out. 'Hey man, hang ten,' our RA told me, held the door open. 'Chill on.' Surfs at least twice everyday and purposely doesn't like The Beach Boys."

"Unreal. They invented snowboarding."

" 'Happy Norman's Birthday!' Walked upstairs and saw Mynor in the hallway, where we played extreme spoons on Thursdays, so I asked if I could borrow his Psych book. 'You smell like the mall. And cookies.'

'Those are good things. There's a book? Oh yeah. *Oh*, shit. Yeah, you can take it. It's all gonna be in lecture though. You smell almost as tan as Sterling.'

'We have to do chapter assessments.'

'Who decided this?' Was actually a mini report we had to do too." Investigate how self confidence is related to athletic injury recovery. Design a study and an experiment to do so. Also, since it's the last week, think of the career you want to pursue and describe how the knowledge and the practice of sport psychology affects that career. It might not be interesting to you, but we find it very interesting, so share any story that comes to mind, whether it's funny or meaningful.

Or both. "Mynor couldn't open his door all the way. Chase is a total mess, superficially. Has at least a four point one, no one has figured out how. Every assignment put in his backpack is never found again. Dude proves entropy, also has the neatest handwriting I have ever seen. No one visited their shabby room, looked like it had a warm smell, like someone just burped." Rather have a roommate and a mess than neither. "I did tell him to organize his life once and he asked, 'Why shower now when I'm just gonna get dirty later?' Yeah, why eat now when you're just gonna get hungry later?"

"You're not gonna have your job forever, might as well quit now. Is he still delivering dessert pizzas?" Coming up on Thousand Oaks it took extra energy to sit and be awake.

"Yeah. His idea of taking a shower is putting on a hat. Keeps everything, like a pack rat. Last Halloween he dressed as a salad, a Christmas present, a squid, and no one remembers what else. Here, this'll answer your first question. Walking away from Patricia into the Parsippany, from the same Sterling who likes to go to bed right after dinner and wakes up with the sun:

Got back first! Thanks for being such a bueno friend, Kleytjen. Appreciate all the times you've listened to me and all the times you shared your thoughts, I do. Thanks for being there and thanks for becoming one of my best friends this year. I could not be more grateful to have you as a roommate. Love you man.

"Unconditionally, as you can see. He's nicer in person."

"The condition was he took your bike, dumbass."

"The day before, he got a maximum wage offer to be a music instructor downtown, so he would have had to cut extracurriculars," officer in nine clubs and captain of the baseball club team. When he missed the strike zone during practice he ran a lap around campus. "Asked me what I thought, I said it was his decision, he said that was irrelevant. So I told him he can make his own place and offer the same service ten times better. I was surprised, no one asks me for advice.

The only other insight he sought was from the fifth graders Carson tutors, more interested in sincerity, curiosity, and the ability to detect hypocrisy than wisdom. Whatever he does, he really does. He was all set to be an RA and I waited until that month to sign a lease, only explanation is I had too many options, like Amie's. Was told to get it finalized pronto, natural tendency to rush things. The house he ended up at doesn't have a downstairs, like a fresh air mission. Nuns used to live there, bathroom has its own phone. It's about the people, not the place."

"Let's hit golf balls into the ocean from his backyard. Is yours more per square foot?"

"No one cares about that. The only reason we were roommates is he had a change of heart, backed out of a lease and decided to stay on campus another year. Last day last year, 'Sterling, I don't think you know how much I'm gonna miss you. I understand that's my fault.'

He said I'm full of crap because there's no such thing as a former roommate. 'We'll arm ourselves with pool skimmers and belly putters and forcibly take back our room!' I hope whomever lives there, whoever they are, I hope they took the screens out. We did our first day to fully enjoy the view, even though you can fall out the window and then get fined. Our RA said not to. You hear the ocean roar either way, but it made too much sense for us not to. Which is exactly what I thought when Mason called me before I left tonight, after the end of the tour.

'Hey man, we're going for ice cream. Join us. I didn't send a group message, I know you get those now. What's new, what's life?' Never answer that well, need to stop being so secretive.

'Better than I give it credit for.'

'I thought you gave it all the credit in the world.'

'I do. Ice cream is the best, I'll see you all over there.' Figured he'd be out of money or forget his wallet or something weird. Dressed in a pink pocketed shirt, and pants. 'You want anything?'

'That's okay, I don't like taking money from people.' Say Hey was the active song. 'You should get yogurt.'

'You're not taking money from anyone, I'm offering to buy you something.'

'There goes Kleytjen trying to be noble,' Chase said. It's the logical thing to do.

'So now it's a date? Damn. But thanks. I'll pay you back by next week.'

'You can just buy me a house or something.' Took it outside to where Jordyn had a table. 'How was your date?'

'Borderline awful. She has deep reservations about me.'

'That's fantastic, everyone else she doesn't have to think about, moves on immediately. You're in. Jordyn, I got you a signed Zac Efron poster.'

Andera inspected it. 'It's signed by you.'

'Yeah. It's signed. We also made that list of what's wrong with you, as you asked. It was hard to narrow down.

She read aloud, 'You tattle. Your microrhytyhms are all off. You purposely incriminate yourself. You have low viscosity. You tie your shoes when you're drunk. You like bug bites. You think selflessly. Your phone can only receive calls after you dropped it at the imperfect angle. You have quiet strength. You're very verbose. You have a recombinant vice grip. You're just like a maze. You're a plebeian. You think Portugal is twenty three hundred miles away. Your know less than forty five state capitals. You know less than forty states. You squint all the time. You're leaking fake tears right now. You at one time held the record for. You don't use watermarks. You intentionally mean what you say.'

'And we got you a card.' Jordyn slash Norman: You are very sexy. Jordyn, you're okay too. Redeem this card for a free shot of apple juice.

'Like you would let us take you out for drinks on *your* birthday, Kleytjen.'

'Make sure to share that. And you can just get me a smoothie.'

'We don't even know when your day is. Anyone wanna get a cake?' Chase is Mynor in metabolism, ate a whole gallon of ice cream in one sitting, standing at the table.

'Dude, how hungry are you?' Carson looked over, 'Kley, how come you didn't go to dinner with us?'

'I had to eat.'

'I feel so fat with you right now. You don't wanna spend ten dollars, Cars? That's less than a prostitute in your hometown.'

'Okay, how bout later? What flavor you get?'

'Nighthawk.' Lemony. 'When in doubt, whatever we say, it's not true.' Including what I just said."

All you care about is talking

I responded to Amie around noon, when I got my phone back. "Yeah dude, doubt the doubt."

"A new crew sat at the table next to us, as Jordyn pointed out. The girl behind me is on the team. The one who kept losing the ball, remember? :))

'Kleytjen, do you see our commencement speaker at all anymore?'

Carson answered since I was texting Amie about when we were maybe leaving. 'Sterling turned into a *mor*on or something. Is he still getting over the Super Bowl? I've never been able to say my team made it that far. Why can't he just like every team, he likes everything else. Did you guys know he quit the internet just to return and invite Liz to a party so she would maybe realize its significance? If he hadn't left, he'd know that she was gonna break up with that dude. Which is funny. I fight with my parents all the time, you don't see me change to my status to Orphan.' Just because she was right doesn't mean it was a fight.

'The only ones who change their status on that site are the ones who change their status with that site. Jordy, let's go see *The Lorax*. *Letters to Juliet* was fun when I didn't find my seat.' Last year we went to see the *The King's Speech* without knowing the other was there.

'And the awk moments when we would both reach for the popcorn at the same time. I already saw that though. Let's have movie night with Liz and Marie, I still haven't seen *Midnight in Paris*.'

She actually did that on purpose. 'One time I had lunch, that was awkward.'

'That was the worst movie ever. At least I hope there's not a worse movie than that.'

'You're lying.' Chase only had an opinion that cause it didn't work out with that girl."

"You should relate. You haven't been to another party since you want Norman's to remain the worst."

"Carson hasn't seen it either. 'You're my favorite recipe. Here, it's an unknown number."

"Hullo? This is her." Asking what Jordyn was doing after, every known number just texted. I regifted chocolate from Klurton, mostly unmelted. 'What's this?'

'Are you kidding? It's Swiss chocolate, it's amazing. Want some?'

'What is it?' It's no Twix.

'It's Swiss chocolate, it's amazing.'

'Okay. Oh, wow.' No one believes me the first time.

'Anyone else?'

'I don't like chocolate.'

'There are doctors for that, man. You want Norman's number?'

'I don't think you should be giving out someone else's info. I thought Liz would be here for me. I said, Wanna meet up at Caje. And she said, Cake sounds perfect! Stupid auto incorrect. It's been a long Wednesday.'

'It's Friday, boo.'

'It was Wednesday when I woke up. What's going on after, Carson?'

'Surprise party for Norman. Drinks will flow.'

'Nice, drunk Mason is one of my top ten favorite people. Ahead of Lincoln, I think.' She hasn't even seen Mason drunk.

'Mazel tov, everyone. As exciting as this is, I'm gonna take off now.' Chase looked all around down and up. 'What's that noise, is there a helicopter?'

It was Mason thinking. 'That's me thinking. Damn it. I'm really tired, but I have to party tonight.' Can't catch a break. 'I'll go if Kley goes. Kleytjen doesn't commit.'

'Sure I do. But I'm having a hard enough time keeping up with just you guys.'

'You like house music?'

'Who's house? Your mom's?'

'Don't be agnostic about these things. I'm up if you're down.'

'I'm down if you're up. Let's do this thing and get it over with. Jordyn, you wanna go with? It'll be, like, cool.' She had work. 'To*night*? I thought you weren't working the rest of the quarter.'

'No, my fourth job.' Goes out even on nights when she stays in. Always says she won't, just to break the monotony.

'We'll meet you there. Mason, I don't wanna go to jail or anything, I got a test Tuesday. If I get laid tonight, it's your fault.'

'Salt your worry, Kley.'

'Really, I don't do all this anymore.'

'What do you do then?'

Ahoy Kleytjen - your phone just called me. Nice music

I checked to see when I'd last texted him before answering Jordyn. 'Actually. I'm going somewhere else first. I'll stop by after.'

'Yeah dude, it's gonna be mad chill. It's right across from our place.'

'Where's that?'

'Three, streets, down, from, the, ocean, Jordyn.' Two from there.

'Where's the ocean?' Doing her best Marie impression.

'Don't be a cartographer.'

'Well I'll let you know if I'm going.' Didn't say she would let us know if she's not.

'Good. And I don't want anyone to talk you out of it.' Since he talked her into it. 'It's gonna be crazy.'

'Good crazy or bad crazy?' Andera wondered.

'I don't know of a bad kind.'

'Where at? I'll probably be inundated with large sums of copious amounts of alcohol, not gonna lie,' Chase said.

'She *just* asked that.'

'You know I'm too cheap to pay attention to what anyone says. Just text me the address.'

'I only text girls. Sorry.'

'Kley's just kidding. He's not sorry. I thought Norman told everyone he was back!'

'Only in a vague sort of way, Mason.' Post online is what he did.

See you tonight gumpazz trick hoe.

When you don't go out and then you say you might, word spreads fast. 'Let's skedaddle.'

'Shall we? Let's shall. Happy half Jordyn, Birthday!' I already wanted to go straight to bed, but we can't be in two times at the same place, now that is a lie.

Reach out touch face ~ Martin Gore

"It's hard to judge ourselves accurately. What's particularly normal is we all know this and yet do not think it. I hung around in Yolk, ordered another glass of melted ice, then walked out to the dark side of the road and called Antonio, he told me on Friday:

Gon get messed up right now. If I'm alive tomorrow I'm goin to the Mes. Last final done lol.

'Kleytjen. It's me.'

'Yeah me too. Whereya been, whataya doin, whenya goin?'

'At the usual place, brah.' His garage. 'I'm done.'

'How you feel?'

'Done.' Cryptomaniac."

"Like you." Exactly like me. I'll say, My uncle from the only city with a building designed by each of those four architects, instead of saying Buffalo, not the Wyoming one.

"Antonio's too cool, 'My favorite color? You probably never heard of it, it's this really underground one called turquoise.' Also wants to beat the system, whatever that means. Told me he got a negative score on his Landscape Architecture final, passed anyway."

"He should play golf."

"Everyone should play golf. 'It's cause I couldn't think of anything.'

'Is that all you had to think of?'

'I didn't have the orange calculator. It wasn't really that big of a deal, just took up a lot of brain space. Like, literally. Mechanics went better. Wanna take shots?' He's great at signposting.

'You're doing summer school?'

'Oh yeah, summer school. Ye.' That's who I got it from. And I'm not giving it back. 'I'm taking Dynamics. It's like a physics class, it sucks.'

'Not the way I'd take it. Take a poly sigh class and have Palm write your papers.'

'I don't know why they call it a science. It's the art of getting nothing done.'

'That's a science.'

'You still got that pirate costume?'

'You still got that money?'

'Yeah how much, hundred thousand? I wanna go up for Halloween this year.'

'The one in October? I'll have my people meet your people.'

'That's what I'm talking about. I could probably go with Paul unless he says he's out of money again. He spends what he doesn't have, so I don't feel bad for him.' He'd be rich if he had more money. 'He won't reply to me because of the whole giraffe incident.' Nobody said it was hard to save."

"*Lots* of people have said that."

More light pollution filled our view as we reached one side of Oceanside. We made it to the other a few couple minutes later, which is like six. Antonio responded to my notification of impending arrival with a voicemail: "Where you is dog? Um I guess that's it. Those were my main points. Did you hear Paul needs a little bodywork on his car? He calls me this morning he's like, Hey I just got in an accident I'm not even joking I'm being totally serious right now. I was like, Why would I think you're joking you get in an accident three or five times a year. He's all, Man I almost fucked up. And I'm like, Yeah again that happens it isn't that unbelievable. Let me know when you here."

"Everything okay?"

"Everything. 'There's *no* way Mason was sober and told you about that day. I remember what I did, just not the sequential order.'

'They're just details. Torrey was in a mood. Well that's how he described her, which is different from how I think of her, which is different from how she actually is. It's darker than usual here for some reason, you know that? I know it, but I don't understand it. I want to get one of those transportation operated inductive light emitting transducers.'

'A skateboard with wheels that light up?'

'Just watch out for the people who don't share the sidewalk. I hate them.'

'No you don't.'

'So yeah I guess we kind of - might've.' It's in his contract to qualify everything. 'Sorry, I have a cough.' Part of his ever present personality. 'Kley. Call Paul if you haven't lately and ask him how it's going. He already has a Paul story to tell you from a few days ago, or a couple months ago. Actually, it was last year.' Conversation ended right there, he had to go cook a salad. Senior year we met up and he signed: It's the end of the world as we know it and I feel fine. So he was crestfallen. Least I got his autograph. Took myself to the movies again, this time on Fourth, the Horton Grand, for the chance to find something more topical than enduring. *Water for Elephants* was an option but you told me to read it, so I figured I should first do that. It's hard to tell. *Cuckoo's Nest* is one of three movies ever to win all the awards, and the book is sixteen hundred times better. So I thought I should watch it first to enjoy it more. I do like Reese Witherspoon."

"You can't be afraid of comparisons."

"And obviously there are more movies that are better than the source, like *The Graduate*. I'm so accustomed to going to things early, too early." Not too early enough. "The next showing wasn't for an hour so I left."

"What shirt were you withholding from your sister?"

"Oh, I wanted to buy a gift for Grace from Nick's Nacks right by Broadway Pier." Typical sundries until I found a shirt that told, Movies will make you famous, Television will make you rich, Theatre will make you good. "The more you look at something, the less you want to buy it." Solana Beach's Hideaway Cafe needed to replace the lights for some of its letters. "Wasn't the least expensive shirt in the world, but I was shopping for a gift, not a price. Also got a postcard for Marie. How I imagined it would happen when I gave Grace the shirt: This is the best thing ever, you have *no* idea! How it actually happened: completely differently. Right before my purchase Carson sent:

I put 5 dollas on dallas to win it all at the beginning of the year. Also, stop spending money.

"The man is an oracle, has a twelfth sense. Liz put down a hundred, makes sense since she makes twenty times as much as he does. And one from Jordy, so it was likely Carson again:

Where you at? Video chat? Pillow fort this Friday

"All the above. I walked along the marina, didn't see any gold fish, red fish, or blue fish or regal blue tangs, which has a good fossil record, like penguins. Or anything else with no body fat. I did see that the waxing moon had already risen and watched it roll the tide in." The commercial on the radio was for fresh fruit and dried fruit.

"Maybe if you were open to watching good shows you'd learn something about having a focus." That was a heck of a thing for Amie to say considering who began the detour.

"I'm not disagreeing with that, I just think the definition of *good show* and the definition of *stupid* are the same. You'll just have to mind the gaps.

Babys got nothing to do with me ~ John Mayer

'Am I interrupting your grooming session?' No one answered the door, he was out on the balcony. Had the same clippers, his own set now.

'Kleytjen! You're not interrupting, you're adding to it. How'd you know I'd be out here? Sorry I've been out of contact, my mind's been untuned. We're in such a funny period of life.' It's more like a paragraph. Mason sent this:

Lol. Freakin chick birthdays. Guys don't know what to do.

'There's nowhere else you'd be. Is Mynor not around? I'm making a quick San Diego run again.'

He had to ask, 'What makes you ask?'

'I'm venturing off into the unknown. Last time I did, he asked when I was gonna change my major. "Why would I do that? Thanks." Psych book has a picture of a girl running a marathon.

"Yeah, you're lucky. I lost my physics book a few days ago."

"Where'd you lose it?" I was still pretty sauced.

"If I *knew* I would go look there." Their room was a toy box. "Let me see yours before we turn it in." Shook on it. "I didn't do the last one right because it was too easy."

Whatever that means. "You could also look at the book." During our final Mynor looked at my answers, climbed over a few rows to get there. We had to retake the class, he talked the vice chancellor out of expelling us. A good grade is fine, a good friend is everything. "It's an easy assignment. I'll do it tonight or on the way back up." Or the alternative.

"Oh I see, thug life. I always wonder how you get your shit done, you never look like you're busy." What waste of a word. Doesn't even mean anything.

"That's because I do things right the first time." That's very false, but it seemed like the right thing to say.

I do know it saves time to take your time. “Oh hey, can you still edit my thing?” Back in the hallway where we could hear singing in the shower. “Maybe Monday?”

“Yeah, sure. After the show.”

“Cool cool, thanks mang. I’m done with it, I just need to add facts.” Chase walked by, wearing the same raggedy shirt for the sixth straight day, decked out in his finest.

“Hey guys. Think I’m gonna take a fat nap right now,” fell into papers on his mattress.

“So, you’re going to bed? We still going to Norman’s?” He changed his mind nonverbally and walked out to go in the bathroom. “How come the toothpaste you use is illegal in most countries?”

“Don’t worry about it.” Twice Chase used one of those blood pressure monitors at the store and his pulse reading was zero.

“You ready? You don’t have to floss that much.”

“Only floss the teeth you wanna keep.” He felt the mirror staring, “Don’t hate dudes, just step up your flossing game. Hold on, gonna check that chick’s profile one more time. You know, just in case something happens to me.” ’ ”

“Your network is your most valuable resource.” Palmer didn’t comment on Topanga Canyon.

“Actually it’s cause his dad joined. Never talked with each other more than they do now, much to Mynor’s disapproval, ‘If you’re not using it to get girls, you’re doing it wrong.’

‘I’m seeing if Liz is going.’ Instead of just asking me who was there.

‘Checking her pictures? You already know what she looks like.’ Minute later he walked back out, sans shirt. ‘You don’t need a shirt?’

‘Shirts are for other states.’ He was in an enviable position.”

“You don’t miss junior year, you just miss having one more year of school.”

“I do have another year. Chase’s not as smart as Mynor most days, but gets better grades. The way he aced American

Transcendentalism, we had to memorize thirty two poems, was he went down the hall the night before the final and recited a few to each girl. The next night went even better for him. Everyone I hang out with is much smarter."

"Good thing it's transitive. Or it's that you see things your way and we see things as they are. Where did you get into school?"

"Or, the average topic I bring up just isn't intelligent. Sterling's speakers are the same, the playlist similar too. 'There you are Eddie, right where I left y'all. Dude, this song keeps shuffling up, and I keep skipping it.'

'It wants to be listened to.'

'Okay, you convinced me.'

'That was easy. You know what it's about?'

'Are you kidding? I know my Vitalogy.'

'I don't. You know who it was written about?'

'Your moral high ground has been lost! Wait, really? Didn't you make it past fourth grade?'

'Only know what I'm told, like if the songs all sound the same.'

'Isn't that what you want from a band you know you like, a good bass line?'

'Are they as good live?'

'Some are artists and some are entertainers. They're both. So road tripping tonight, no way! Can you crank this out, bro?' Nodded toward some papers in his room through the window. 'You'll like it, it needs a lot of improvement.'

'Of course, I've never seen you struggle with anything. What is it?' Was glad for the lack of wind.

'Commencement address.'

'Oh. I'm already working on it.'

'It's taken me twenty two years to write. I definitely feel more pressure than four years ago.'

'You rushed it, it took Lincoln fifty two. There's not more pressure on you, there's just more people who know there's pressure on you. The best speeches are the ones where the audience knows the speaker knew they would win. What's the best part?'

'How I got good grades. Just kidding. Law of averages: Some of you will get in car crashes tonight, some of you will get arrested. The last game doesn't matter, it's the whole season that counts. If you really want to know someone, ask for their top three thousand songs.'

'That's a bit much, eh?'

'Quantity ain't bad, all it does is increase your chances of finding quality. If you're into that kinda thing.'

'Happy songs with implicit sadness make up eleven percent of mine.'

'There are no sad songs. Who's your favorite photographer?'

'My grandpa, and there is no second.' His favorite picture is me from my fourth birthday.

'Who's third? There are always influences when you're absorbent, like a succulent. When's your launch time?'

'Sometime tonight, I guess. Before midnight.'

'You oughta know the planley Stanley. Who ya goin with?'

'Amie, midnight trolley. Seems to be the way everyone else gets around. I don't think she's in a hurry. Biking back to the apartment Tuesday, I saw her backpack going inside Casey's, but didn't follow. This morning,

When should we leave?

'Two hundred minutes before you wanna get there, I said.

Don't look at me like that. You are not going to decide for me, are you?

'Typical conversation between us. Then she wasn't sure.'

'Ah, you're going with *And*relchik. How's she doin? She still cool? Still gives you a no decision?"

'Good one. We got this relationship: I ask if she wants to do something fun, she says No. She asks if I want to do something lame, I say Yes. Wasn't always that pattern, continually invited me to a cappella shows, but I never went.'

'What about riding on her handlebars going fast, like two hundred miles per hour on Saturn?'

'I thought Saturn used the metric system.'

'The way you think about her and the way you feel about her have ceased to be separate. What do you listen to when driving?'

'I'm beginning to find there are those with dream pursuits and those with real pursuits.' The difference between a roof and a ceiling. 'She only has one kidney.'

'Why did she tell you that?'

'There is no why. It's *nice* when somebody tells you about their kidney. Every time I get a cold I remember when I went to get medicine from her.'

'You never get sick.'

'She told me her aunt just had a stroke, so she had a much worse week than I. I never have medicine anymore. After Mynor and Chase left, she picked me up in the parking lot by Ziegarn and Segundos in her red Cruiser, lusty Patricia. "What's up Double A?" Has a pillow shaped as an A. I thought she should have two, she told me that would limit her options. "A little night music, huh?" *Serenade* is what I was looking for. We just listen to music, no podcasts.'

'Limitation is the greatest form of focus.'

'So much for being late, "You're so slow." I didn't even stop to have a drink. "But nice shirt." She bought me that shirt our hall designed. Drove away and my camera fell off the roof, the only thing I didn't put in my backpack, I'd set it there to open the door. I think she ran over it too, but I didn't know either of these at the time. I was so damn drunk.

"Thanks. Thank you. Nice hat." Brown beret. Also pink pajama pants, dolphins on the bottom. High waisted shorts, actually, so flesh on faux leather. And nothing on her feet except a birthmark. You take the surfer off the beach but can't make her wear shoes.

"If you want something just say, Amie I'm hungry."

"Still wanna make some drank?" I had those lemons sitting in our room waiting to be used for strawberry lemonade tequila. "I'm glad you texted. I didn't want to text you because I felt like I shouldn't be looking for a way out, but once you did I figured it was a good time." As we got onto The Camino Real, before the Funk Zone, Amie turned the air off and the heat on, passed Chesire Inn, Casablanca, train station. I had a question, it's just she was singing along with whatever forgotten amplitude or frequency, driver's discretion.'

'What'd Chasen say today? Are they still together?'

'No one knows. He said, "You have inspired me with your pictures to take a hand at it. Would appreciate your opinion," handed me his phone and promptly fell asleep. Seriously, not even Jordyn knows.

"Hey, you wanna take Enviro with me so you can hang out with the cool kids? And me?" It was the closest to her apartment and her Tuesday wasn't until the afternoon.

"Yeah I don't know about that. But how are you doing this quarter? You're taking five classes, right?"

"I'm gonna get all As, too. Oh, come on, my best is your average." We had Methods of Cultural Analysis together, where we met, I turned in our final paper two weeks early, got it reviewed, turned it in again a week early, got it rereviewed. She showed up the day of, didn't realize it was assigned, wrote it during lecture. We both got a ninety five.

Big smile at that. "By the way, I'm not gonna triple anymore. I'm just gonna double with French." Canadian doubles.

"Really? When did you decide this? Do you dream in French?"

"I dunno. Last quarter."

"How come you didn't tell anyone?"

"I did, I just didn't tell you. People in the know knew. My bad. How do you like *Outliers*?" She's the one who lent it, still has my *Pi*.'

'Récits are meant to be shared.'

'Amie put her big sweatshirt on, fits me really well, backwards, only covering her arms. "Not sure what his final argument is, so I like it a lot." Always does her hair and paints cats on her nails while driving. I wish I could multitask. Even when she drives on the wrong side of the road or somewhere, or with the emergency brake, I assume she is perfectly justified. Who wants to be a backseat driver? Still, must've given a look of bemused befuddlement, she told me not to judge. Are we listening to Must Be The Money on loop?'

'You say that like it's a bad thing. How do you know all the words and not the title?'

'Jordyn told me she has no idea how Amie thinks he needs saving. It's his previous girl, but what Amie doesn't realize is he's the one who made her skankier. "Correct. Nice haircut, by the way. Well I had a busy day today, what did you do?"

"You first."

"Lotsa homework, went out to dinner. Activities. I made perfect oatmeal today."

"I cut my hair."

"Never would've guessed. Whose party did you go to?"

"I already told you, homegirl."

"Okay, *that* helps."

"Norman's. For his birthday."

"Oh cool!"

"It is cool it's his birthday."

"No, cool that you have friends. Wait, Wagmeister? He still dating Liz?"

"Correct. I don't think they said much to each other, maybe she's holding out."

"No way, he wouldn't still be dating her."

"Maybe he'll be like Bradshaw."

"Brad's not single anymore. I thought I told you! I thought I told you, because then you made a funny comment that I agreed with. Not to be conflated with me thinking you're funny."

"Yeah, that doesn't sound like you," in her sultriness. "Well I'm gonna look her up on Facebook and since I didn't already do that, I don't think you told me. You know, the website. Oh, do you mean Emily?"

"Yes, stalker. You know Mynor? This guy already asked if we could be lab partners for the fall." Mynor would have been a better person to ask, he'll find anyone's profile. The last time we went on a run she wanted to go around the lagoon and I wanted to go to the pier, so we compromised and ran around the lagoon.'

'You don't have a problem with it always being her way?'

'Maybe her way is better. Anywhere you run is good.'

'So you're stayin active?'

'Yes, I'm still running.'

'Run your race.'

'When I run by my lone my imagination runs away with me.' From what I don't understand. 'In circles.'

'Yeah, we haven't had to run for thousands of years.'

'Haven't we? "So are you ready to take care of the incoming freshman?"

"Yeahya. Orientation is zipping by and gets more fun," every day.' She was in RA training before summer, with Sterling. I would have schooled summer too except they'd make you graduate early for taking so many units. 'Amie continued, "Jordy and I have been watching Ginger Rogers movies like madwomen the past few days."

'What was wrong with accounting?'

'It's the same class twelve hundred times, Money Value of Time.'

'How'd you do it, Kleytjen? They don't let you change majors that late.'

'I didn't change. I added. Couldn't choose, so I just decided to do everything.'

When asked if all my effort meant anything in her book, Klurton said, 'Not in my grade book. Kleytjen, I'm not worried if you drop these sessions after learning what it's all about. I was worried if you were to not learn anything, and decided to continue.'

Anyway, "Guess who else likes her."

Amie doesn't like suspense, craves anticipation. "Tell me!" A la me. Patient, don't like waiting.'

'For that exact reason, I like it a lot. Weird thing for her to do as one who doesn't like the past. She's the least sentimental person you ever met. Her mom told me that.'

' "Good guess. Brad. If you don't see anyone after next year, who are you gonna remember most?"

"Don't be stupid. Do you know when you're going home? Like, right after finals?"

"Huh? Oh. Yeah, I think so."

"You should stick around for a week or two so we can hang out."

"My lease doesn't start until July though, so I might sublease."

"You can sleep on our sofa. Or the empty bed in my room. It's only one subleaser and I for summer." Sueno, way out in the goonies where you're not allowed to have parties on the roof. "You'll have to get our spare key. Are you gonna do more school?" So only operating at half capacity, and I knew her roommates better than yours.'

'Yeah, you gotta wait. Like when you want a new look by growing out your hair. Would you choose the same again?'

'I would. "Only if you are."

"Ha. I'm not sure yet." She wanted to get in to med school, so she got in to med school. Always beats me at Scrabble and crossword puzzles and anything else involving words or obtuse language or intelligence. "I don't think it's actually analytical. It's rote memorization." '

'You do see eye to eye despite the height difference.'

'So much for what her mom says, "Well whatever we do, if we end up not living in the same city, let's make sure to stay in touch. Not just saying that, I'm an experienced long distance friend." I bet she is. Monterey's only two hundred minutes north.'

'It's more than that.'

'Two thousand. It takes however long you want it to take. "Sounds super good to me. Let's go to at least a hundred concerts a year." Bought The xx tickets for herself and Chase for six months later, she knew they were still gonna be together.'

'Hold up, Kleytjen. Do what makes you happy, not what makes you feel good. The difference, if you want to know, is the former will be there tomorrow. Don't focus on her, concentrate on yourself and then you can measure up with anyone.' I just wanna deserve to. 'You act like she and money are different to you. They're not. Neither could be any more indifferent to your affection.'

'You don't like her?'

'I wouldn't let you think so. She's so.'

'Chase's *nat*urally nice. Amie has the capacity to not be, yet she is. She was crazy about those goldfish, we finished them in five seconds.' "

"You're not nice, Kleytjen. You just try so hard to be." Animal crackers were almost gone before Camarillo and as we cruised down the Grade, the hour marker, without Palmer letting up on the gas, dark water returned to sight and burnt rubber to smell. Dude drives like he's being chased. He probably is.

"What's the difference? 'She's going to visit her best friend. She's in the Sierra Club. audited Basket Weaving or something. The reason she decided to go down this weekend is to avoid Thanksgiving traffic.'

'Good for her, dude. I've been told crazy ridiculous lies by girls, but nothing eats your soul like sitting in traffic.' I don't have to tell you about the whole car ride. She dropped me off at Parsippany at three in the morning."

"I like traffic, less speeding tickets. Before I say anything, I just wanna say, your fashion has the - were you actually at that concert?"

"What? Oh, Sterling gave this to me." Pearl Jam's ninety four tour.

"I knew it would happen. You can tell Torrey I'm totally fine if you want to."

"If you knew this would happen then what's the big deal?"

"I dunno, she's already talking about this other guy. She kept talking about him, then I finally met him and was like, are you kidding?

Everything he did done by someone not *cute*," air quotes, "would be creepy. Ain't fair, ya know?"

"And you still wanna be with her?"

"All I can think of is No Rain and Good Girls Don't."

"Those aren't alike at all."

"Yeah, but to me now, every song is about the same person. My uncle in Colorado always calls this place Oxford and I never correct him."

"Sounds like no one else has either. 'She knows how to be happy.'

'Happiness is independent of the decisions you make. You can't buy it.'

'You can sell it. And rent it.'

'Well, pretty soon she'll scrounge her next.'

'That's not a nice way to put it.'

'You'd think it pretty nice if it's you she scrounges. She gets it while she can.'

'She always can, Chase pretended he would do anything in the world for her. That's way too limited of an offer.'

'You're gonna get it together now or later, so it may as well be whenever. I think of it this way, Kley. There's the girl you used to like and the girl you will always like.' There are always more than two."

Look whos laughing now youre wasted ~ Jack Johnson

"Like you're blindfolded, a couple hours after you left me I didn't know where I was going, I just wanted to get there. From Middletown, Little Italy is close, there's a great place there that only serves spaghetti." Menu choices: small, medium, large.

Amie noticed, "You walked off a hangover it sounds like."

who's the target?

"I've never had one. To stay awake, seek a place with live music, like The Break Room. Of course there's The Casbah, which The Rage and The Fury frequents, but it's way up on Kettner. I'll have to go there the next time I go there. What were much closer was Hard Rock and House of Blues, both on Fifth. Also The Tipsy Crow. A few bands in town: Sirus and Iris, The Talon, and some other third act. Nothing was open, my favorite. Some people were already on twilight runs, and there I was walking around half asleep. That spotlight didn't care if you looked at it from the front or from the side, like a portrait that makes eye contact with you from every possible angle. It never seemed to get any closer. When I saw the sign for some boulevard, the exact street is eluding me now, I turned west where all the construction is instead of continuing north to Old Town. As any good city, San Diego is never finished. Went to the airport for an inconspicuous bed. Took so long to walk the length of Lindbergh Field."

"What does Charlie L have to do with San Diego?"

"Exactly. Grace is the only one of us who's been to Georgia, Atlanta's Hartsfield Jackson. This airport just keeps going, like a one take movie. Stumbled all the way down Harbor, things always look different from far away. Or cropped. Not even that big, only two terminals. Almost thought I should just keep toward Rosecrans and make my way over to Sea World since I had already gone so far, felt I could walk that pace for ever, simultaneously felt I was going to pass out cold alone in the gutter in the middle of the street. Should have hailed for a taxi. My nose felt weird."

"Pick up the pace. Don't skip too much."

"The whos who work at airports get there so early, I don't know if I'd get used to leaving for the airport at three ante meridian and not have a flight to catch."

"Just because you're used to it doesn't mean it got better."

"That's what I'm saying. I only slept a couple minutes at most. So crowded already, put my feet down, didn't look like I was waiting for a flight since I was backpackless. Sterling always woke us up with a song he picked out before bed, but the playlist at the airport seemed thoughtless. Crossed my mind to call Palmer to see if he stayed the night in his car again, and if he could give me a ride, but even if he had he wouldn't get up that early for anything. Including his own wedding. I knew I could borrow Jen's car if I explained everything to her, or if I didn't. Was expecting it to go to voicemail so I didn't know what to say. Already left a telegram on her phone about borrowing it but parts of the airport have no service. 'Not sure who that is but sure. I have my keys though. I can't believe it's been nine months!' And now it's been more, but whenever you're with her it feels like zero days have passed since you last were." Whenever you're without it feels like a thousand years. Whatever that feels like. "She was referring to Mesa's football game when I saw her walking, tried to say Hi from afar, she didn't hear me, or if she did she would have had to yell back, and I don't think she's capable of yelling, so I phoned. Don't know how to whistle either.

Haha aww dang it! Well now I'm saying hi back! :]

She came and found me, I said we must not have been cool in school otherwise we wouldn't still be there. 'At least we admit it.' Shared the rest of her nachos.

'What time do you have work? Noon?'

'What's up?'

'When do you work?'

'Twelve. So I could drive and meet you or whatever is easier for you.' I never know how to answer, with girls everything is a test. Like, Do you think she's cute? Or, How many classes did you have today? Also the difference between, Nice dress is it new, and, Is that a new dress it's nice."

"Don't complement the *dress*."

"That's what I mean. 'That's alright, I still need to eat and stuff.'

'Well just let me know when you get here so I know when you got here.' Thirty eight second conversation, felt less than half that. And thanks to all that being alive stuff I was hungry, long time since way back at Segundos. There was a bunch, like grapes, of kids running around in the security lines which made me less groggy, one almost ran into me."

"Lack of sleep gives energy. Respect the unexpected."

"Back on North Harbor, which turns ninety degrees south once you're clear of the runway, tried to go to The Lion's Share to fill my belly. I walked right by it, no one goes there, there's always an hour wait, like when an avalanche of mariners show up. 'Is it exactly about an hour?' Right by the Maritime Museum and the *Star of India* where all the sailboats dock. Do you need a boat?" She shook her head. "Right behind me someone asked, I think another student, 'How come we can't afford no boat?' "

"Everyone whines about how much money we have to spend on textbooks and all and then you find out their parents gave them eight credit cards. How do you complain about spending all your money when you're not spending *your* money?"

A la me. "Palmer knows what you mean, before junior year I was encouraged to take Stats instead of Calc because it's more practical. Sure is. The material's far too boring for any of us, so we educated ourselves on probability. Queen overthrown: Dude this year has been sick, playing poker in class is how I eat. Bonne chance next year and beyond

"I got a four, Palmer got a two, felt guilty. I just know he's willing to bet on anything. Year before: You bet you're gonna win your bet? That was all luck that Salem is the capitol of Oregon and history was pretty tight this year."

"Does he have a gambling problem?"

"No one has a gambling problem. He had a losing problem. Thought it was Eugene so I won five bucks. We were just like how Wyatt Earp and that other guy made San Diego popular thanks to gambling halls. What was written for Antonio, in Bio, taught by his dad - he'd been with a girl for five months, asked her to be the first one to sign. 'I started reading it and realized halfway through that she dumped me.' And no one else signed it. What he wrote in mine that year: If you ever need a door opened call me up. He always went to class early, thought the door to be locked and waited in the hall so everyone did the same, finally I just turned the handle and discovered it wasn't locked. But back to our bets. I got lucky, my parents talked with Escanola, she was a counselor that year, and we didn't have to pay for the Exams in full."

"Your bets are all win win. Either you win so you win or you lose so you refocus."

"The latter has never happened. It's nice when you have something to give away, but money is too cheap of a way to try to make people happy. It doesn't require any thought."

"Anybody who says money won't make you happy has no money."

"Yo no soy muy dinero. Everyone I know is broke, or at least they say they are. My parents, my school, the state, the country. So I don't see the big deal." We're products of financial aid. Completely subsidized; not by my parents, not one cent, even though I was in their economic sphere of influence.

"They have no funds to threaten you with, that's awesome."

"Is it?"

"Like scamming a scammer. Remember if you didn't drink before you turn twenty one your grandma would have bought you a car?"

"It's just a car. Zodo's with Marie was out of the question, so I went in to Lion's, which was undercrowded, overpriced, and worth it. As soon as I entered, the hostess greeted me with a good morning, which sounded really weird, and found me an open seat near a window. The waiter I had, Jessie, had a friendly demeanor. Flaunts it.

Look for him whenever you go there. Polo hair. 'Aye man what it is. Sorry to keep you waiting.'

'I understand.'

'Some don't.' I don't get how others don't get it.

'I've never been here before. What should I get?'

'Coast Toast is a must. You'll love it.'

'What's it like?' Could have just looked at the picture of cat shaped waffles.

'You want me to tell you or you want to find out for yourself?'

'The second one, definitely.'

'I like your attitude, Bob. Mind if I call you Bob?' I don't mind. 'Don't just do something, sit there.' I kept the menu while he waited on two other tables. They also have a ham and egg sandwich called a Hamlet, along with a hodgepodge of assorted yumminess, which got me thinking. Luckily Jessie walked back with the apple juice and getting into random conversations is his way of paying for school.

'What are their names? Gilligan and Rumpelstiltskin?'

'Rosencrantz and Guildenstern?'

'Rosencrantz and Guildenstern, yeah.' Took until then to mentally defrost."

"You always forget their names." I always forgot their names.

"We prefer Timon and Pumbaa, and that elephant graveyard. There's a group that holds, You'd have a decent play if you'd get rid of the opposing thoughts, and I'm in the out group on that one. Besides, I'm more interested in his friends. 'I think they were in with Ophelia the whole time.'

'Hold your bets, let me put your order in.' Jessie carries twenty five plates at a time and still walks frighteningly fast. Told him that I noticed his careful alacrity upon his return. 'Good use of alacrity. When I was a freshman I always walked a special someone to her class. A few days before homecoming I walked into her classroom, sat next to her in some other dude's seat, and asked her to the dance in front of everyone. She said Yes. I tried to be smooth by walking away slowly with abundant confidence when I lost all balance, tripped over a chair, and slammed my head on her desk. Now I walk with care. I would like to be a funambulist.' Good use of words.

'It's awesome how excited y'are for what you do.'

'You should have seen her,' pointed toward a tie dye tie. 'Better than I am. She was employee of the night last week, bought a new car with all her tips. And that's in spite of her severe case of shabirititus.' It's contagious.

'So, employee of the week?' Like Andera every day.

'Sure. Anything you want to get good at?'

'Underwater photography. We don't have a major for it, but I like it anyway. Or that's why I like it.'

'Who's we? You have any experience?'

'Nope.' Everyone opens up to him, like you open a door.

'Room to learn, good. No one can tell you you can't do something without your consent. Even professionals, who pay the mortgage with nothing but their pictures, get their pieces accepted maybe ten percent of the time.'

'Yeah, there are so many. Usually I sift through about six hundred to find one that's really good.'

'That takes a lotta time.' Like a long exposure.

'It's something I enjoy doing.' Like Annie Leibovitz said, I am impressed with what happens when someone stays in the same place and you took the same picture over and over and it would be different, every single frame.

'I'm really good at that stuff, scouring through things. It's too bad I don't like it. But art, I think it has to be strange in some way to be beautiful. Does that make sense? It's weird.'

'I think so. Could you tell me what makes us choose to do things for ourselves? Shouldn't we just donate blood and join the Heart Association?' Sterling's pledging a dollar to them for every point his team scores this season."

"He has that kind of money?"

"He doesn't have heart problems. 'I don't why - I don't know why. It brings more attention and scrutiny, but there is always a path to success when it involves your passion. I'll be out with your food in a minute.' Up until then he had answers to questions I didn't know how to ask.

"So, really was only a minute, though the hour changed, my splurge for strawberry blonde French toast brought a little taste of the good life. Doesn't everybody deserve to have that? Like the professor in *Twenty Thousand Leagues*. And Charlie from *Algernon*. Palmer didn't finish that one, didn't like reading. 'If you don't want to read it, play the game.' Sitting there hungry's when I realized I should remajor."

"I thought it was because for your final report you read *Fight Club* instead of watching it, so you didn't pass."

"That was the first time. And I still passed. Palmer also took Video Productions, we just had to make short films, like a yearbook. Only a few of us participated, there was even a couch for anyone who didn't sleep enough during Stats. As per protocol, he walked in fifteen minutes late, said his hellos, 'Fuck school, right Kleytjen?' Never sounded like a good idea, but I didn't say anything, he changes the topic every three seconds. 'I'll admit, Kley, when I first started having sex, I was addicted.' Then he'd detail the sexual tension between us, which I was completely unaware of."

"Right Kleytjen?"

Right then another Antonio voicemail came through, even though it was from just after his first one. "I told Paul you were here but he says he's gotta get something. Fuck this guy he's doing it again he's like, I'ma come to your place, and he doesn't, so I'm gonna ignore him I think for like a month and then see what happens, so let's go to Vegas. Oh also I made some bomb tacos tonight they're the greatest." We were close now, La Jolla and her destination coming up on both sides, houses to the right that won't be there after a few more years of cliff erosion.

"Right. I might never understand this phone. You asked about Sterling? I told him while we were outside his room, 'Palmer was on our football team, always got injured, a la Motley, don't know if he ever played a full game in four years. Played linebacker even though his personality is all offense. He's a year older, knows Ravi. That year he had just graduated and moved out and I freaked out about what I would do. I always *knew* I would know, I just stopped caring for a while.' Anyway, Ravi is enjoying it back east now.

'Of course you knew, you were born on a campus.'

'I was born young. That summer Jen was told about a man, don't know how I feel about that, just know that I'll always have known her longer.'

'She didn't meet him first?'

'That's like asking what comes first, one or one thirty.'

'Why do you measure everything in time? It's so subjective. There's a certain amount of misery with the position we're in.'

'You're lucky to live sad moments.'

'I've never been to a funeral. That's luckier.'

'Knew it before it happened, but acting on inside info is illegal. She ended up saying he was pithy, that she was definitely a test run. As an objective person, I could have told her that eighteen months sooner.'

'Objective people don't exist. But you should never make an objective decision, make your own. Subjectivity is a beautiful thing.'

'You just said - whatever. Don't make no difference what nobody says, when you like someone, you like someone. I just know that they don't talk with each other anymore even though they ended on Good Terms, whatever those are. The same summer that averaged a hundred eleven degrees, not Celsius, so hot you could burn a disc. Everything is degraded by heat. The valley got the worst of the drought, nine months without a drop. What a drain. I've told no one else our house foreclosed, we moved.'

'So all that happened at the same damn time.'

'After the first day at my new school I skipped an entire week. Only time I've ever been absent, might as well have transferred to Rim of the World. Sometimes it rains so hard it's funny for four weeks.' And muddy."

"Nine parts dirt, three parts water."

"I'm sidetracking. I was able to meet people, so there's that. 'Bob, you like Greek food?' Jessie walked over with the bill.

'Is it food? Then I like it. This I liked a lot.' Paid cash, it makes me feel rich."

She itched her nose. "If you didn't pay for things you actually would be."

"There's no consolation for being rich. 'Good man. If you're looking for lunch, Paradise Cafe is a despicably wonderful place. On Tuesdays everything is half priced.'

'It should be Tuesday more often.'

'Sign the petition. There's also Flour Power Bakery if you find yourself in Cajon.'

'Which one's better?'

'Paradise. Ask what the Deal of the Day is. If it's the Frontega Chicken, get it. If it's not, get the Frontega Chicken.'

'Which one's worse?'

'Neither.' His hair was messier already, before the crowd.

'How about here, you close at eleven. Does that mean we leave by then or we just have to show up in time?'

With a hint of a smile, 'Ten fifty nine is just fine.' Get it on the go. I thanked him and got back to the Parsippany all ready to borrow from Jen her car, but then I saw her."

Alameda

Everyones a winner were playing that game ~ Mathangi Arulpragasam

I pushed the seat back as far as it would go to stretch my legs. Mulholland, Reseda, Ventura signs had ceased, like you're driving through a Tom Petty song backwards. Palmer thought about waiting at Golf n Stuff til it opened and asked about the hotel he ordered booze and hookers to. "With magnitude and frequency inversely proportional, this is more meaningful than my original assessment, yet in the interest of brevity I'll just say all that occurred once I got there is I went up to my room and rain is the best thing to fall asleep to. Rain makes you think better. I think I think too much. Woke at six, always wake up right before my alarm. Having a bed was amazing. Something airports should consider including."

"It's called suprachiasmatic nucleus. Dumbass. You still don't drink coffee?"

"When I wake up, I'm awake. I always shower. It's great to get up early, all I could hear were the dawning birds. The room even had a dishwasher. From the window I saw the marine layer burning off revealing a sliver of some sort of refracted light diffraction illusion. There wasn't actually a line on the horizon, that's just how our eyes interpret it, like you're in a painting."

"Or Mystery Spot. That one you can see visually."

"The stairs I took to the lobby, checked out and knew the thing to do would be to go see my sister, figured that one out just by sleeping. Checked my backpack at the front desk and left a message asking Jen to get it for me when she got off. She was already out of school, except she was taking classes up in Linda Vista, first time she stayed for summer. Before leaving I went for the free continental breakfast."

He started laughing. "Cheesebro? Dude, that's what you are. She's like gold buried beneath a cemetery: not worth it." We'd passed that exit twenty miles back.

"Outside, bright and sunshiny, some dude walked by with an open cup in each hand, pushing a stroller. Pushed it with his belly, 'I feel stupid. Do I look stupid?' Seemed smart to me. Walked up to Park and G Street bus stop, the thirty two showed up. The whole transport took over an hour, stops every minute.

At Fashion Valley a passenger got on without stopping to pay, headphones in so obviously didn't want to talk. Shadow of the driver's hat on her arm, 'Are you listening to *mu*sic in those? Pop one out so you can listen to me.' Looked like the lady from outside the hotel. Library on Salmon River is the closest stop, where there's always someone on the corner selling bonsai trees. Malcolm X down by Paradise Hills, closer to downtown, is my favorite. So I walked the home mile and a half, a stretch of sun cooled land right between the ocean and the mountains. It's the best soil around, so much mulch. Now houses are built on it, lots of concrete.

I didn't even realize what song was on until Sterling said, '*Elephant*'s my favorite album. Did I tell you I'm not going to San Diego for summer? I'm staying up here.'

'You did not. No summer camp director extraordinaire?'

'I went to the first week of regional training, and some will say that leaving is taking the easy way out, but I realized I would be way more a coward to stay than to leave somewhere I didn't want to be. It's so spaced out.'

'It's much easier to get a job than to quit a job.' Looked like there're a million hairs falling through the air.

'Thanks Kleytjen. Forget last year, like how I forgot Andera, think about two years ago in Bio when we didn't know each other. And we thought the other guy was a jerk.'

'And then I found it to be true, thanks to Mind and Modernism: Your presentation of Aquinas and your conclusion approach claims. But, you confused two objections which makes the paper not perfect.'

'How do you even remember that? I'll take hilarity over clarity every time. Who wouldn't be able to get along with someone?'

'You still like Andera? She's back in town today.'

'Dude, I don't know who I like anymore. I think I'm starting to get a little crush on Liz. She and I, we've texted two hundred twelve days in a row.'

'Your knowing that is far more impressive than any streak.'

'She overwhelms fact.'

'I coulda told ya that, facts are cheap. She gives the best texts. I totally get it when we like girls, I don't understand girls at all.'

'She's better in person. Man, dude, you gotta shake it out. Tell you this though, if you were I, because people only figure out personal things long after they've been obvious to everyone else. The difference between girls and relationships is that you understand girls more than a lot and you don't understand relationships, at all. You know what's great about music?' I do. 'There are always new songs.'

He looked sharper by the minute. 'Sterling, I have two things to tell you. The first one I forget. The second is I've been doing what you said, about investing in people.'

'It's not about in*vest*ing. It's about relating. See, that little tweak in your brain is all it takes. Creating and repeating the right mental vocabulary is the first step to success.'

'That's pretty punctuated, where'd you hear that?'

'Deck of cards. Second, be the opposite of a situational person. I walk in a room and say whatever I want. You walk in and try to determine my mood before deciding what you'll say or if you'll say it. You went to office hours that one time, right? You don't do that - you reacted to your situation. It probably wasn't effective. If you had taken that time you'd spent there but writing the paper, be*fore* it was due, that would have been effective. That's up to your personality. If you put in the time, you'll be fine. I'm sure of it. You're way more detail oriented than I am.' Hard to tell if that's true, he makes a list for everything, precious time meticulously crafting each day. 'Dude, if I wrote I know who I want to take me home, I never would have sung it that way. That's what's great.'

'I didn't go to office hours for *my* paper, remember. I'm reading that *Peaceful Warrior* book.'

'That's mega. I met someone who knows Socrates. Which part are you at?'

'Page ninety nine. Who knows him?'

'I mean, what's happening?'

'He just broke his leg.'

'How'd he break his leg?'

'I know you know the answer's a motorcycle accident.' Mussel Shoals has got a swell, huh?" In One Ear entered ours.

"Cut the crap. How was Jen?"

Pulchritudinous as ever. She looked different but she hadn't changed, something we recognize and don't analyze. Palmer switched lanes twice without anyone in front of us, like he's avoiding turtle shells or something. "After reading that text from Sterling I realized my rookie mistake. My reservation was for Saturday night. It was Friday."

"That's what happens once you know you can, you don't think about if you should."

"Small sign declared a lack of vacancy, how biblical. Holiday weekend trap. A strange reality to be faced with, something I would blog about if I had one. 'Are you sure there's nothing available at all?' Would have taken the penthouse if they offered. 'Well how early can I get my room tomorrow?'

'Tomorrow? You can check in anytime you like. After noon.' Sleep Inn was probably all booked by then too and I didn't want to go anywhere else and spend money. Mason once stayed at a three and a half star hotel and said he was roughing it. There's also the El Cortez, but Hernán always attracts a crowd. 'I can't let you stand there for the rest of the night.'

'Sorry, I'm a little distracted, my roommate was texting me.' My mind was stuck texting Jordy, that's why I didn't respond to it right away.

YOU WOKE ME UP FOR THAT

'He sounds like a pleasant person.'

'He's smart, too.'

'Is he? How tall is he?'

'I don't know, five eleven, five twelve. Is Jen working right now?'

'You won't find her here tonight.' She had to check someone in, so I called up Antonio. I had no way of getting over to him, the trolley stops running at midnight, and I doubt he would get up just to drive downtown and pick me up. Then I reremembered he was already done with school, wasn't sure if he had gone back up to Mesa. I'd've called up Grace just to talk, she goes to bed late on Fridays, yet she didn't have a phone, if you believe that. I walked away from the desk, stood in the lobby where there's a shimmering fresh fish pond. My eyes gravitated toward mirrors on the ceiling a hundred feet overhead. I'm surrounded by water. I know there's a hotel nearby that has a pool on the roof, I don't know how late it stays open."

"Let's go there now."

"Shuffled down the corridor and into an elevator. Some attendant was in there sleeping, standing. 'Going up?' He pushed all thirty six buttons, so I got out at the second floor and switched. That one only went halfway up, so I was switched again at the nineteenth. Should have taken the stairs. Good music though. The wonders of the modern hospitality industry, built in nineteen sixty nine. Actually there's a thirty seventh floor, no button for it, any reasonable hotel has a secret top floor. Even unreasonable ones. Unobstructed by fog there's a great view, but all I saw was what someone printed on the ledge: You must be afraid my friend. That is how one becomes an obedient citizen.

Whatever that means. 'What are you doing?' Out of nowhere. 'You're not allowed to be here.'

'It's okay, I'm with the band.' Didn't know what to do, he stood in the doorway of the stairwell.

'Relax, Max,' said the night man. 'You don't have to explain yourself.' And walked away. 'To anyone.' Just like that. Made my way down to the first floor by way of the stairs, nice to have gravity on your side. Last thing I remember I unleashed my backpack and checked it at the front, don't need a room to do that. Brandi, according to her name tag, said so. Before that I took out one of the shirts I packed and put it on. Two shirts, twice the fun. No jacket. That was it until I returned eight hours later.

Post hug Jen showed excitement through her smiling eyes. 'You went shopping without me?' Sweet like candy.

'You know I can't help myself.' "

"Of all the hotels in all the San Diegos."

"Her idea. With girls I go for the more complicated, it just happens that way. Like there's two best friends or three roommates or something like that, or twins, the one I like will be married. Oh well. 'When are you done with school? I probably already asked you that. You wanna walk around outside,' she interposed, 'so I can get my blood to circulate?'

'Cause it doesn't do that naturally.'

'Precisely. I love this song! It's so happy.' Somewhere Only We Know. I thought to ask about goldfish, but I already knew the answer.

'We're done in one week.' Feet headed northeast toward Gaslamp.

'Are you coming down here then?'

'For a couple weeks or so.'

'Delightful. I'm throwing a party for my roommate on the thirteenth. She's moving out, she's engaged!' Only reason I know them is Jen, nexus. 'I'm gonna make cookies and we'll watch a movie.'

'Sounds good, just let me check with my lawyer first.'

'That's been taken care of. Everything's legal.' Looks at me like she knows what I'm about to say."

"She's inside your head. Why do people even live here? There's a mudslide every nine years."

"The view though. 'Well now it doesn't sound like much fun. What movie?'

'A good one.'

I just smiled, 'That's not what I asked.' Get those mirror neurons working.

'Well I told you anyway. I'm not supposed to say.'

'Says who?' Girls are always keeping secrets.

'It's just supposed to be a surprise for everyone, that's all.' She could tell I wasn't good crazy about that answer. 'Okay Kleytjen, how about this? I give you five guesses. If you get it, I'll make an extra batch of cookies. Just for you. If you want to risk your streak.' How could I tell her no? Like the time she had us make a bowling bet.

'It would be an honor and a privilege to lose a bet to you.' Gambling is fun when you're with her.

'It would be better if you win,' with a wink, it looked like. Back inside now, 'So do you need anything in particular or are you just here to get me fired?' Easily baffled, hardly surprised. 'I'm kidding!' Handed me silver sidewinders.

'Thanks Jen, I owe you big time. Like at least a picture.'

'Don't even worry about it, Kleytjen. I trust you. It's a dirty, filthy, disgusting car.' Word for word. 'Oh, and my audio cord broke. Sad day.' It's always funny when the happiest person you know says that. Jen Joy Wafel. Important syllables if there ever were any."

"There never were. What makes you say she's happy?"

"Monday is her favorite day. 'There are some records in there, though. Feel free to use whatever. Driver side window was smashed last Sunday, trunk was popped and it was taken. Everything important was on the passenger side, still is.' She had me burn some songs for her mom once.

'That's the provolone. I really will listen to anything.' A little rasta.

'Oh yeah, guess who just found her original *Raiders of the Lost Ark* soundtrack!'

'Well, that seems like an easy question. Too easy. It's probably a trick question, so I will say: I did.' Just a fool.

'Dang, you are good!' Such a great laugh. 'It's Saturday, right?'

'Yeah, but to me it's Thanksgiving.'

'Saturday is a good day for today. I'll see you when I'm off?'

'I'll try not to skip town.' Wasn't easy, either. 'Seeya.'

'Later.' Sooner. Jen went back to her shift and I meant to reclaim my backpack from the front desk with Grace's shirt in it, I think

I was thinking about our overnight trip for National Honors, end of junior year. We had an uneven gender distribution and Torrey and I got a room with one bed.

Talk about a clerical error. 'Okay, this doesn't have to be weird or anything, just tell me what side you want. Top or bottom?' "

"That part actually happen?"

"She was cool about it, even tried to offer to take the couch. On the bus ride up to San José Jen slept on my shoulder the whole while, circuitously."

"Why the hell do people slow down just cause the shoulder is closed? It doesn't change a damn thing."

"Soon as I got outside I figured everyone watched me from their windows until I heard a kid singing on the way to finding where Jen had put her car, walking with his grandparents it looked like, 'All the monkeys aren't in a zoo.' Found Carmen in the employee parking lot. Easy to find, a shiny purple Beetle, looks great with Jen in it, her favorite color. Got me from K to J and back. First time driving it, like a maiden voyage, so it felt weird, good weird, like when you get something unstuck from between your teeth. Cleanest car I have ever been in. Goes from sixty to zero in less than three seconds. There was mixed music in there featuring The Cure. I thought of plays I've read and never seen, *The Big Bonanza*, *Anything Goes*. Just as I started I rerouted, right down the street is the stadium de los Padres, they were set to play the Nationals at one. Less expensive tickets than for Grace's play. The last time I was at a Padres game my parents adopted the notion that it made sense to leave in the ninth cause they were down by a run. While trying to leave the parking lot we heard them tie it up, then walk off."

"What I get from that is your parents took you to a baseball game. That's fantastic."

"I told Sterling about Grace's play before, so, 'Back at Parsippany, after five when I arrived, she had just walked outside. Lucky her thingy was stolen, I had a station all lined up, Just Like Heaven. Weird Al's One More Minute followed. "Oh, you're right on time!"

'So? And so much for being late.'

'In all my punctiliousness. She never waits too long. Unbuckled but Jen said I could drive. Happiness perfumed the air as she sat down.' Smelled like blueberries. 'I thought she was done for the day, turns out it was only her lunch.' Least she didn't have to work the night shift. "How goes it?"

"Great! Ah, the tank is full. You didn't need to do that. Claim it on your taxes."

"Was your boss mad you had a visitor?"

She took her phone out of her purse. "Huh? She wasn't mad, she just takes her job seriously. She's a funny girl."

"What's funny about her?"

"She's just really weird."

"Funny is weird now?"

"It's all right, you have permission to be peculiar. She's weird, we get along gorgeously."

Started looking at pictures on my phone, "Here's your castle. I'm pretty sure it's a symbol of our collateral."

"Right! I kept getting a call from this random guy yesterday." I apologized. "No worries, my little brother told his friend to do it." We drove nowhere. Thought about going to Balboa, to the zoo, to check on the elephants and see if they remembered me from a third grade field trip. Monday they let all the vets in for free.

Alone in her car, "Anything particular you want to accomplish in forty four minutes? Like have lunch?"

"Already ate. You know already, spaghetti. Let's do something crazy!" Voice got higher as she talked. "We could go sky diving really quick. Or we could do nothing." '

'No, yeah, you're way too analytic for that.'

'Not analytic enough. "Jen, I'll do anything for you. I won't do that. Okay, let's do it. The diving part. We could also scalp Sea World tickets, study a smack of jellyfish." Seemed like a good idea at the time.

"I was just thinking that in my brain!" Asked if she wanted to stay for a while after her shift. Alas, Jen revealed she was having dinner with someone at nine. Sinks to the ground. They went to Elephant Bar, already too late. I'd've chosen to be third wheel instead of doing something fun, which is perfectly stupid.'

'Sadistic. Don't censor yourself.'

'Just hope they didn't meet at a party, no one knows why the thought alone drives me crazy.'

'She's in love with the world. It seems to me.'

'Rolled the windows down just to feel the rain. "Tomorrow I could take you from here or pick you up and we can hang out near the station before you have to go. Want to? The rain is a traveling friend I realize I've missed as soon as she returns." '

'That's an expensive ticket. A lot of work to have fun.'

'Was the transportation any less effective? Next time I'll sail. "I already have a ride there. But yes anyway."

"Oh no, saying yes begins things!" Like improvising.'

'But it's not the answer that motivates you.'

'It makes you smarter. "Ha, I want to meet her! Is she a looker?" I always go with whomever I say yes to first. "Why is my phone singing?" She's a great singer.

"It's feliz."

"Just as the sun - hold up. Hello? Oh hey! Yes. I'll call you then. Yeah!"

"Dunno if this will affect our plans, but it's supposed to rain still."

"You don't shower with an umbrella, do you?" I don't even own one, she'd always give me hers.

"There was talk of fireworks and I might go see the water at midnight. When we get to the ocean - "

"I'll be bundled up in bed by then!" That makes sense, which is why I didn't think of it. Crazy en la cabeza.' Have to realize that the plans all through my head don't match the plans in - Yes?"

"You were gonna say, Like Katy Perry. Right?"

"If I were going to, I would have. 'Let's just see what the day brings. Savvy?'

'Yes. Yeah, let's do that. That'll be great, like a really bad taco.' She reached over and tapped me on the opposite shoulder. Right in the middle of a friendly conversation.

'What what?'

'Nothing.'

'What else?'

'Santa Barbara treating you well?'

'Better. You know it's perfectly legal for you to visit.' Hundred dollar laugh."

"Are you crying or are you getting an eyelash out?"

"It's still in there. 'Torrey has been begging me to come up! I will.'

'I'll sway you when I think of an applicable movie line. Which language did you take? Chemistry? Let's become multilingual.' "

"Polylingual. You're bilingual when drunk."

To lift your heart in case youre hip ~ Anthony Kiedis

When you see her you'll understand. "This is as I said the rest of what I was telling Sterling. 'There are many things that I would like to change.'

'Just because it's not perfect doesn't mean it wasn't worth doing, too often we risk very little. The more you think about it, the more you'll like it. I want to see what eventuates, if you can tell it like it is.'

'I'll take it to its illogical conclusion. Drove back real quick after Happy Wings, listening to the radio I thought of what Kabiting told me, which you know already. We've been told by everyone how to prepare for life, they forget your life has already started. They tell you to wait and be rewarded. We're still waiting. When she called at the smoothie place I told her to meet near Bunny Park, off Bacon Tree, right next to Maplewood. Parents still weren't back but I wanted to stay outdoors and watch nature sprout up, ours to discover. Takes them a minimum of ten hours whenever they go anywhere, even if it's just to the post office. I kept the sticky note up. Didn't know it was the last time I would be there. From our driveway to the park I started to continue looking for a breakthrough. I couldn't remember the last time I went a day without drinking.' Just a sec."

Someone asked Paul to do this drug deal. My thought is he should probably hear from someone that that's pretty awsful.

Before responding to Antonio I asked Palmer if he was free to chauffeur. "How's their new place, by the way?"

"They tell me it's ferociously nice. Someone jumped off the swings, like a baby butterfly, then looked through the other end of binoculars. End of May, June in bloom, hundred degrees outside, hot in the sky, and they were wearing jeans. Allergic to Vitamins. I counted only nine clouds. Nine or eight, like an Irish dozen. I apricated and got sunburnt, the sign of a good thing."

"Only nine, really? You need more fingers."

We passed the city limit elevation forty two feet sign. "You know what they say about the young. Between the park and the school there was writing on the wall: Failure prevails why bother. Stigma about young folks being too idealistic to be taken seriously. Cause we don't know how. I wanted to paint over it, even beige. Like Noel Gallagher said, That's fucking rubbish. Kids don't need to be hearing that nonsense.

"Or maybe that was his brother. That, and the professor who interviewed me for the section leader position, 'The praise you should give to kids is limitless.' She has ultimate power, to hire someone, so I commit to that.

"Where were we? 'Sitting on a park bench with its share of dried bird poop and squirrels asking for food. Waiting, wondering where she could be. Wishing I weren't so tense. She was there when I thought of her at the house and she was there when I thought about her at Lost Hills. To think she didn't see the signs or it was a bigger earthquake and the epicenter was downtown. Or that when I texted she was driving. Or maybe a hurricane got her. Thankfully there were just enough distractions, thanked you for a text earlier saying it was the highlight of a precarious night.

You're very welcome Kleytjen, the words mean a lot. If you ever feel off, remember to talk with your friends. They are great. Always got love for you.

'I sent that!'

'Everyday, in your element. Everyone else I thank:

Lol your response time

'Kept wondering that it would run out of chemistry in its battery, must have used it lots over one day, yeah. Always underestimate how long it takes to get to where I am, my own fault. Whenever anyone tells me five minutes, I can't help feeling they mean five minutes, when really they mean three hours.'

'The best things said come last.'

'The first girl I wrote a letter to she is, like an initial public offering, short as it was.'

'Or not like that.'

'Either one. A real letter. Hard to break apart the right words, but she still has it. She just acknowledged its existence, suspended judgement. Necessary and insufficient, the same week another dude wrote her a thrice as long letter. Everyone did, come to think of it. I can't imagine why. All the girls around her say she was lucky, but no one ever means to be in a position to disappoint. Made me realize pictures are better, no captions. She was smitten but didn't go for him, he signed it, Rationally yours. I can see a way it's got nothing to do with me.'

'Any type of letter is crap, you have to *say* it. Here's what I see. You spend your time thinking about the small picture, like the difference between delayed and instant gratification. There is none. They're just adjectives. Gratification and disappointment, there's a difference there.'

'There is no disappointment, only reevaluation. The guy's full of crap, a few weeks later he went out with Torrey. Apparently that's called waiting.'

'You're not waiting either, you're lying to yourself.'

'Okay, Sterling, tell me if I'm wrong. You get a favorite song, you hear countless songs after that you like a lot, some are even better, yet your favorite song remains.'

'I get it, your first always takes your innocence. The thing is, it only happens at first sight.'

'We'll see. Phone vibrated once more, excited me thought she texted. It was Palmer calling.'

'Exciting enough, he rocks to his own song.'

'Without letting me talk, "So down to hang in ten summers. Let's go to Hotel Coronado July twenty sixth, one twenty seven Hawaii time. Kley, never take advice from crazy people." We'll just go with that. Also wrote a special letter when he was after his own heart. Her response: You didn't give me a self addressed envelope, so I assumed I could recycle it. "You might *think* you'd rather have her say no than not ask, but in reality, you're doing just fine without knowing. It sticks with you." Happened again, this time Carson.

The radio just transitioned from Werewolves of London to Kyrie. Happy almost Memorial Day indeed p.s. I challenge you to mini golf

'Almost got sick just sitting there, feverish, like a big deal. Probably my low blood pressure. All at once she finally showed up, like a magic trick, so for a moment no time passed at all, like you're a photon. Was there ever any doubt? She got out and came a little bit closer so close everything started going really fast like Santa. "*Notting Hill*?"

"I thought you were gonna wait." Sweet like vanilla. "Guess it's not yesterday anymore." '

'The finest of the flavors. How did yesterday happen before today?'

' "Oh yeah, guess what!"

"Whoa, what?"

"You're not gonna guess? I didn't find any tickets to Sea World." A redundant name.

"Good, I didn't look for any. You're so bright today!" I was wearing neon, stopping traffic. She: happy face earrings, fancy that. "Why so snazzy? You ready to go?" The sound of barking. "I have your backpack."

"My mom told me not to get into cars with strange women."

"No worries." She turned around. "All I can suspect is you've had a strange day, and it's still going, but if you get in you'll be on your way back to whatever normal is." I did, without visible excitement, wondering if I could return to the status quo, like a cartoon. "You have something in your hair."

"I always walk into spider webs." She successfully tried to get it out. With expendable time, Jen suggested Seaport Village, while she cracked my knuckles. Started the car, made a you turn, and we headed to do just that. "Are you done for the day this time?" What is it?'

'I was just thinking, Jason Mraz said, The greatest challenge is to write happy and positive music. We should make that as easy as possible.'

'It's about that vulnerable creative spot. "I'm done for the month!"

"What are you singing?"

Jen answered quite slowly. "A song."

"Oh I see. Does it have a name?"

"Yup." Could show everything to me. The drive took exactly as long as it should have; much shorter than anticipated. All of it I spent looking out the passenger window and the sunroof. Thought we'd talk, but Jessie was there, the mood all changed.'

'That's not the reason.'

'Yeah but it's true. He wasn't aggressively nice like at Lion's.'

'What'd he say?'

'Nothing. "*The Princess Bride*?"

"Two down." We parked. "So is there something particular you want to talk about?" I didn't think it would be around all these shops or on a crowded avenue. The station's on Kettner and West Broadway, place to reminisce. Jessie feigned sleep, she and I resolved to go on a walk.

"I think so. I thought so. May I? There were a couple things I was gonna say, but instead I'm gonna tell you about my day yesterday, if you have a minute."

"I thought you didn't like boring." World's most entertaining guy. "I'll jump ahead to my closing statement: this won't be a recurring event.'

"Recurrent. How was your sister's musical? She's quite the thespian." We circled the menagerie carousel merry go round fun horsey house built right before nineteen hundred. Lots of other hand carved animals, and a couple chariots. Last month there was a contest to see who could stay on the thing for thirty consecutive hours and the winner won ten grand. We ran out of space, only leaves you guessing. Came back to the start so our conversation ended, she raised her eyebrows and opened her mouth to laugh. All you need.

"Good point." Even when she deviates.

"It's just a talk. You like helping people laugh." I offered to go for a second lap, but I really wanted to be face to face, like to say to you. Forcing the issue is like riding a bike with one foot.'

'Especially when you stutter. No one's gonna tell her.'

'Stomach all tangled up, collapsing on itself. I wouldn't have it any other way, makes music more intense. Had her hands in her pockets, at least she wasn't wearing sunglasses. Just for one day.'

'Our carousel, the one downtown, was originally from San Diego.'

'Jen asked if I wanted to get something sweet and spicy, not the other way around, at Lettuce Feed You. Wasn't hungry, not even a little bit. I definitely should have been. Heart beat fast as a hummingbird's, like when you touch something hot. It's good to care, until you don't know how, like when you learn to juggle with eight and you forget how to with seven.'

'Is that what it's like?'

'The line was long and we weren't sure what was on the other side of the pizza place, there was a wall in the way, brick wall made of steel. Standing by the wall, along the railings and the fences, a seagull landed on Jen's shoulder. "I'm pretty sure this needs to be documented." Took out my phone. If I had been all in as photographer, I would have had my camera instead of letting it fell off Patricia. No more detours as we walked quicker to the station. Glad to take the train, by then I really just wanted sleep, should have eaten the apple Grace offered. There was an increased spattering of clouds in the sky, the stormy kind, stolen from the sea, in between the waves of sunshine, just as predicted. Even still, sweat ran down her face. "Strange weather."

"Oh but I know. It's sunny somewhere." Is it any wonder?

"Coronado," at the same time. I looked up as doves dove down to the water. As we're walking on by, "Is it only supposed to storm today and tomorrow?" '

'Empty question.'

'Yep. Progressively more clouds landing from over the ocean, going into the grey. Looked like November. "I'm sure it will sometime in September. It's a beautiful day Kleytjen, the weather's just not sure what it wants to do yet." I guessed *Say Anything*.'

'You really are old fashioned.'

'Gotta be fashionable someway. You know when that's from? "Hmm. Maybe. I like your thinking!"

"Cause I'm neurotic? I'm all out of focus, I still need to do homework and everything."

"Weird definition of everything. There's no such thing as everyone or everything."

"I round up."

"Just think about breathing and you'll be perfect for your interview. We're all teachers." Obviously the white elephant in the cage, no wise words to change that. Thought it out in my head so many times, things don't go the way I think they will.' Not so many times enough.

'Thank goodness. What you expect doesn't make any sense.'

'It's more organic that way too. I get too flustered, you've heard it all before. I thought about not going back. At all. Does that make me crazy? If I didn't tell her I could leave, in spite of these deficiencies. "*Edward Scissorhands*?"

"I'm actually really glad you said that," she said over my shoulder as we changed direction.

"I got it right, right?" So impulsive. I'm still saving my last.'

'Wait, it took you a year to *not* figure this out?'

'I stopped thinking about it. "We have our soccer game tomorrow." The one with Brad and Torrey. I'm Batman was our name. Hers was Robot Love. Our schools played each other in September, the last Friday of the month. Home game - match. Don't know the meaning, nor was I sure it had one, but Jen originally said she wanted to drive up for that.' That was the one we almost broke the attendance record again. What is it?"

"Seriously, a year? All this time, how could you not know? You know, you should look into voice acting. It's *Wall E.* Is it *Tangled*?"

lol not tonight dude I'm with the hottest girl ever

Nice of Palmer to be descriptive. "It's not. She does like that Dave Matthews song though. 'She said, "You still need to buy your ticket. Read your options carefully and get the right one." I just looked for the one that's better than everything else. You know how it's always quicker going back? This time was unequivocally longer.

"You know I don't know what things mean." Think it was everyone who said, Anyone who isn't confused doesn't understand what's going on. "What do you get in business class? Foot massages?" In coach you be who you are. "I'm not cool enough anyway."

"Everyone is sometime." It didn't take my twenty, probably all the blood on it. Silly nose. Then put my room key in by mistake. "See, it's a good memory! Being who you want to be is far superior to knowing anything."

On the platform as she's walking on by. "Perceptions dictate."

"So so what? Let someone else's opinions become your reality? Keep doing your crazy funky thing." I know it's cliche when anyone else says that. "Thank you for all the laughs. We'll see each other. Soon."

"Hopefully." What a thing to say, it sounds so unsure. Yes we will, yes, might have ended it right there though. "Maybe even sooner." Felt a drop of water on my head, so passive.

"You know I'll do anything you ask, but I stopped reading minds a few years ago."

"Just let me know if you quit your job and stuff." Trying not to look at the ground.

"I have a - "

"Me too." That didn't go the wanted way, the words wouldn't.'

'I miss you saying that.'

'Me too. "Okay, you're about to say something crazy."

I know it sounds absurd. "I know it sounds crazy; it's not crazy. It's the smartest thing I've ever done: realize how wonderful you are."

She just stood there, not unhappy, not smiling. "That's very sweet. We're still the greatest, Kleytjen. Happy Birthday." '

'Are you serious?'

'Better belated, don't worry about it.'

'You said it's during the dog days of winter! How come you never do anything for your day?'

'Better chance of having a surprise party. I got used to my parents never doing anything.'

'The surprise is for everyone else. Maybe she doesn't want *sweet*.'

'Maybe too much. I could hesitate no more, at least deserved the truth, she did. What was I gonna do, wait another four years? I spun around again, should have kept Ballroom and not dropped it for Biz Econ. "Take the sunshine. Let it burn." She meant the train was about to leave. It was. I tuned around and got on board without another word.' No elixir."

"What am I looking for? Persephone?" Her voice knocked me back to the present. Of the dozens of drives down there, this definitely went by the fastest, so slow.

"Parsippany, Amie. It's the one right next to the Hyatt across from the Wilshire, third tallest building in the city, used to have a different name. We should study. You provide the being smart and I'll provide the Cheese Its."

"I'm not there yet. But, I won't be hanging around Geisel the entire weekend, so let me know when you need a ride to the station on Sunday. Or if you decide to stay an extra day and want a ride back." All I could hope to hear.

"Whoa, let's not get carried away."

"Don't make too much of this, I'm sure there are a lot who listened to the same fifty six songs we have. You care a lot about your stories, but do you really have to to give every detail that comes to mind for preservation's sake?"

"The past makes me happy."

"No. The past made you happy."

All I know is, whenever you tell someone about anything, it makes you feel a lot better.

I can see us lying arent we ~ Gwen Stefani

There's so much time in a day. We were running almost two hours ahead. "I think the longer hair you have the less time it takes to cut it. 'Kleytjen, my muscles are down here.' That laugh again. 'What's the biggest compliment you can think of?'

'You sound like Zeppelin. My parents, they're smart and friendly, that's for sure, they just like to worry. Like if the refrigerator is open more than one second, or if the price of gasoline goes up by two tenths of a cent, or if you cough and a hospital isn't close by, or something crazy like this, or if the yellow light turns red, there's an app for that anyway, and if there isn't anything to worry about, which is undoubtedly the case five weeks a month, then they make things up. Naturally, I didn't want them to know I was running around town unpreparing for finals when I was about to be dropped from Honors. I talked with them the weekend before and they told me how it was too bad I would miss Grace's play and all that that's life crap. Yeah right. Too bad to be true. I emailed Grace saying what I would do, it was easy once I figured it out, and told her to not tell them.'

'Did you get a good one? Still taking landscapes?'

'See for yourself. They just seem a little weird, like I always call them, they don't ever call. They think they're bothering me, a highly irrelevant consideration considering the concept of phones. Comes from only filling your days with work, even though they didn't have anything steady. What a bunch of garbage. What it is is I just wish they would say "I love you." I already know they do, but it has passed on. So simple for everyone else, I've inherited an inability to say it. Instead they say "be safe," which always sounds strange, even before considering you can have safety, but you can't *be* it. Another thing is I knew I would see them in a week or anywhen when finals were over. An other thing: I get bored sleeping at home. Here it's always different. You went to bed before me one night, but after me the next night, or Mynor came back super late, or you just finished printing a paper, or something, or we both stayed awake for a couple hours talking about kangaroos. I don't know how to explain it, obviously, but it's always different. They especially would get worried if I showed up at three in the morning. Three eleven.' We always have a squeaky front door." You get near Carp before the temporary eternal flame and it's a speed trap. Nothing to do but go fast. Palmer's still doing ninety and there were two cops waiting as we mobbed by Rincon. They didn't move. I'd been awake almost one Earth rotation by now and thought he put some weird station on where the songs were a little slower. In actuality the songs just sounded slow to my brain. "I think this is Razorblade.

'Boredom isn't day to day, it takes years. Did you first meet during the day or at night?'

'It's different for you, your parents call to tell you what they had for dinner. It's a little bit funny,' what a weird word, 'all the thoughts you have in one second. I left to the Gaslamp area and Jen swirled, even with that Who song still stuck in my head, connections, and shared events. The greatest thing since the invention of color. Trying to remember where it all began. Way that I met her was algebraically, you'd say. Trigonometry actually, our lowest common denominator. On the third day we graded each other's diagnostic quizzes, first thing she said to me, first time we saw each other on a Friday, "Wow, Kleytjen, you are one smart cookie." A gross overstatement, seeing as Trig was so easy. Our final instructed us to do only one of the ten given problems, I did all. I got a negative eight hundred percent.'

'Hold on, is this chronological?'

'There's no logic to it. It's complicated, simple as that. First time anyone asked me about her I heard myself say, "Really attractive." Has a lot to do with it, but it's not the first cause.

"Yeah, she wears magnets." Back when Mason wore a suit everyday.' The way running entered Jen's life is she missed cheerleading tryouts. Push em back, push em back, way back. To be honest, the unoriginal reason I joined is my friends, so their judgment's not to be trusted, kept telling me how every girl who runs has great legs."

Palmer noticed that about Torrey, got the top grade in Trig cause he liked it infinitely more than the rest of us. Also told me, "Some people who are excellent with numbers have no common sense, even if they have a thousand million more synapses than average." Then he made a top ten list of his favorite songs, "That'll make it an even fifteen." The way that he got good at talking with girls is sixth grade his brother moved out and conference called his girlfriend and him every week, always fell asleep when she talked, so Palmer had to carry on the conversations.

" 'Our senior captain told everyone new and unnew, "We are uniting as a common cause under a team where the throwers and runners come together and conquer the valley of evils with our wit magnanimously." Apart from them but a part of the team. She and everyone else made the decision for us all to do a midnight run in January and water balloon us at the end, our initiation. Now they call that called abuse.

Mason, when you ask him how fast he is he says it's relative instead of just saying he has a sixteen hundred time of four thirty one, "You like her?" We just called him Turtle.

"What does that mean? I hardly know her."

"You like her." Friends are always right.'

'You're innocent until you deny it.'

'She's the exception.'

'Exceptions are convenient. Is she a manic pixie? You know, you could eat every meal for free.'

'I don't even know how you know that term. Affection mixed with economy of desire, progression toward the mean. Even her friends offered to put in a good word. I was actually good at hurdles, one of the only things I've ever been good at. Coach Escanola's motto: If you're not tired you're not really running, or, Run til your teeth hurt. She always asked us, "What's the most important thing in acting?"

"Delivery? Timing?"

"Practice. What's the most important thing in sports?" Later she was my Government coach.

"Athleticism? Ethic?"

"Practice." No one skipped practice without a notarized letter. Practice breathing from your stomach. Practice perfecting your stride. Escanola is from Loveland, Colorado, some place I've never been before, I've never been anywhere I haven't been, and always wanted us go to Leadville to train and build up our aerobic capacity. Not at a meet, but practice, I tore my left hamstring. Who knew running a thirteenth of a mile could be so hard? Heard it before I felt it. Jen, being who she is, helped me back to the locker room, no one else knew if it were serious, least of all myself, without wasting words. Everyone else, rightfully, focused on Mason's last hurdle, he landed the wrong way, and his fibula landed outside his leg. Can't help it if I'm lucky like winning a raffle she remembers that too.' Never stop, like numbers."

"When you actually care about someone, you never have to tell them."

"You know they're a liar. Care means you change your life. 'No one took me to get it fixed. When I was able to really run again, two years later, she had switched over to soccer. She does everything, like a mustard plant. Even though she didn't rejoin track, we had fun, just the two of us:

Let me change first slash I'll be ready in five!

Are you home? Where are we gonna do this?

'Had to find her headband. I constantly think I'll reinjure myself, that's all.'

'Yeah, it *has* to be something mental.'

'Explain yourself.'

'Our senior meet against our rivals, Mynor and I finished first and second, and one of guys on the other team was yelling to his relay partner, "Dude, just keep going, it's all mental!" We just laughed.'

'A crazy run that destroyed me and my cruciate ligament, but Jen gasped for more, "I like that one, it's all uphill and then gets steeper." Everyone, I'm never sure who, knows someone who runs up mountains for fun. Anyway it was a good choice for her. We both know it. She's superb at soccer.' We run like a river.

'Did she keep playing?'

'Didn't matter anyway. My dad lost his job, the whole oncology department was ditched, so we didn't have nor could we afford insurance. You're not allowed to play a sport or get your hamstring fixed without it. But no, for reasons still unknown to me, Jen turned down a Santa Barbara scholarship.'

'You've never finished a race, and you've never said why. Wrong use of anger?'

'My first meet back I was disqualified, false start. Next time I stubbed my toe in warm ups.'

'That's bogus, you were dis*qual*ified? No warning?'

'The whole idea of that race is based on the assumption that the difference of four milliseconds is recognized. It couldn't be more fair.'

'You're overdue like a library book. I wouldn't change anything, keep rushing to the start, it's better than starting late. You can afford to postpone the least since you're already behind.'

'Never have to try to hear her funny laugh, just comes naturally. Plus she knows everyone. One Tuesday, we were walking and talking, and I was horribly happy, not in the abstract sense, but that feeling you get in your stomach. Except every seven seconds she got a call or text, so we barely talked. "Hey. Have you ever thought about getting some friends? Then you wouldn't be so lonely." Maybe she's just a big drug dealer.

"No it's a good thing. I don't have to turn my phone off when I go to the movies." She makes me laugh.' "

"Doesn't sound like much. Do you think movie theater popcorn is the most expensive thing in the world per ounce?"

"I think a ten thousand dollar bill is. Another time, a Wednesday, we - whatever. Insignificant things are always the most significant. She thinks I'm a commiserative, and that's really just derivative of being agreeable. Well, she doesn't actively think that, she just said it once. All that thinking took a lot of time and there was hardly anyone around anymore, still didn't know where I was going to sleep, didn't know *if* I was going to sleep. Horton Plaza, home of Mad House Comedy, would have been perfect, except everything was closed. Horton is the first dude who asked for a public park to be developed. Some say he should get a memorial or a monument, but an outdoor shopping mall requires less paperwork."

"I thought he was an elephant. Fun with your friends never closes, Kley."

"Back by Parsippany, once the blood was circulating I checked what my phone said.

What are you wearing? I have nothing but good things to say about meeting Brad. Props to getting trashed!

"From Torrey's phone, whether it was she, or Mason still had it, or who knows what:

Urban wine trail tomorrow you are welcome to join if you want! Tenaya, me, and a bunch of people you don't know. Sounds fun right lol.

'You crack me up. No one gets that concept but you, Kleytjen Coral!' Untrue, still flattering. We sat down and ideated what to do over summer, like leave the west behind. 'That sounds expensive. I'd need a new boyfriend.' She crossed her legs and twirled her hair, all kinds of mixed messages. 'Did you bring homework with you? I thought you were a study stud.' Desiring to get all As has nothing to do with wishing to be studious.

'Yeah, it's in my backpack. Did summer session just start? So you have homework to do too.'

'I know! I need to do a lot of things.'

'Do you still - nevermind.' Writing utensils.

Wind kept blowing her hair in her face, over and over. 'Anything going on with your parents?'

'Nothing at all. I'm boring, so I don't want to compound that by going home.'

'Well remember boredom is a matter of choice.' I do remember reminding myself that." It's trickier that it seems. Palmer, he gets bored driving slower than a hundred in Carpinteria, but he sits on the couch for four hours doing nothing, watching garbage, and is perfectly restive. "She gleeked, said she had to go back. 'You didn't bring a jacket?' Felt like a six minute talk."

"If you talked slower you'd've had more time together."

"Didn't want to make her late, I didn't know any better. 'Well we'll talk before I have to go so we can figure this out.'

'Perfect plan!'

I wanted better. 'I might even be able to stay out of trouble in the pouring rain.'

'Think about everything that's happened and how lucky you are to be alive.' Obviously she was referring to how stable your alkaline levels have to be."

"Or how many asteroids almost hit us. If you change any action more than six years before you were born, you wouldn't have been born."

"I'd say six months. 'Tootles. Save your room key, it's a good memory.' Soon as I disembarked she slid across the seats and I thought, which I wasn't mentally prepared for. Thinking by yourself is dangerous."

"Of course, when you like everybody."

"The way you tell is you get extra nervous, just anticipatorily. When you're there with her, breathing, there are no nerves. Like Abraham Lincoln could have said, People who like this sort of thing will find this is the sort of thing they like. Sterling commented, 'Stop anticipating things and start reacting to them, I thought by now you'd realize the outcome of habit. You need more accidents in your life.' Reactions are no more an accident than losing your arm after sticking it in an alligator's mouth. You don't know when it'll snatch, only that it will.

'Before the airport, I walked to the some theater to spend my time.'

'Now that's purchasing power.'

'Besides, where else besides a theater can you go to sit and think? The Gaslamp Fifteen, the one on Fifth near The Melting Pot.'

'California's more of a salad bowl than a melting pot.'

'Plurality of moviegoers this weekend, it kicks off summer, not solsticely speaking. My choices were *Kung Fu Panda Two*, liked the first one lots, thought it had a great chance of winning Best Picture but not Best Animated; *Something Borrowed*, didn't know what that was;

and *Hangover Dos*, wasn't going to see that by myself since I didn't see it with Brad. Also *The Tree of Life*, but it wasn't showing late in the night, only the newbies. I stood by the concessions thinking about gluttony and the ones who get the chance to do it for art. Arthur, Hoffman, Benigni.'

'The guy who played Eminem in *Eight Mile*. You're confusing chance with probability.'

'Wallet out for whatever happened to be showing next and then I found a picture of Mynor, right in between my righteous dollar bills. Must have done that when he was at my desk. A couple walking back to the lobby from whatever they had just seen was so good they forgot to eat their popcorn. "I liked it a lot, great story and superb acting. But you can tell it's an indie, it had tone and pacing problems." I don't know what that means but I'm sure it's true. Pretty much changed my mind thanks be to that and was about to walk out. "It was epic!" Last time something epic happened, people weren't around to see it. "The best part is when he gets the tattoo. What's even better is when they steal the boat." My grandpa even likes *The Pacifier* and not *Mystic River*. At first I thought that was straight crazy, then I figured, they're just movies.'

'You figure out some deep secrets.'

'When he was ten the only thing he had to eat one afternoon, they usually didn't have dinner, was a box of Oreos. Ate all thirty two, hasn't had once since.' Doesn't mean he never will. 'This was before he met my grandma. I used the bathroom, where someone was playing piano, before going back under moon and star. Seconds after stepping out I got into a conversation with, not two, but one girl out in the street who also just abandoned the theater. Knew she must have been about twenty two, I guessed. Club couldn't even handle her, trying to get people to church, nondenominationally. There are worse things to do in the middle of the night, but I hadn't thought of any. "Sleep is for the privileged," she spoke. At least she was inclusive. Besides, maybe she already converted the daytime crowd. Who knows? Not me, I didn't ask. "Is it alright if I ask you a couple questions?" Good people, the city's filled with them.

"Is it a quiz? Knew I should have studied tonight." No reaction. "Go on."

"You buy insurance for your car, right?" How innocuous. "Well, church is like that, only it's free. I'm not going to recommend where you go, to me there is no actual difference, it's just how they are named, so long as you are aware of the options available to you, if you're not already." I didn't know what to say. "I know you might not care, but you have to understand that other people care a lot. We must individually. Religious people are very down to earth. If they're not, then they aren't religious, they're hypocrites."

"That's debatable. Earth is such a small sample size."

"I don't know, it would be a really quick debate." '

'Hypocrisy is useful.'

' "Depends on the moderator. Like Moses said, He has heard your gambling.'

"Did you just say gambling?"

"I remember it differently. Moses was stoic, how come he got to be the one - "

"He looked in the right place."

Babbled on. "He could have done a lot better."

"Than bringing guidelines to us in stone?"

"If they were more optimistic, in order to make sense. Lists should include everything that *is* acceptable." Otherwise they're negotiable. "Why would you let someone you don't know affect how you live?"

"Why would you not? There are more tomorrows than yesterdays. It's a cosmological certainty."

"Are you from around here or are you on a mission or what?"

"Thanks for asking. Only here for the weekend, making the most of time." Visiting from Portland, said she had to go help the rest of the world. Spunky, wearing boots that go all the way up past the knees, you know, in case it snows, and other zooty attire. 'Where did you say you were from?' Then, in my mind, I went back to her place and, I needed to sleep. I be crazy like that, most things I think about never happen. Would have been nice to keep some company. Portland had to meet some saints she said, across from Lenny's Leftovers and The Greasy Spoon. "Thanks for talking, you're helping me live forever. Peace and trees." We walked in different directions and my lone thought: Norman's party's probably just ending.'

'Sponges live forever.'

'Really? Jen's deeply cool, like an eight pointed star. Whenever it was cold she let me wear her gloves, enduring chill. The best thing about Jen is she's imperfect.'

'Everything you do is like riding a bike.'

'Someday it will all fade into random access. Decided on a place that's open at least twenty four hours before last call, Coyote Chaos, right next to Chris's Card Shoppe, which always plays Something. Two thousand pounds of playoff highlights for everyone who already forgot what happened two minutes ago. Dallas won, that was good for the world. Boston, not the band, beat Tampa, so Mynor was ecstatic. They couldn't prevent him. Earlier I asked Carson how Tampa did:

They won.

'Wasn't a massacre, two thousand to one thousand, so most talked about basketball anyway. Made me wanna join in, but I didn't sit. "Being a Miami fan is emotionally complicated. Coaching especially becomes more complicated in the Finals."

"Calling it complicated would be oversimplifying it." Couldn't resist.

"That's ironic," all nasally like that.

"That doesn't even make sense."

"Why are you whispering? Things don't have to make sense to exist. Girls exist. What kinda chicks you into?"

"Albatross, Shearwater, pelicans." Mason was right, so much for being unambiguous.

“Really? Good for you. You might find some flying around if you go back outside. Just be nice to the first person you see and they’ll lead you in the right direction.” ’

‘People will tell you anything when you’re nice, you just have to ask.’

‘Best thing ever invented. He just talked about balling, with disregard to all else, like a honey badger. “If you look closely, LeBron travelled.” There are ten top ways to respond to that, instead I listened and went outside to walk Eleven and a Half.’

‘I know what you mean man, you should always tell someone. You don’t know when you’re gonna forget it, only that you will.’ ”

Cuanto escucho esta cancion ~ Selena Quintanilla

Everyone has a car except me. I mean that categorically, not descriptively. If I get a job in a city where I have to commute and get stuck in traffic twelve hours both ways, I'll just be happy to have one. "We're basically there now."

"It's after midnight," she noted turning down Market Street.

"Where? Well, I might as well finish about Palmer, been in four relationships from two girls. Always getting back together, like Humpty Dumpty. Or Taylor Swift."

"I'd faint if I ever met her."

"Palm would ask her out. 'It's easy. Buy an item on her wish list, get her follow on Twitter, take her out on a thousand dollar dinner, bam. Literally.'

'Figuratively. Twitter's real? I thought it was a joke, stop idolizing strangers. Did you know all her songs are about the same person? You come here every week?' I assumed he did, he lived in City Heights."

"You should always make assumptions, otherwise you're not thinking."

" 'Often enough to know I always end my night here. What have you been up to?'

'Still doing the whole econ thing.'

'I know that. You're a boring major.'

'What do you study, geohydrology? With comparative anatomy?'

'It's better than it sounds.' And it sounds really good. 'No, I never studied. Facts are cheap. Good to have backups, things can go wrong.' Take lessons from him, you can fall upward.

'I'm well aware. That's why they won't.'

Those who are logical and those who are sensible. 'Dude, failure is *al*ways an option.'

'Nobody said it was easy. You wanna look at some of my pictures and let me know what you think?'

'Yo I just came here for the chili burger. Ultimately my advice is find a professional. Yes, it will cost you. Friends are nice and all that shit, but it doesn't mean they know anything about lighting, contrast, dimension, angle, rule of thirds, and basic proportion, not to mention subject. I don't think you comprehend the magnitude of work anything worthwhile takes.' Like anyone doesn't know that. 'How's the brother doin? Gonna move down here?'

'Lower Manhattan. It was either them or The Angeles and they bought his love, he said. His first gig is a tech intern, also found his way into a role this summer. Dartmouth Two is his character.'

'Oh that's big time. Manhattan, is that with the big building?'

'Torrey's good? I'm glad y'all are together.'

'I am too.'

'And you're not seeing anyone else?'

'I'm not even seeing myself.' They were steadfast, you could tell. Called me every week to bask and after four hours says he has to go have his date with destiny. Palmer's like family."

"I thought you liked him."

"He says all the right things, does none of them."

"At least he says them. He drinks, smokes, and sleeps with lots of women? That's awesome."

"*Aw*esome? That's your descriptor?"

"Better have done less. Makes enjoyable mistakes, so it's hard to recognize when he does something right. He just wants to have fun, like girls."

"Then what makes them better? Anyway it's unsustainable."

"So is the sun, I wouldn't worry about it."

"When he agreed to be Torrey's boyfriend he made her sign a Summary of Risks. 'We need to get you on track. If you don't have girl problems I feel bad for you son.'

'I thought you were gonna say, You don't need a woman you're doing fine. I got a pick up line for you: How much do you weigh?'

'One Szczesny. I don't do quotes, those aren't the lyrics anyway. Remember the year I was your Valentine cause you knew I wouldn't say no?' True story except it happened more than once. His empty glass was taken, 'Hey, how you doin? Someone came by but said I could only have one IPA at a time so if you could bring another nine that would be great.' This request wasn't acknowledged. 'When we first started out I'd look around and say: Hot chick, ombre hair, three oclock. Now she points them out.'

'How many one more chances are you gonna get?' "

"You didn't tell him Torrey's a swinger? Someone's gotta tell him."

"I told him, he knows. 'Listen, whenever you do anything for a reason your life becomes complicated. If you ask to go out for dinner it means you want the same thing but are interested in making it long term. This might be seen as taking it too fast though.' Too slow. 'Strong because he wouldn't, weak because he didn't. You have the potential to gain something. I know you won't, but you should ask. Only reason not to is if you're afraid of no reply, but that's stupid, fear wakes you up. Don't tell me you agree with Murphy's law.'

'Second, a law is something that's always true.'

'Unless you're driving on the freeway.'

'First, Murphy's guess is always wrong. Things are in the last place you look? Then you don't have to look anywhere else. It's all a bunch of crap.'

'No it's not. It's classic grade A bullshit.'

'At least we agree on that.'

'Pure propaganda people buy, like species evolve only when they have to adapt to their environment. How else would you have something say one dollar on it and not be worth one dollar? It's worthless. Its value is artificial. It *lit*erally grows on trees.' Cotton and linen, figuratively. 'Everything's politics.' His yes got really wide.

'How's that going?' The way Palmer became interested in politics, in fourth grade, was Lewis Black, same as everyone else. Smear Campaign Manager was his aspiration. The National Young Leaders Conference vigorously invited him the spring of sophomore year to explore Washington, he declined because he didn't want to miss any basketball, not even the replays. It would have been during the playoffs, so, obviously. The Conference reacted to this diplomatic situation by conspiring with league officials to make the Wizards a playoff team. It was kind of exactly like Taiwan declaring itself an official independent nation and its subsequent relations with China. Anywhere, his favorite classes at Mesa, where Neon Trees is from, were Future History and Nap Time."

"You lived in Utah?"

"Who? I like astronomy because it's apolitical. 'I'm on my way. Good at flip flopping and mixing in the important with the unnecessary and pointless. Repetitive. Redundant as well.' Just like Natasha, kept checking on us cause we were sitting on the same side of the booth, otherwise he kicks you.

'All good speakers are.'

'Yeah that's true. In my opinion. So if you ask to get lunch, it means you wanna take it slow and get to know her.'

We never talk about the same thing. 'Do you like the proposal to make streets out of something that lasts, cobblestone or brick?'

'That shit's expensive.'

'Anything more than free is expensive. It's *more* more expensive to repave the streets every five years. I read if our state increases taxes on the above five hundred bracket by two percent we wouldn't have to pay public tuition.'

'I read today's Tuesday. You're not in any position to judge the merits of legally stealing.' My grandparents were glad I didn't apply to Berkeley, even though I told them it doesn't matter how you think of them, they register less voters than we do despite having twice the students. And it's Tuesday somewhere."

"That's not how Tuesdays work."

" 'I don't even know what that means. I'm in favor of things that make sense. Like Chris Rock said, republicans are idiots. Democrats are idiots. Conservatives are idiots and liberals are idiots.'

'Anyone who doesn't flip flop is an idiot. Don't listen to him, make up your own damn mind. I need to ask you what you actually think about taxes.'

'I like syntax.'

Natasha glowed, 'Everything all right here? Can I get y'all your check?'

'No thanks, we won't be paying tonight. We're on vacation.' He hadn't used any silverware, all wrapped up in his napkin like a sleeping bag. 'Kley, you have class yesterday?'

'Not since Thursday.'

'Fuck you.' Natasha waited for an answer. 'Sorry, we'll take the check, but he has a gift card.' She turned away and rolled her eyes, you could tell. Only five dollars on it.

'Yeah, this quarter dude everything's packed in. Why don't you finish your fries?'

'No. Tell me what not to do and I'll do it.' Only logical thing to do. 'Wanna watch the meteor shower?

'That's late, I didn't sleep last night.'

'Oh come on! I haven't slept all week, I been busy. And drunk.'

'At the same time?"

'No further questions. Even your answers have questions. Ready?'

'You're having another beer.'

'My car won't drive itself.'

'You're driving?"

'Who else? Anything else no one's ever asked you?' Palmer drinks hot sauce, increases the metabolism. Not as conscious, easiest form of philanthropy, as he should or claims to be. Brad was the same, first year we had the same room his uncle had twenty two years earlier. Big on the environment, whenever I got back to our room he'd've left the lights on, like a motel, always trashes paper, and he burns coal for fun. He took a class that said every part per million of pollution is caused by corporations, not individuals, which is a really bad reason. Or he just didn't give a polar bear. Attributes outweigh imperfections, so that stuff ain't important. 'Have this.' Pepper sprout. 'Doing things at three in the morning is a good time to do things. Where you living today?' I pointed outside. 'I'll order some booze and hookers to your room. If you ask to get coffee that's the most casual route and means you don't really want much out of it, you just wanna hang out for a few minutes. Make no exceptions.' Without exception there's an exception to everything. All Palmer asked Torrey: Wanna go over there? 'What day is Friday?'

'Day after Wasted Thursday. I'll be asleep before they get there. And I don't drink coffee.'

'No, the date.'

'The third.' "

"You and Brad were the most random pair."

actually yeah girl is done let's go. I got a ticket lol

"At the beginning we were. By the end of the year it made perfect sense. 'What's gonna happen Monday anyway? Bunch of veterinarians are gonna parade around?'

'That was today, there's gonna be rain.'

'Well I just spent my last dollar so I'll let you get back to your night, and have fun in your precious Sanna Barbara. I bet you'd be *ham*mered if you were up there right now.' "

"You're the reason for our school's reputation."

"Palmer is even better in a different setting, got accepted into the Daniel Freeman Paramedic Program. Turned it down. Natasha walked by and whispered, 'That was awkward.' I thought it was great."

"Admitted, that's what he got. Turn here, right?"

"Left. Palmer went to meet up with Antonio in a crowded empty bar, The Fleet Wood, right across the way on J Street. Used his phone's map to get there, uses it to get anywhere, like home, even when he's already in his own drive way. Traveling by foot is great, had my walking shoes on and didn't want a ride. Nothing understandable about taxis, posted rate on the doors saying a sixteenth of a mile is two hundred dollars. People know we walk that in twelve seconds, right?"

"Palmer is crazy. You can learn from him, if you want to."

"Not crazy enough. He got pulled over for speeding on the autobahn. Everything we talked about was a repeat, Palmer forgets what he tells you. Or he likes to say it all more than twice." He's who I get it from. "You don't have to park. You can just drop me off out front again."

"I'm staying with you. There's no way I'm driving any more."

When we first find our plans are different from reality it takes time to recalibrate our thinking. Stepping out of the car didn't leave behind any music, Hang Loose dispersed through the automatic doors. "Hey Tore! I'd like to check in." Sleeves were biggest at the elbow.

"Do you have a, reservation?"

"Sure do. Would you por favor tell me the next time Jen is scheduled?"

"She doesn't work here anymore. You're in room two twenty one. Last one." The last sentence was directed at a bottle she returned under the counter. Immediately I told Jen my location.

Sounds like we switched. I leave in the morning before 8 if you got something to say

I was trying to phrase how I would be at Alameda park before eight. "Here Amie, two twenty one, on me. I have to go."

"You're a terrible liar."

"There's no such thing as a liar who's good. I'm going. Friends can always make it."

"What in the *hell* are you talking about?"

"I need to be somewhere else right now. I hope you find it in my wallet to forgive."

She grabbed it before I realized I had no grip. It had the last room key still.

"You know how to get it back." *Where*, she meant.

"Keep it. I'll see you on Monday or Tuesday."

Second half of a laugh. "Adios forever. You won't get very far."

"Okay, Tuesday." And that was it. "Torrey, you're drunk." Wearing rings with diamonds, and a long miniskirt, elegant but not eloquent.

"I'm not that." Leaning on the air, where I'm from they call that drunk. "It's weird. You're a lush!" Bright blue voice. "It's okay, I'm leaving now too. Think I should call a cab?"

"Is there a more expensive way?"

"We could take a limo," she walked outside in front of me.

"Last time I was here, at night, there was this lady who asked, 'Do you have a nickel?' With a sign next to her, She wanted to say something clever here. Wasn't a ragamuffin. Nice scarf, smart phone. In omnia paratus, if you will: bottle openers on her belt and bottom of her shoes. Speaking of which." Looked like she had fresh styles.

"How many sides does a circle have? Two. The inside and the outside!" Pirate laugh. "What you don't know can't help you. Do you have a dollar?"

"I don't have my - hold on, here's ten." Always have money in my backpack. "Invest wisely."

"I don't need to invest. I go to sleep on the beach, I wake up on the beach, and people give me money." She was also not on the beach. "I like the outdoors, they allow pets." Turned around. "Collect unemployment and surf." And couch surf, the natural progression.

Torrey didn't wait to say, "That's *so* annoying."

"Yeah, it's so annoying to be asked a question, but it's more annoying to be homeless."

"It's different when you're a guy."

"It is. Still, I maintain being *home*less is worse than almost anything you can throw at me."

Passed by the Omni on the way to the end of our walk. It was twenty five to and we were still standing on the side of the road. "Kley, could you imagine there were no hypothetical situations?" I imagine Einsteins would not. Walked past twenty-six sleeping apartments, the sky was pretty starry. If there were perfect symmetry with the celestial and the mundane, like when the stars fall from the sky, would our center of mass change, or would we move with them and not perceive any difference? Down on the corner, Fluxx on 4th, every man in there wishing. Wanted to see if they had a capacitor, although I don't look like I belong at a hip hop night club - my diagnosis, but it's verifiable.

So called problems. At the crosswalk of Island and 4th, Torrey kept walking around with her phone on her shoulder. Hefty heels that make you a couple feet taller, already reached terminal velocity standing. Now I see how wearing those requires assistance, like how we can't tickle ourselves. So after an hour and a half we finished step one of crossing the street, right in front of a blue car, honked and woke up the whole block. "Wherever, wherever, I cross where I want!" Doesn't know how to talk, only know how to yawp. By the intersection of Broadway and Park near Spreckels Theatre suddenly exclusivity is bad. We turned toward 3rd and the Civic Center. "Are you even listning, Kley?" To hey chica catcalls. "Here. For my sweet birthday eve my friends and me went to see *Hot Rod* then went, we went to this island where I had the most awkward carnival ride with my best friend. My best guy friend. There was also this ride that we rode three times and on the third time Jen threw up all over the guy, working the ride. Then we went to her - to my house and my friend threw up in the plants. It was!" Sentences all broken up, like Eminem on the radio. "This is nothing. One day I had hiccups for ten years." Another day she kept sneezing for three days straight in a row. "I was the late bloomer in my family, I didn't start drinking until twelve. Most see it as one of my flaws. Also I have a big blister on my foot."

"Just one? Do you ever wear sensible shoes?"

"It's ohkay. I can even walk backwards" A bit off balance, only wearing one earring. "The first time I drove we went inside and when we were done eating she asked me if I had her keys but I didn't and were they locked in the car, no, they were in the ignition with the engine still sprinting! Her mom had to drive down two hours and unlock the car. It was!"

"Excuse me if I fall asleep." Only half awake.

"Go for it, it's good for you. I'm a small doses friend. Not the greatest of stories but at least I had wheels. It was really lame, it was cool. Gawdy outlandish overdone demented questionable taste in fashion and the best hour of music ever. I hope my boyfriend's still awake. What do you think about a chance encounter."

"Are you asking me? I'm certain it happens all the time."

"Competition makes you want something even more than you knew." Once you stop competing with the past.

"Are you cold?" Not that I had a jacket to offer.

"No I'm from the Northeast. Everything's colder in Maine!" Really proud of her home state but not stately, like a devout Texan; rustling her wavy hair in the reflected moonlight, fighting the fixation. "You like what you saw?"

"I like what I see."

"Are you gonna slalom up and down the avenue, with me? You are?"

"I didn't really hear what you said so I just nodded."

"Please? I really need to pee."

"We'll pass a church along the way on Ash Street."

"I don't know streets, just say what bar it's next to." She mentioned her former faith and how absence is evidence. "We're almost to where we're going! But it's really far away."

"If you're a leprechaun."

"That would be bad. The good kind of bad." Up then over or over then up. Destination on Columbia, only a couple streets away. "I can't decide which is worse, so I'll go whatever way you go." After anything that moves, like a duckling.

"At least we don't have to walk over to one of those islands." Past Point Loma and the military dolphins.

"You can't even see that far," she talked so loud with all the silence around.

"Yeah you can. You can see the moon." Told her what only a roommate knows. "Sterling's favorite football team, favorite sports team, has gotten to the Super Bowl twice since we met. The time they lost, his former favorite band was the halftime show. Hasn't listened to them since, he listens to their winning Anthem performer all the time. He also skipped his midterms that week, only went as far as Segundos. 'Next year's gonna be great, which is that way.'

'We weren't playing for next year.' That's when he decided to stay on campus another year, 'I know a lot of friends and you know a lot of people. I at least wanted a close finish.'

'You wouldn't say that if *they* had the lead. You'd want them to keep scoring. They're not any worse for losing.' I won ten dollars on it."

"I have a better roommate story than that but I forget what it is. We're there." Slipped off the curb thirty-nine steps away. "Why does he care so much about them?"

"He was born that way. At his graduation, Sterling ran from a possession ticket, got away by hiding up a tree. 'It's because our speaker was full of lopsided thinking, congratulating the top third for continuing school. That's not good.' If I get caught, I want to be very caught. For tragic relief.

"Our RA visited right before Sterling took out the recycling, put the screens in first. Glanced at the empty bottles, 'I hope you guys weren't drinking.' That's *all* we were doing. End of finals week I received: 'On the basis of the information gathered from our conduct meeting and case documentation, the following decisions have been made for each of the alleged violations. Seventeen A One, Alcohol Under Twenty One, Not Responsible. Seventeen A Two, Concealment of Violation with Complicity, Not Responsible.' Only way to think that's accurate is if you're unfamiliar with the evidence."

"Wrong person took the fall?" It would have been my third strike, with expulsion to follow.

"Got that right. Then they asked me to be a tour guide, so I requested to do it without pay."

"You're joking."

"They have to pay me. Originally, Sterling won a raffle for a seven thousand dollar travel voucher, laptop, and twenty five hundred dollars of gift cards, for living in the dorms with no damage done. This decision revoked it. And he wasn't allowed to be an RA. That's how tall he is." He was okay, he'd signed to live on the Playa way back in January as a backup. Too, he thrived on change. It was sudden but no surprise when we arrived at the burnt orange apartment.

"Do you want to stay out longer?"

"Not at all." My feet were getting sore, imagine how hers felt.

"That's more than me." Primed for bed when it started to rain. "I smell bread!"

"You're just hungry."

"Negatory! Guessing is good. I feel this was good for everyone involved. The both of us? Thanks you, for helping me so much. Is there a secular term for blessed?" Amazing how easy to please we are, and how nice it is to assist. I can't decide which is better.

"Torrey, you're pretty. That's the simple part. No makeup, neither. Usually people look trashy when they're trashed. Palmer said so."

She tilted her head. "My Palmer?" My Palmer.

"Can you tell him I'm here?"

Torrey stumbled inside without words. Generic one bedroom, ten bathrooms; previously owned, not used, I stayed outside. Thought about church just for the sake of divinity. Had better things to do, I just didn't do any of them. Brad, Jordyn, Norman, and I went to the Mission for Easter first year. Queen, a la Beyoncé, of the Missions. It's a great place, whether or not Ortega or Portolá have anything to do with it. We'll go back. Bradshaw, well he got drenched in Holy Water instead of just getting a few drops from the palms. We all agreed that's exactly the thing that would happen to him. Mynor didn't get the memorandum, "You guys went to *Church*? I thought everything was closed on Sundays." Escanola asked if I go to church. You can tell when anyone asks whether the hope is for a yes or no. So I said yes. Obviously once a year counts, wasn't a total fraud. Astronomy midterm, one of my answers was: Because all matter and energy in the universe was determined before 10^{-37} of a second passed. All Halkirk wrote: I didn't know we could know that. So those offset. Proper study of a deity is done by a deity, the. And so I tell myself but nobody knows for sure. All I saw inside was a furry feline. Cat was asleep, her tail was awake, right next to a cactus. Every guy, at some point, the only plant he wants is a cactus, so he doesn't even have to water anything. Torrey was having a full conversation with her, which seems legally insane.

Termination shock reached me this way: Jessie walked out. A woman's man, you can tell. Torrey must have put her foot in her mouth or her tail in her ear. "Who the hell? What the fuck?" I agreed. "What is this?"

"I'm making sure she's okay, if that's what you're asking. She needed help getting back."

"Didn't look like it. You're telling me someone would go out of their way to do something like that?" I didn't know this was a problem.

"I was just helping her get home." It's easy to think we give an explanation when we only restate, used to do it all the time on tests I didn't prepare for.

"Why?" Same reason everyone else does. Boring questions fail to yield interesting answers.

"She could only read and walk at a first grade level." Sometimes I find myself stupid when I'm smart. Not stupid enough.

"Looks like we have different opinions. How come my girlfriend keeps talking about you?"

"Don't worry about it. She's not your girlfriend." No sense of humor, slapped me and hit my nose. I didn't look threatening. "Dude, it's not even like that." Torrey was exponentially more sober now, still wasted, and back outside with apologia, explaining everything, partially, after originally being rendered speechless.

"Vamos, go! It's all right." Now wearing a beanie, covering the luscious locks. Had to keep my eyes from the rest. "This is totally like the time with Antonio and the giraffe."

This wasn't like that one at all. "Boo, you can't be messin around like this." That's what I'd told her. "You said he wanted to take you upstairs."

"Is that what I said?" He walked out of the picture. "Sorry Kley. I don't know what the hell we did, but we did it. You laugh, but if he actually broke your face that would suck."

"Well that didn't happen, so it's funny. You have a new roommate, eh?"

"We should have told you a long time ago. Palmer and I broke up. We never expected it to last." She waited. "It's the truth."

"I'm looking for something more believable." Doesn't matter anyhow, anyway. There's a good reason for it, I just don't know what it is. Mea culpa. No real reason to stay, or pretend ones, so I sprung backward out of the area, despite its inviting presence. Kept toward the harbor, the seaside my lodestar. Called Palmer and was starting to see I should have brought my charger. Straight to voicemail: If I didn't answer at three fifteen in the morning, what made you think I would answer at three thirty?

A car stopped and its windows rolled down. "Get in the cab?" I did. Better laughing in the rain than staying inside, sometimes you laugh so much you hurt yourself, but that never hurt no one.

"After this plaza, make a left at Front and just keep going." I was just guessing. Thought I was about done talking for the night, so nothing more was said until the driver dropped me off by a driveway I'd never seen before. Paid with the rest of my cash.

Made another call, Grace answered instead of being asleep, which made me feel even worse for interrupting her sleepover. "Hello? Are you pranking me?" Home is where you don't have to knock.

"Hey punk, I'm outside. Not a prank. I need you to bring me Dad's keys. Quietly."

"What? I don't think I should be doing this." The blinds in her window moved.

"I'll write a note on the garage door. Like last summer."

"I guess that'll work."

"It did work."

"Okay. I'll be outside in a minute." Twice that. "You're not gonna have enough gas."

"I don't have my wallet."

"You really haven't thought this through."

"The thinking's all I've done, it's time for doing. Tell them it's for an interview." We hugged. "Have fun!" I got in the thing and answered my ringing phone. "Sorry Palmer, I didn't know about Torrey. How'd it go down?"

"Last time we saw each other I bought her groceries, and a cheese cake. I spent my last dollar."

"If I'm ever hungry I'm gonna break up with you."

"She's a sell out."

"I can't wait to sell out, I can't even buy in."

"Her family took me to an Angels game last week. She was mad about that. So now I'm mad. I'm even mad at you. You took school loans for four years to teach yourself how to zoom in and out? Everyone takes their own pictures, your career's extinct. More photos have been taken in the last year than all time before."

"It's still a very new profession, but I'm lying to myself saying that's relevant." He went silent so I thought he dropped his phone. "I hashtagged your mom last night."

"Does it sound like I'm smiling? If you want to do this just buy me some food. Did you know Anthony really does have two birthdays? Where he was born it was yesterday, but here it's today."

I straightaway asked if he wanted to take a trip up north. "Palmer, check it out. I have a car. It's a nice car, well maintained. Five springs ago my dad needed to get the ignition remedied - repaired, which cost upward of nine hundred. Predictably that was a big deal, even mentioned again this year. If that's not funny, I don't know what is. You don't know the true cost of something until you sell it, so I volunteered, 'We wouldn't be any different today, you would've found somewhere to spend those nine hundred dollars since then.' Tell me when I'm wrong."

"I'd have to interrupt way too much. You know you can always chill with me, as long as it's three in the morning. Anyway we're not taking that car. Don't take your family's fucking car, Jesus Christ. I've never even seen you drive, I'll pick you up. Just stay where you are. Where are you?"

"I thought you got a ticket."

"So what?" A whole three minutes away from the house, I parked the Accord, meant to text Grace where.

"Well what was it for?"

"I'll tell you when I pull over. I was explaining a situation!"

Palmer makes it really easy to have fun, because he never holds any expectations.

But I dont wanna wait ~ Brittany Howard

You know how some people take your breath away? Jen rips your lungs out.

"I've come to decide you only regret the things in your life you don't do."

"Tell that to every person in prison." Palmer flipped the wipers on as if it would push out the fog.

"I looked over at Sterling after telling him I got on board. 'Well, that's it, so.'

'That's the end? That's so stupid! You never say anything. Way to be anticlimactic.' How lucky. 'You lack, propinquity.'

'You think if I asked she would have said yes?'

'Kleytjen, think what we're talking about. Call your bluff.'

'She's his and his alone.'

'That's all? Double down. Put your cookies where your mouth is. Do you even know if they're still together?'

'Those are the last words we exchanged. I take that back, I wished her a happy day when she blows out her candles.'

'You don't like talking about this.'

'I took all this time doing just that.'

'You don't *like* it. Finish the dinner part. I like those shoes, by the way.'

'Oh yeah, they're half off now. I have til midnight to get a price adjustment. I'd had a gift card for Yolk, otherwise we would have ordered off some drive thru dollar menu. Palmer's grandma told me, "The longer you live, the better chance you have at living a long time." Don't know whether that's wise or stupid. I'll go with wise. She also said there's no sense in being stupid.' So, nine o'clock on a Saturday, I didn't know you would show, you kept calling it the Broken Soul. 'Our conversation would have differed if we had talked just a day earlier, and here you say he can overcome time. Parked way over on Market, he has an aversion to parking anywhere where you have to pay,' you prefer to pay for parking tickets, so I waited.

'If I were going to say that I would've said it.' Trying to keep my place. 'That's a full day. You care a lot about things most people don't.'

'The people I care about do. What are you gonna be famous for, music? Athletics? You have all their gifts and few of their faults.'

'No sports, no music.'

'Charm and good looks? You have them, whether the idea appeals to you or not.'

'I think education. Early education, preferably.'

'Education isn't a famous thing.'

'Not yet.'

'Well good, I like it, teaching one person and knowing countless more will benefit.'

'Say that again.'

'The idea being, if you're a teacher, and you connect with your students, they'll be excited enough to go and tell everyone else what they learned, right? Teachers share. Ouch.'

'Salud. You have such a recoil. Is behind this ear okay? Bet you didn't know I'm bilingual.'

'Just say you lost a bet. On purpose.'

'I left my laundry card in the washing machine, right after I put thirty bucks on it. I didn't even notice until I went down to put everything in the dryer, and it was still there! No one else had been laundering.'

'Or no one took it.'

'Are you gonna answer that?'

'I'm already talking with you.'

'You have a weird concept of phones. Anyway, that's why I do laundry on Fridays.' Last Friday of the month, he meant.

'Last year, second week, all the dryers were in use, I'd took the last one. Got there just before Chase, he was in a big hurry. Half hour later I checked on it, "Hey dude, it ended but some stuff was still wet so I put my card in for ya." That's why I do laundry on Mondays.'

'Hey. If girls were with terrible guys, you would stand a chance. They're all with great guys.'

'Every single one. Even when you don't think they are, like the ones who don't update their nominal status. When they do, that's how you tell how much you care.'

'They exist just to spite you. But that's not how, it's when they update that it's over you act on it or you don't. You have poor judgment if you're gonna go for a girl in a relationship, I'd never like a girl who would fall for a guy.'

'One percent chance with her is better than ninety nine percent anyone else. Sue me. And I know there's more than those two options.'

'You don't get that it's not about numbers. You only play out of your league.'

When you are watching a basketball game what are the little yellow marks below each team's score?

Marie already knew. 'True. True. But I don't know what that means, and even if I did, ambition is sexy.'

'Who told you?'

'What? I know everyone gets a phone for their first birthday now. I just got this this week.'

'Nice! Parents' present?'

'Self's present. After Yolk I walked to the Parsippany. It was kind of cold that night, nearly got hit by a car. Driver said, "You may have the right of way but you don't have the right to do something that stupid." Right. If it were the driver's fault I would have thought it was Palmer. Remember our driving test, we're allowed fifteen minor infractions? Most make one, some make two; no one makes more than three. Palmer made fifteen.' And that was back when you drove slow. 'I paid no attention, that spotlight caught my eye and I thought about things we don't have anymore and how much your life can change in one day or how much you can change it or is there any difference.' It was bigger when I couldn't see it.

'Was it a lighthouse? For me, I took my great grandma's car, the instructor got in, moved the seat back, and nine beer cans rolled out. That phone, you'll dig it. Just don't get sucked in too far, outside's where the beauty of life is. Dude, it is the best. It's so stunning. Have you been picturing? Looking for that tonal variation? You know, get some color.'

'The good day's gone when I don't take pictures.'

'Awesome. There's only so many times you can listen to a girl talk about how unfunny her boyfriend is and then you listen to her laugh at all his words, each and every one.'

'Exactly. For the most part. Where ya goin tonight?'

'We're gonna watch *Perks of Banging a Wildflower*. A nature documentary?'

'They haven't even prescreened that yet.'

'Carson's mom's friend's sister's cousin's friend's daughter gets them. The last one, all I did was read the subtitles, even though they didn't need to be there. I saw *Moneyball* with Liz.'

'No you didn't. Pitt's character went to my sister's school, Maplewood Middle.'

'She's still in middle school? You told me she's the smartest in your family.'

'Sure is. Did you like it?'

'I like watching movies with her. Why'd you tell me that part about Jen winking?'

'All I do is look between the lines.'

'She's not there. You have bad luck for someone who's never lost a bet.'

'I don't have bad luck, I just don't bet enough. I'm happy every second I'm with her.'

'So? You were born that way. You're so interested in this topic, such a waste of time.'

'If Adele sings about it it must be important.'

'You know how lyrics are stupid until they're put to music?'

'It's interesting for the same reason you have a favorite team.' I just realized I lost my bet with him, that I'd never pull an all nighter."

"You're not sure if you're in love with a girl or in love with school. I don't think you'll ever know."

"He said the same thing, 'Are you sure you don't have brain damage?"

'Depends on who you ask.'

'I'm asking you.'

'You gonna shave? Your hair is darker.' Colors matched. 'You think if I asked she would have said yes?' We walked inside.

'Yours gets lighter. I know that sound, you have a new voicemail.'

'Okay, I'll shut up.'

So are you ready? I'm leaving in five minutes, not six. Maybe 7even. You don't have to

"Except for all the parts I left out, that's what happened." At last the sun was waking up, the Channel Islands were rising out of the ocean, civil twilight. It's great to stay up late.

Keep the car as long as you need it. Just be safe

Corvette stayed above eighty eight. The last game doesn't matter, it's the whole season that counts. I called to tell Sterling, but sometimes when I talk with someone I save things, thinking there will be a next time. "Hello?"

"You're awake?"

"It's sunrise somewhere."

"About your speech. I have varying degrees of recollection about what I want to say. My phone's gonna run out of battery, too. You don't need to write it down, just use your fake lyrics."

"Those aren't fake. They're mondegreens. Did Mynor find them? No one's supposed to see those. I'll send you one, but no one will see the rest."

"Today is my last day here. Look at that row of houses in front of you on the beach. That's where I've spent my last year. The path we rode our bikes everyday, in pouring rain and playful sun. There's something magical to its layout. Tomorrow is the first day of our long term adventures. Thank you to everyone who has shared a moment with me. All your minds have shaped mine. Friends: for the past four years we have been learning about average. It's harder to dazzle us. It doesn't escape me for a moment that we are more than average. You all did more things right to get here. I've earned the best grades and won phenomenal games, neither made me a better person. These years were spent finding an inflection point between earned runs and grade point. There's no honor in not going up to bat. John Masefield said, 'The days that make us happy make us wise.' Let life happen." We passed my favorite Next Twelve Exits sign.

"Who cares about honor?"

"You can't be *any*thing. This is the issue confronting us. Name who you like most in this world. Redo the list if you didn't put yourself first. Sincerely, I attempted to make every interaction with each of you a nice one. We bring our own talents and preferences, neither represent success. I don't want to take up anymore of your time, I will simply say this last year was different, there was a different approach. Instead of doing things I've never done, I did all the things I knew I would miss. Without lag of enthusiasm. We have - hello?" That's when my phone was done. "Aw, roar. Probably fell asleep anyway." When it came to I saw what he sent. Wasn't even from a song.

Time takes so long, I replied. Like taking a look back when you notice the stripes. Doesn't mean anything, makes for a good line. Over by an exit ramp the engine stopped, only halfway out of the lane, right as it reached two hundred nautical miles from the start. Dude behind us jumped out of his car and asked what the hell happened. Golden hour.

"I always park like this. Kley, you should get out and run the rest of the way. If you wanna get there." Would be glad to see Mynor, Marie, and that smooth horizon, but I didn't move. "Get the fuck out! I'll see you tonight and we'll go to a party," and unlocked the door.

"Thanks for caring so much about my story."

"What do you want me to do, hack the mainframe? You don't *have* a story."

"Alright. I'm leaving all my stuff here." I left the door open and everything. "Just don't lose the camera."

What I remember most about that run is wondering what goes on between two lungs and looking at the ground. Started by hurtling over a French drain and going away from that rich hill with the spinning sun rising right on it, straight past the harbor to the ocean. The best sand to run on is where it's intertidal.

Birds were singing like it had just rained, but they were dry. First two miles were the worst. After the fourth I finally got into it, way over a hundred twenty beats per minute. Once I saw another person running I was getting faster. Better than thinking alone. After the birds were silent all I could hear was the distant sound of a truck backing up.

Instead of thanking the breeze, I got mad at the wind for slowing me down. Nothing to do but listen to myself breathe and to the sound the water makes when it recedes over the rocks. Tasted the blood in my mouth when I stopped being able to breathe through my nose.

Who knew running thirteen miles could be so easy? Campus Point was half draped in fog and I couldn't feel my legs. But I got it right when I caught her with the sun in her eyes.

All we care about is talking. You look at her and the way she moves, you see she's never faked a smile. "Morning sunshine! Actually - what? Did you know there's a sunflower here? What is it?"

"I love you so damn much."

Printed in the United States
by Baker & Taylor Publisher Services